Chasing

MIRACLES

-WEBB

Chasing
MIRACLES

TOMMIE WEBER

Library of Congress Number: 2002090699
ISBN: Hardcover 1-4010-4912-5
Softcover 1-4010-4911-7

This book was printed in the United States of America.

To order additional copies of this book, contact:
Xlibris Corporation
1-888-795-4274
www.Xlibris.com
Orders@Xlibris.com

-WEBB

DEDICATION

This book is dedicated to my six daughters. They lived with me while we were all trying to grow up. Thank God we didn't succeed. They are all beautiful young women who will put back into this world more than they take out.

ACKNOWLEDGEMENTS

CHASING MIRACLES took fourteen years, a blip in time. It appears here because Marge Naso remembered the efforts of a friend helping a writer. Susanne embodied all that is good in humanity. She lost her fight with cancer. I, the writer, she edited for free and tutored in unselfish love, am forever changed for having known her. She is comfortable with princes, paupers, and everyone in between. I thank Margie for thinking of me fondly when she remembers Susanne Luz. I dedicate this book to these two women and all others who strive each day to nurture our world into a better place to be.

Kyle and Barbara Magnusson. Without their support I would not have had the opportunities I have over the last five difficult years.

TW

PROLOGUE

Trees stood, stark naked, on a frigid March afternoon. Bristling in the wind, they held their ground, like sparsely clad soldiers shivering in the cold. Standing solitary watch over frozen earth, they waited anxiously for this long devastating winter to end.

Those few precious weeks are etched in my memory, as clear as air on a brilliantly sunlit, winter day. They are unforgettable, as is a favorite movie watched over and over, or a melody sung so often that hearing just the first few notes drives us instantly to song.

Ten years are gone since I left Springfield for college. Ten years, God I wish I could tell you where the time went. I return now only to visit and remember. Like many young people, I was anxious to leave home. I wanted to explore what life held in store for me. Because of the events in early spring of that year, I face each new morning expecting to find joy, no matter where I am. Each breath I take is a renewal of my life. Happiness is something I work at everyday. It is a lifelong study, never to be taken for granted. Happiness is available to all of us, wherever we are, whatever our situation, if we look for it. Everyone has hopes, dreams and expectations. All of these dreams can come true. Every expectation we have will manifest itself as naturally as taking another breath. The universe provides all the resources we need, though it might not offer everything we want.

The people in my hometown know the importance of searching for joy in each new moment. We studied happiness and sadness, as a group. We came away from that study more learned people, wise people, if I may be so arrogant. We are well prepared, as a group, for our individual earth walks, because we walk the earth within each other's ethereal plane. There is something to learn from every person we meet, and a blessing to offer for them as they pass. We are part of a universal awareness. Wishing someone well adds power to that awareness and increases our abundance, while the reverse is also true.

We walk around in the greatest machine ever created, the human body, rarely caring for it as well as we care for our treasured cars. It will take me this lifetime, and several more, to explore the body-mind's wonderful possibilities. Each of our seventy five trillion cells thinks, knows, and remembers. All our organs participate in that thought process through enzymes passed in the blood stream. These lessons had their seeds ten years ago and are still taking root. I don't know what each of you are here to do. That unique lesson is for each of us to explore alone. I am here to heal, and help others discover their body-mind's capacity. That is the essence of my life, along with one other important thing. It is an integral part of any healing journey to learn to love unselfishly. I don't know how to take, I only knew how to give. If I hadn't begun to learn this lesson ten years ago, I would never experience the gifts others have to offer me. It is, perhaps, the greatest lesson any of us gets to learn in life. We must allow others to feel special. More than that, we must make them feel special. We shouldn't make anyone feel small or unworthy, just so we might feel more important. We are all connected, whether we like it or not.

My family and I had the great good fortune to discover this simple wisdom collectively, during those few weeks in March. I regret it was after my grandpa died. He would have added to the experience. He lives in my heart everyday. He was a special man and is a special spirit. I say this freely without reservation. I know it is true. Oh, I can't prove it, except I remember his face: every line, every mark, and every wrinkle. I close my eyes and he is standing right in front of me.

Do you remember a friend or loved one you might not have seen for years? Can't you see them smiling? Can't you hear their laughter? But how is that possible? There is no physical stimulus. Over the last six months your body has created an entirely new set of cells. You are brand new. How can you see, or hear someone who, for all intent and purpose, does not exist in your physical reality? How do we remember? How are these images so real? Our mind draws out of pure energy, as we were created out of energy. All energy exists. My grandpa is still around.

Einstein said, "I want to know the mind of God, the rest are details."

Grandpa used to say, "Life can be like carrying around fifteen pounds of dog do. It gets heavy and starts to smell. You have to put it down, for a while."

Einstein understood simplicity in life. My grandpa knew life was to enjoy. It only became a burden if he let it, so he didn't. He was blind from birth, but saw better than most.

Springfield is a community of ordinary people from all walks of life. We are forever meshed in time and space, altered by events none of us could control. Today, we remain hard-pressed convincing others that the stories in the tabloids about our town were true. We are, as a group, as diverse ethnically as America itself.

This is a story I need to tell. Much like the Apostles in the Bible, this is not my story. It is not about me. Perhaps a half millennium from now people will call me, Prophet. I hope so, not for my sake, but for all of us as a race of beings with unlimited possibilities. The story has a life of its own, existing as an event within the universal time continuum. It will touch lives and hearts everywhere, if I tell my part half as well as some of the others are telling theirs. They've already begun to network their feeling of hope.

Springfield's inhabitants didn't fall instantly in love with one another, one day. We aren't even now, and we don't all believe the same things, but we did learn to listen without pre-judging each other. When that lesson sunk in, we began to accept our own weaknesses, which created a short step towards patience with others. This sounds so simple because it is. We began to experience life based on respect and love, rather than greed and envy. Reason allows humans to make decisions. Ideally, we would always control our animal instincts with reason, but we are not perfect.

In Vedic Science there is a guideline for life. "Live each day in a state of non-judgment. Judge no one, ever."

The Bible states the same philosophy where it says "Judge not lest Ye be judged." or, "Let he who is without sin cast the first stone."

The American Indians suggested, "Walk from one full moon to the next in another's moccasins, in order to know their feelings, their dreams."

We all met Zebedia during those few weeks. He lived according to the letter of the law of love. He is the only person I ever knew, who never expected any return.

Our town grew to be chock full of people trying very hard not to cast the first stone, after Zeb arrived. Many of us picked them up, and were quite ready to let them fly. More often then not, we put them down. I've cast a few, hurt some people, and will again when I lose my temper. I learned to forgive others and myself, and to begin again trying to emulate his ways. Perhaps, that is why I've waited ten years to put those long ago events to paper. Its taken me this long to begin to understand. Now, I need a refresher course of my own. A simple man and a complex woman taught the original lessons.

As it all began in Springfield, we groped to accept each other at face value, something America professes, but hasn't perfected. We are all fortunate to live in this country. It's as if someone created America as a design for what the world might become. America has the world's people. Every ethnic group on the planet is represented here. It doesn't work all that well sometimes, because we can be a hateful, maladjusted bunch, but it does work. People of every different background are learning to get along.

Even in Springfield, where we experienced miracles on a daily basis, we harbored and hid our prejudices. Change takes place over time, usually as old people die off. I realize change doesn't seem to happen fast enough, but think of the advances humans have made over the last seven decades. To someone living those decades they seem very long. But to someone younger, looking back at seventy years of history seems merely the blink of an eye.

Young people embrace new ideas, while older people cling to tradition. Balance needs to be found. Springfield became what America wanted to be as a child. The town was open, caring and fair. We lost it as quickly as it came. Over the years, we went our separate ways, but the people of Springfield search constantly for what we lost, no matter where we might be. The search isn't in vane. Love is not an illusion. Happiness is a study and a work of art. Investing life into life takes time; it must be done carefully without measure. Jim Rohn, one of my favorite speakers, says this often. Investing our life into the lives of those around us is the most important investment we make. This is our story.

CHAPTER ONE

I was the first of our group to drive. My dad let me use the new family car whenever it was available, which was pretty much whenever I wanted. I didn't appreciate it. I was at a defiant age, believing he was anxious about his car. My seventeen-year-old emotions didn't allow me to understand he was concerned for my safety, yet loved me enough to trust me. Some of my friends saw this better than I, but I didn't listen. He cared about his new car and that was it. At seventeen, martyrdom is still very much in vogue, especially for the richest kid in town. I had no trouble getting people to feel sorry for me.

Zebedia walked past the forest green sign with bold white letters announcing Springfield's city limits at about five o'clock in the afternoon. Normally, budding leaves and flowers announced the rebirth of spring; not this March.

Puddles along the curb were sealed closed by a newly formed layer of night ice, as the temperature dropped with the setting sun. Zeb stopped to get his bearings, thinking he'd missed a turn somewhere.

Glancing at his written directions, then up at the street sign, and back to his directions, he scratched his head and chuckled at his inability with maps. He thought of himself as a geographical moron. During a later conversation, he told me it was a good thing he passed up the chance to be Christopher Columbus. I didn't think anything of it, at the time. Now, I know he meant physically being Christopher Columbus, and I also know it isn't far fetched. Zeb rarely hurried, feeling much life is missed by scurrying past it, but he was a little behind schedule, and had to hurry now. He needed to find a place to stay before starting work the next day. Reaching down, grabbing firm hold of his duffel bag, he hoisted it up over his shoulder, just as I drove my father's brand new BMW around the corner, very close to the curb. Sweeping through a deep puddle, we splashed mud, water and ice all over Zebedia's threadbare pants, and mustard colored, canvas coat. It was his introduction to Springfield's hospitality.

He heard us laughing, as we sped away. He saw the girls point at him, standing there covered with wet filth. Zeb watched us go, and I noticed his eyes in my mirror. They were steady and full of sadness. I felt a little tightness in my throat, but shook it off. His shoulders appeared to sag.

Hoisting his bag back down, he removed an immaculately clean towel, old and frayed at the edges, matching his pants. Just as he finished wiping himself dry, we rounded the corner again, hit the same puddle and covered him with filth once more. This time he glanced up quickly, and I was caught in his gaze an instant before his eyes were blocked by our second shower. Still no anger played in them, as you might expect it would. There was something else though, a look beyond rage. Pure wrath maybe; reason, battling fury. His face was a horrible mask, instilling in me a sense of utter despair. I will never forget it, as long as I live. My heart sank, and the others lapsed into silence, so I knew they felt it too. His glare was all encompassing. His eyes missed nothing. Through ice and dirt, I saw him shift his stare to the car. Our engine died, and we coasted to a stop about five hundred yards away from him.

I was watching him in the mirror the whole time. I don't know if he willed it, or if it was a coincidence the car died, but I was scared. I was scared, not because I was wrong, but because I was caught at it. To this day, I believe Zeb willed the car to stop, but I can't prove it. I know it happened. I believe it happened for a reason. It was my first run in with faith. Not Catholic, Protestant or Hindu for that matter, but Faith as Webster defines it. Trust, loyalty, believing on the strength of trust alone without proof. It was my first inkling; faith would play a major role in my life.

I wasn't easily convinced then, and I'm not now having, a head about as hard as cement. Faith was strictly for weak willed fools looking for an easy way out, until that day. Zeb wasn't weak. He was quiet, like an empty church or a graveyard, and he was confident. He was no fool. I knew this intuitively, as if I was getting a message inside my head. I heard him without any sound passing between us. I knew he was speaking to my heart, yet he was five hundred yards up the road. I knew he was sad and disappointed. For a cynical, insecure seventeen-year-old, this was just a little more information than I needed without talking to someone.

Zeb glanced down at his clothes and up at me. He took his time wiping himself down, slow and deliberate for effect. Hank, my best friend, was in front with me. Our girlfriends were in the back, leaning forward, screaming at me to start the car and get the heck out of there. I knew instinctively there was no point. He wasn't allowing us to go anywhere. My legs began to tremble uncontrollably.

As Zeb approached, I panicked.

Glancing sideways measuring his progress, I began frantically turning the key in the ignition switch. I didn't want a confrontation. I wanted to run away. We all did. Zeb walked towards us, slowly finishing wiping his face and arms, and I warned him in my best man's voice from deep in my stomach. "Stay away. My father is the mayor. This is his car. If you damage it, you'll pay for it."

Hank chimed in sarcastically. "That sounds real scary."

Zebedia chuckled and kept coming, as my heart sank along with whatever courage I mustered.

Zebedia's eyes sparkled with amusement, and he asked, "Why did you deliberately splash water and dirt all over me?"

Finding my seventeen-year-old voice, I replied, "We were having some fun with you. Can't you take a joke?"

"I don't see the humor in scaring someone and possibly ruining their clothes. Perhaps you or your friend here could explain it to me. Your car won't start, by the way, so you can stop running the battery down."

"How do you know?" I began to calm down. His silky deep voice had that affect.

"That new BMW has a problem with water splashing up through the under carriage. You were lucky the first time."

"You know about Beamers?"

"A little. I know more about washing clothes." He joked.

I softened. He seemed like a nice guy. I apologized. "Sorry, man. It was a perfect set up. You were standing right next to the puddle."

"Twice?" He answered, evenly, no smile this time.

"Yeah, right. Twice." I laughed nervously.

"What if I were a madman?" Zebedia asked, allowing his voice to lower, becoming menacing. He hadn't shaved in nearly three days, and appeared thoroughly dangerous. My friends shifted uneasily in their seats, as if bugs were crawling all over them. For some reason, I was no longer afraid.

He continued in an eerie whisper, "If I went crazy, and killed all of you right now, would your prank have been worth it? Would your father, the mayor, be of any assistance?"

None of us moved, and one of the girls, or Hank, began to whimper. Zeb realized he was scaring us, and stopped, as quickly as he started. His smile returned the air of intrigue evaporated.

"I never hurt anyone," he added, to further quiet our fear. "I scare the hell out of people, sometimes, but I never hurt anyone." His pleasant attitude was contagious. He wasn't angry. His clothes would dry. He was either very stupid, or very nice. In either case, we were very lucky.

"Pop the hood." He ordered, and I did without a moment's hesitation.

Hank grabbed my shoulder from the passengers seat and leaned close. "Are you nuts, Rog? The guy is loony." He whispered.

"Maybe we should jump him," Hank added. Zeb replied, "That would be the biggest mistake of your young life, Henry and I'm not loony."

My mouth fell open, "How did he hear you, Hank? I barely heard you myself. His head is under the hood."

"How am I supposed to know? He must have ears like a dog or something?" Hank whispered with the veins in his neck bulging.

Zeb chuckled at the thought of having large floppy ears like a dog, but didn't say anything. We sat quietly wondering what he was doing, not moving, not knowing what to expect. Zeb dried a few wires with a rag, letting us sweat some, then slammed the hood down and strolled back to the window.

"You're all set. Try it." He said.

I turned the engine over and it roared to life. I glanced in the mirror at the girls, huddled against the opposite corner of the car.

Then, I spoke, thoroughly chastened, to Zeb. "What now, mister?" Hank was nudging me to drive away.

"You go on your way." He smiled. "But drive around the puddles, especially if I'm standing next to them."

The girls slid more to the middle of the seat, and leaned up trying to get a better look at him. They sensed the danger passing.

I didn't laugh, but I didn't leave. I didn't want to.

"We splash mud all over you, douse my dad's car; you fix it, and we can go. No yelling or cursing, just like that?"

Zebedia's brow creased, and he grasped his hands together at his waist. "What would yelling and cursing accomplish, which I haven't already. You will think twice before you do something like this again. You may still do it, but you won't get any laughs. You won't feel good about it. There is something you can do for me, though?

"What is it?"

"Actually, two things; First, as I just said, 'Think' before you consider doing something mean or stupid again."

"We told you, Roger." The girls interrupted.

"All of you thought it was funny. I saw you laughing and pointing at me from the rear seat, until the car engine died." Zeb chastised them gently, and the girls blushed. He turned back to me.

"Secondly, direct me to County Memorial. I'm lost, can't read a map worth a darn."

"We'll drop you off there." I saw Hank shaking his head back and forth out of the corner of my eye.

"That isn't necessary," Zeb replied. Hank shook his head that he agreed, pulling at my arm. I pushed him away

"Neither was fixing my dad's car. C'mon. Get in."

"Thank you very much. It is kind of you, but no."

"I thought you weren't angry about our prank?"

"I'm not, a little sad, that's all."

"Why?"

"Because you wouldn't want someone to do it to you, Roger. If I was old or sick, you might have scared me to death. How would you feel then?"

"I can't feel like much more of a jerk than I do already."

"Good! Then, we both learned something."

Hank asked, "What did you learn?"

"That I wouldn't like having ears like a dog."

Hank replied, "You heard that too? Geese, what are you Batman or something?"

"Or something." Zeb returned.

We all thought that was pretty funny, and for some reason I can't explain, I wanted to know if he was staying around, and found myself hoping he was.

"You're new around here, aren't you?"

"I got off the bus from Stewart, in Fayetteville, and here I am."

"You walked from Fayetteville? That's seventy-five miles. Why didn't you stay on the bus?" I asked.

"I gave someone most of my money, because she needed it." Zeb said this, as if it was normal, something everyone did. Hank rolled his eyes at me, drawing circles in the air around his ear, indicating Zeb was nuts. I felt inclined to agree with him. No one gave money away when it meant walking seventy-five miles. No one we knew, anyway.

"Are you a doctor?" I asked.

Zebedia answered, “No, I’m not.”

One of the girls asked, “Have you eaten?”

Zeb patted his bag, “Yes, I have. Thank you.”

He pulled out an assortment of dried fruit, barley greens and a canteen of water.

“Would you like some?” He asked us. I distinctly remember turning up my nose like a little kid. “That stuff is gross.”

You think so?”

He laughed at my reaction. Handing Julie a dry, shriveled Apricot, he sprinkled a drop of water on it. Julie was my very dreamy looking, sixteen-year old girl friend. Slabs of makeup layered her skin, hiding one zit, which she insisted was the size of Mount Everest. She hesitated, looking directly into Zebedia’s eyes. They were light brown, almost tan; the color of deer’s fur. A gentleness played around the edges and the corners of his mouth raised slightly giving him a kind, resigned look. Not quite happy, but far from sad. His brown hair was long and wavy, spreading out from under the baseball cap jammed on his head. She took the Apricot, bit a little corner, chewed, then smiled shyly.

“This is very good.” Zeb laughed.

“It is, isn’t it? I thought they looked disgusting too, when I first saw them, but when I tasted one and added a little water, the sweetness of the fruit melted on my tongue.”

Julie took another bite and offered it to me.

“Not me. I ain’t eating that.” I pushed it away.

The way I contorted my face must have been something, because they all laughed. Zeb popped the rest of the Apricot in his mouth.

Hank asked him if he was a cook and he became animated when he answered.

“I enjoy cooking very much, and I enjoy guests, but my job is handyman or maintenance. Now, if you will point me in the right direction I will be on my way. I start work as a hospital janitor tomorrow and still have to find a place to stay.”

Julie asked, “How will you make out with no money.”

Zeb smiled as if he knew a secret, but said only, "Something will turn up."

Oddly, I knew he was right, or I got the feeling he was right. Not that he wanted to impress us or anything like that, but he did anyway, without trying. I asked him again if we could give him a ride and he gave me an answer, which we considered strange.

Hank thought it was out and out weird.

"No, thank you." He said, "I promised I would walk."

"Promised who?" I asked him, but he evaded me.

The sun, sitting in the treetops, started to lose hold of the sky. It was slipping down into the branches, when Zeb turned away into the gathering dusk. We watched him for a while and suddenly Julie found her voice. "Hey!" she called, "You didn't tell us your name."

He cupped both hands over his mouth, swinging his bag to the side, behind his right arm. The weight dragged him a title off balance. He righted himself, walking backwards, "Zebedia," he hollered back, turned again, adjusted his bag, and disappeared, collected by his surroundings, as if he never existed.

We stood staring after him, wondering what to make of it. If we pulled our puddle prank on any other adult, we would be grounded forever. Zeb took it in stride. He didn't even seem upset, while quietly pointing out why he thought it was wrong, and wouldn't do it himself. We genuinely felt horrible. I usually do when I get caught, but this time I was sorry for what I had done. I learned something. This quiet stranger, who laughed easily, wore patched clothes, and shoes with no socks, was all right. Sitting in the car, our thoughts swirling, created a strange mood. The silence was enormous.

"Spooky!" Hank quipped and got no response.

Usually everyone was talking at once, but this time, as I started to move the car, I could hear our tires crunching over frozen gravel. I don't know why I stopped and stepped out, but I did, and the others followed. We stood staring after him sensing something. It wasn't a bad feeling. It was easy, like the first taste of an ice cream cone, or biting into a crisp apple, but that was too simple. It was more than just a physical feeling. It was like I felt good inside my heart.

We felt peaceful, happy and excited all at the same time. It was like the morning of your birthday, or a big dance, or getting an 'A' on an exam you expected to fail. I glanced over at the puddle I drove through, and then off where he disappeared, thinking, "It wasn't funny. It was kind of stupid." He was right, and I would never forget.

We got back in the car and I punched Henry good-naturedly on the arm.

"What do you think?"

Hank answered, "About what?"

"About the space program, Henry. C'mon. What did you think of him?"

"I don't know. He's a little weird I guess."

"I think he's special."

"I think he's kind of cute. He's got a great little bod." Julie chimed in and Lisa added, "Did you notice, he never raised his voice, but you could feel his essence, and he had beautiful hands."

Lisa was our resident intellectual, very cerebral. I think she dated Hank, because he was a challenge to her brainy friends. My best friend was never going to be mistaken for a rocket scientist, and he knew it. And I loved him; I never realized it before, I didn't even think I was odd for thinking it. I looked at him with a brand new set of eyes and didn't know it.

Hank laughed and chided his girlfriend, "Leave it to you to notice his essence, but I agree about his hands. They were large, and I could feel them around my throat, when he threatened to do away with us."

Lisa frowned, "He didn't threaten us, silly. He pointed out, we took a chance and were responsible for our action."

Julie added, "And also for what might have happened."

"He scared the crap out of me." Henry answered and I added.

"That's a lot of crap to scare." The girls laughed and Henry pushed me lightly.

I put the car in gear and we drove off talking and laughing. A thin layer of ice had formed over our puddle. Animals settled to rest for the night, and everything seemed the same, but it wasn't. It was changed forever. A lone leaf kicked and jumped along the ground propelled by a whisper of wind, blowing towards County Memorial Hospital.

CHAPTER TWO

I could hear my parents arguing in the kitchen, as soon as I opened the car door. All the windows were closed against the cold, so it was obviously a heated contest.

Their arguments were an everyday occurrence of late. They fought over small things, like turning out lights, and large things, like what to do with us kids. They fought about everything just to be arbitrary and didn't realize, or admit it, even to themselves.

I didn't understand any of this then. I began to sort it all out long after I left Springfield. Back then, I was seventeen, angry and feeling very put-upon. Anger fuels emotional blindness, and I wasn't helping the situation at all.

My parents skirted around issues really bothering them, preferring to stick with safe areas. They no longer trusted one another with their souls. I don't know if they ever had.

I slammed through the front door. Both of them called out, but I kept going, not wanting them to see the tears in my eyes. I learned early to protect my own soul. Hiding behind walls of self-pity, I added more than my measure to our problem. Our family was falling apart, and I was afraid to approach them, so I stayed away as much as possible.

As I headed upstairs, they began arguing in lower tones, but I knew it was about me. I hurried past my little brother Timmy's room, into our sister Linda's. They were sitting on her bed huddled together. Linda was stroking Timmy's hair. He had his hands pressed against his ears. I tried to sound cheerful.

"What's up, you two?"

Linda answered, "Mom asked Dad to leave, Rogy."

I spun her desk chair around and straddled it, facing them.

"It's okay, little one," I said quietly and Linda eyed me funny. I was surprised by the gentleness of my tone. Normally I would sluff it off, pretend they imagined things. Tonight, I didn't want them to feel alone, or hurt. I wanted to help and I knew I could, because I loved them. There it was, the "L" word again. Funny, I never really thought about what they both meant to me before. I never told them I loved them. That wasn't, "cool."

Until that night they were just kind of there. As I spoke to them, an image of Zebedia covered with mud came to mind and I smiled. I was seeing my little brother and sister for the first time. I was interested in their feelings. I didn't want them misunderstanding, or thinking I was laughing at them, so I asked Timmy, "What's bothering you, champ?"

Timmy blubbered between sobs, "I didn't mean it. I won't do it anymore. I don't want Daddy to leave, Rogy."

I didn't even tell them not to call me Rogy. I should have been in shock. "Slow down, bud. You didn't mean what, and what won't you do?"

"Whatever I did to make Mom and Dad mad."

He was frantic to stop their constant bickering. I stood, turned my chair and took him in my arms. I rubbed his back as he snuggled against my chest. Tears welled in my eyes, spilled over and formed little rivers down my cheeks. "You didn't do anything. That's not why they're fighting."

Timmy continued sobbing, but he was listening. My attention was having a calming affect. It was my attitude. I felt peaceful and I guess they sensed it. My entire attitude changed when I walked into this room. Linda and Timmy were more important than the hurt I was feeling. Somehow I knew I needed to change. I didn't know how or why I just knew I had to, or none of us would survive. I had an overwhelming urge to connect with them, as their older brother should, which is something I never thought older brothers did. It wasn't cool, but tonight, "cool" didn't matter. Linda and Timmy mattered.

"I won't tell you I know why they fight, guys. I don't. I just know it isn't anything we did or didn't do. Look how nice they are to us when the other isn't around. Its like they're trying to prove something, all the time."

Linda interrupted, "Mom took me shopping three times last month, Rog. She asks me questions about all of us. It makes me nervous. I liked it better when she was being Mom. What should we do?"

I didn't have to think about it a minute. I told them my idea. "I'll toot the horn twice when I get back. Wait for me."

They wagged their heads up and down, traces of small, brave, unsure smiles shinning through spent tears still shinning on their baby cheeks. Then, I raced downstairs and out the door feeling better than I had in a long while. Mom and Dad heard, and hurried into the living room, in time to see the door slam and hear the car engine come to life. Elizabeth, my Mom, called me from the door, but I was already out the driveway with the radio blasting, so I never heard her. She closed the door slowly, flipped her long blond hair back over her shoulder and moved back to the living room, believing I left again, because of their fighting, which was only partially true.

She sank down into our new, wrap around, white leather sofa at the center of the room and Dad settled across from her. A circular, two tiered, glass coffee table with polished brass edging and legs separated them, while two pastel ceramic lights shone brightly on end tables in opposite corners of the room. My grandfather refused to enter this room. He called it our plastic people room. The horseshoe sofa arrangement opened on a movie screen size television, covering almost an entire wall. Behind Dad a decorative archway led to the foyer and our expansive dining room beyond.

Mom stared at the dark television set for several minutes before speaking. "We're ripping apart every good thing we ever did together, Benny."

Dad sighed, leaned back and closed his eyes, "You're right, Beth. All this bickering is destroying our family. We're destroying each other little pieces at a time. Maybe I should move out for a while."

She didn't answer and he continued, "It just seems awkward, and I don't really understand why."

Beth shifted uncomfortably, "You know we all appreciate what you do for us, Benny. But, I don't feel like we're part of it. Can you understand that?"

"Not really. I go to work and I come home. Once in a while I play golf or cards with the guys, but for the most part, I'm here. I'm not having an affair, and yet, I know you're not happy. We rarely touch each other or talk without arguing. What is it, Beth? What do you want?"

"That's just it. I don't know. It seems I've spent my whole life here. I've raised our children, and I feel I don't exist. This was going to be a partnership when we started out, but it's not. You have your life at the office and I have mine here. We know very little about each other, and except for sporadic love making, we rarely connect."

She was crying, and Dad had tears glistening in his eyes, too. He felt useless, because Mom wasn't happy, and he did love her. He asked her the question, eating at him for more than a year.

"Is there someone else, Beth?"

She laughed a small, sad laugh, which hurt him and he hid his face. A few moments passed in desperate silence. The air in the room was electric with raw emotion and silent anticipation. They were sailing uncharted waters, exploring each other for the first time in years. They were passed the point of no return, walls would fall, and worlds were colliding. Dad felt everything he loved slipping away.

Finally Mom spoke, quietly, in a hesitant frail voice.

"There was someone a year ago, but it wasn't serious and it never went very far."

I often wonder at the fear grabbing at her guts. Telling the truth, faced with humiliation, she persevered. Exposing her heart, gambling everything to save her sanity, she risked her life with us to make life better for all of us. It is a courage few of us muster. She wanted, more than anything, all of us to be happy. She opened her secret heart, trusting her moment of weakness with my father, and he didn't handle it well at all.

His face went bright red, eyes bulging, "Why, Beth?" He squealed in a voice coming from some tormented demon buried deep inside him, piercing the growing silence, like the howl of a wounded animal.

Getting the answer he feared most made him furious, hurt, and confused, all at the same time. He tried in vain to control his emotion and couldn't.

Rage took over and he exploded, "How could you do that to me, to the kids, to us?"

He stormed out on the most defining moment of their married lives. Mom let her walls fall and trusted him. Dad disappeared into a well of self-pity, and male ego, completely missing the courage and trust it took to tell him the truth. He missed his chance to love her unconditionally. He couldn't see passed his own needs, to glimpse her loneliness. He missed an opportunity to be her hero, her knight in shining armor once more.

I would miss it too, even today, if I am honest, I know I would. Most of us don't trust love. We live life in shadows, half truths, and fantasy. At seventeen, I didn't even like my girlfriend looking at anyone else. I rarely missed an opportunity myself. In ensuing years I began to comprehend the strength, courage and absolute love it took for Mom to face her fear, for all of us. Without her selfless act, our family would not have survived.

She sat afterward, deep inside herself, listening to his tirade somewhere in the distance. His anger flowed over and around her like water cascading over the rocks at the base of a waterfall. She thought she would feel terrible. She wanted to, but she didn't. She wouldn't fight back. She didn't have to. Her most important battle was over. She had won, not over him, but over herself, for her and us. It took all her energy to confront her fear. She was relieved, as if a tremendous burden were lifted from her shoulders.

She hadn't done anything nearly like Dad was imagining in his mind. In mere seconds he had blown it all out of proportion, already writing himself in as the victim. She had gone on a couple of picnics, with a friend. Her mind increased her guilt exponentially, making a good friendship into something more. Admittedly, it could have gone further. She was attracted to Peter and he wanted her. That was a normal, healthy physical response she hadn't acted on. She understood Dad's anger. He had a right to be a little angry but not off the wall. Most importantly, she was free of her shame.

She remembered talking to Peter of all the things she dreamed of doing and he listened. It made her feel worthwhile. He was a little younger with long hair and an earring, "My God, an earring. How decadent and exciting." She remembered his face.

When Peter told her he loved her and pressed her to make a decision, she retreated. Lunches were fun, a diversion from her everyday existence. When he kissed her she melted away. His hands were new and strong, and she felt like a woman. That only happened once. It had gone no further, and she was guilty for more than a year after over her body's trembling reaction. Whenever she thought of it, she was transported back to a world of romance and sensuality, not with Peter, but with my father when they were young. Dad asked and she answered truthfully; about something she believed she could never tell. Her spirits lifted and she wanted sing.

She wanted to tell Dad, "I trusted your love for me, Benny, can't you see? It wasn't Peter I wanted. It was you and I and our dreams together."

Peter was a catalyst, an adventure, like taking a dare in school. She hadn't connected emotionally with him. Their friendship awakened feelings she and Dad used to share, but it taught her something important. She wanted us, but she wanted to change too. She wanted to be vital and alive. She wondered why she and Dad allowed emotion to fade into the background of their everyday lives, living separate existences together. Feelings were exhilarating, so much a part of life, of who they were together. Why lose such a vital part of life, to work, little league, and acquaintances. For a brief couple months, she felt all of it again, and she wasn't sorry, but she would never say that. It was mean, hateful and unfair to all the sacrifices she and Dad made.

He was blind with rage, refusing to understand. Mom was being reborn. She wanted to share it with her husband and children, and she wouldn't turn back. She couldn't. He slinked back into the living room, and she looked up hopefully. The scowl on his face dashed her feelings to the ground, before they had a chance to soar, but she wasn't afraid anymore. Her emotional prison was open and she was free. She felt foolish, nervous, and almost giddy. She chuckled unintentionally from nervous energy. Dad misunderstood entirely.

"I'm glad you find this amusing." He forced himself to appear calm, while white-hot emotions had him seething inside. "Perhaps you won't be laughing tomorrow. I made a phone call. I won't be leaving, Elizabeth. The laws in this state are quite clear about adultery."

"Adultery?"

The word hung in the air accusing them both of failure. Mom never considered herself an Adulteress. She sat there, stunned, thinking, "A fling, an indiscretion, a mistake, but surely one kiss is not adultery."

Then, his full meaning hit her and her heart sank. "Ben you wouldn't? Not the children."

"An hour ago you wanted me to leave. I'm not going anywhere, but you are."

She couldn't believe it. She told the truth, and he would destroy her for it.

"This is how you love a person?" She asked quietly trembling squeezing her hands and knees together, refusing to turn back.

"You're right, Beth, we don't know each other at all," was his lame response.

She was shaking uncontrollably, and a wave of nausea swept

over her. She took a few deep breaths and gathered herself, thinking, "I would've been better off lying."

She couldn't go on feeling guilty all the time. Now she was cornered, and frightened, so she lashed out, "Perhaps if you were a little more of a man." She let the words dangle in the air accusing him.

He started towards her, hand raised, but stopped short when he saw Timmy sitting on the stairs with his face stuck between the open spindles. He looked like a little prisoner peering out of his cell.

"Please Daddy. I promise I'll be good." My little brother begged.

Linda walked downstairs, and sat down on the bottom step, hugging her blanket, a small, stained piece of material she clung to for comfort from infancy. It was pink, with shiny frayed satin edges. Part of this satin trim hung loose. The blanket was covered with juice stains and food spots, never to be removed, in a thousand more washings.

"Me too, Daddy." She added, in a small voice, venturing a smile, through overflowing eyes.

"We promise to be good if you and Mommy stop."

Dad looked at them, then over to Beth, who was hugging one of the couch pillows, much the same way Linda held her blanket. His heart sank. He stood looking at his hand still raised over his head. It condemned him and his shoulders sagged under the burden of his shame. Slowly, he lowered his hand, realizing what he was doing to them. All the bravado raced out of him. He slumped down on the sofa, and began to cry softly.

Through open tears he said. "No one is going anywhere. I promise, if that's okay with your Mom."

Mom nodded, tears rolling freely down her cheeks also.

The children ran to Beth and hugged her. "Its okay with me, Benny. I'm sorry I said what I did, you know."

"It's okay, Beth. I deserved it. You were brave to tell me. I'm sorry I've made you feel unwanted."

"You didn't, Benny. It's both of us. It's life itself. We are so busy. I love you, Ben. It's you I think about, but the way we were, not like this."

"I don't know what to say, Beth. My world is falling in on me.

"On us." She corrected him. He didn't answer; just sat staring at the floor with his head in his hands. Mom tried again.

"I trusted your nature, Benny. I want you to know how special that is. We are both to blame."

"I don't know whether that's good or bad, Beth." He sighed and added, "Why don't we put the kids to bed and let everything rest until morning."

"It won't go away, Ben. We need to talk it out. I want to talk it out, before its too late."

"I don't know if I can. I don't know if I want to know any more."

"Stop imagining things and making it worse. It serves no purpose to distort what I said or did." She was angry now.

I tooted the horn twice from the driveway, as promised, burst in and announced, "I have someone I'd like you all to meet."

Zebedia stepped over the threshold, assessed the situation and knew, at once, he was interrupting. Extending his hand, he offered, "Hello, Mr. and Mrs. Crowley. I'm sorry to intrude. Roger tells me you have a cottage to rent. Perhaps we can talk tomorrow."

Ben and Elizabeth looked at me, as if I was from Mars, but I was beaming, and didn't give them a chance to say no.

"Dad. Zebedia helped me get the car started this afternoon after it died in a puddle of water."

"Died in a puddle of water?"

"Let him finish, Ben." Mom interjected. I didn't miss a beat warming to my sales pitch.

"Did you know our year BMW has a problem with water coming from the under carriage, Dad?"

"No, I didn't know that, son. How much do I owe you, sir?"

"You don't owe me anything, Mr. Crowley. I'd like to rent your cottage, but this is an inconvenient time. I'll come back."

"I think that's probably a good idea, Mr. Ah . . . I didn't get your last name."

"Its just Zebedia, Mr. Crowley. I know it's strange, but I've never had another that I know of."

"Dad, Zebedia has no place to stay tonight, and its getting cold. Can't he use the cottage."

"There isn't any oil for the furnace, Rog."

"I'll get the wood stove going. The place will be toasty in an hour. Please?"

"My son is determined, Mr. Zebedia, and the cottage is empty."

Zebedia spoke quietly. "There is another problem Roger neglected to explain, I won't be able to pay you until I receive my first paycheck, but I will do some chores before, to pay for the firewood."

"And I have some money saved, Dad. Zeb is welcomed to that."

Dad's jaw dropped, when I said that. Mom's eyes grew wide as saucers.

"The money you saved for a car, Roger?"

I nodded up and down. Dad turned back towards, Zeb. "You must have made some impression, Mr. . . . ah, ah Zebedia."

I knew Dad was softening, so I threw him a fastball to go along with my first curve.

"Yeah. What's the big deal? Its only money."

"No big deal." Dad said sarcasm dripping off every word. "But you did threaten to remove your brother and sister's hands if they touched that money."

He turned and spoke directly to Zeb, "Mr. Zebedia, I don't know what you said or did, but anyone who could separate Roger from his car money deserves a place to sleep."

Dad was in partial shock from my sudden streak of generosity. Mom was quiet, not quite sure what to say.

I remember yelping with glee, like a rodeo star, further confusing my parents. I raced over to Timmy and Linda, and dragged them up, "C'mon you two."

"You want us to help?" Linda asked, grinning broadly.

Mom couldn't believe this. "What is going on? What's gotten in to you, Roger?"

I answered honestly, "I don't know, Mom, but it sure feels good." I turned back to my little brother and sister," Let's go, gang."

Linda, Timmy and I hurried out the door, and then stopped to wait for Zeb.

He hoisted his bag once more, thanked Mom and Dad adding. "I have some stories to tell the kids, if you don't mind. It will take a while." Then he said something unusual. "Be gentle with one another, while you find your way." Mom and Dad looked at each other surprised.

Mom spoke to Zeb. "No scary stories, Zebedia. Timmy has nightmares."

"None tonight, Mrs. Crowley. He will sleep peacefully. I promise."

Mom didn't know why, but believed him. Zebedia closed the door softly behind him and was gone. Mom looked at Dad who offered, "Who was that caped crusader?"

They both laughed and we heard it from outside. It was the first time they laughed together in over a year. It was the first of many magical moments for all of us.

CHAPTER THREE

Linda dragged Timmy along, walking and running, trying to keep up with my long strides. Zebedia caught up, took Linda's free hand and slowed them to a stroll, allowing him to take in his surroundings and me to speed ahead. Our lawn was neatly arranged with stone gardens passing in and around trees. Flowers of every color and description burst into bloom when life returned in spring.

Zeb stopped. Turning his head from side to side he saw flowers, with bees buzzing, working everywhere, while birds sang and squirrels danced in the treetops. He quietly experienced all that was going on around him. He tried to teach us all to use our minds this way. He joked it was better than Valium, but he was serious. He taught us to journey anywhere in the universe at any time in history. To do this we merely close our eyes, empty our minds, become quiet. In the vast silence we then open the door to whatever adventure we desire. Our connection to pure universal energy creates our images. The power of our unconscious awareness is unlimited. It is where God, the Great Spirit, Yahweh, Jehovah, Vishnu, the list is endless, reside. The destination is the same for all of us no matter what we believe. I would visit the beach or a favorite little rock next to a small stream behind our high school. It isn't as glamorous as visualizing a trip to Europe or Spring Break in Florida, but it brings me peace, like Zeb visiting the void.

Zebedia traveled there often when he meditated. I try to visit everyday in my own capacity. Some call it power of positive thinking, some call it prayer, some meditation; it is much more than all of these. It is an awareness of life, without struggle. It is an exploration of infinite possibilities within us. Gene Rodenberry called space the final frontier. With fifty trillion cells separating within us everyday, we are space and beyond. We are the mystery of the universe. We are an enormous exploration. Call it meditation, prayer or whatever. It liberates and empowers. It works.

Zeb spent a few moments in the spring sunshine feeling its warmth on his skin, then returned to us. The garden lay cold, flat and still; frozen in place, like a picture. Some of the yard was brightly lit, illuminated by floodlights mounted on our house. Further along, where the strength of the lights dissipated, shadows deepened. Only low-level lanterns marked the path through the trees.

Beyond the trees, in a clearing, our cottage came into view, visible against the moonlit sky, sitting on a small rise at the rear of the property. It stood at the edge of the clearing, carved out of the scrub brush and trees, positioned with infinite care, by my grandpa. Zebedia felt Linda's small hand tighten around his own, as eerie night sounds engulfed us, and he squeezed back gently to reassure her. A whisper of air floated through the branches above them and Zeb glanced up. He stopped again. Linda and Timmy followed his gaze.

He chuckled and said, "Oh sure." Looking directly at an empty branch, then paused, listened, and answered, "They know that." He turned to Timmy and Linda and asked, "Don't you?" They both shook their heads eagerly up and down without knowing anything at all.

He looked back up into the branches just as they shivered again with a slight breeze and Zebedia spoke, "I'll tell them. Take care now."

Linda looked at Timmy staring blankly. He had no idea who Zeb was speaking to either, so Linda asked, "Who are you talking to?"

Zeb answered, "You didn't see them? I'm sorry. I should have introduced you so you can see them. I'll remember next time."

"See who?" Timmy chimed in.

"Your guardian angels, silly."

"Really! Where?" They both asked looking up.

Zeb smiled, pointing. "Up there. They intend to take good care of both of you. You should never feel alone."

Linda stared at Zeb wide eyed, "They knew I was afraid." Zeb nodded. "And you spoke to them?" He nodded again.

"Cool! Was your guardian angel here too?"

Zeb grew serious, his soft eyes sparkling, "Mine never leaves me. She knows I need her often."

"Is she here now."

"Right beside me."

"Hello Mr. Zebedia's angel." Timmy chimed in.

A glow appeared next to Zeb. Timmy walked right up to it peering inside.

Zeb and Linda laughed out loud.

He marveled at children's innate ability to accept things on faith. They trust implicitly. As childhood fades, innocence gives way to grownup lessons of doubt, fear, and envy.

I reached the cottage first and flicked the lights on. There were two small windows on either side of a door in the center. It was a cape cod style cottage. A sharply sloping roof began just above entrance, and raced almost straight up to a thin peak. This high roof allowed for a sleeping loft, with two bedrooms, above the main floor.

"Roger's inside," Linda said when she saw the lights blink on, as much to reassure herself as inform Zeb and Timmy.

They broke free of the brush-lined path into grandpa's clearing. It was covered with gardens, full of frozen dead weeds overflowing surrounding low stone borders. The stone borders were cracked in places, while shutters hung at odd angles beside several broken windowpanes. Aside from the obvious lack of recent maintenance, the cottage seemed to belong in the clearing, built to someone's exacting specifications. The entire scene exuded a feeling of gentle harmony. It was put together with great care; attention paid to blending everything to the naturally elegant surroundings. Though in disarray, everything fit.

Zeb walked through the door and smelled must. It went straight to his sinuses, like fresh cut onions to your eyes. Inside was clammy, cold, neglected, but in order. I was pulling covers off furniture and already had a fire blazing in the stove, which gobbled up the musty odor in short order. Electricity was the only concession to modern convenience grandpa condoned in his home. I took full advantage, setting a small electric fan in front of the stove. It rotated from side to side radiating heat from the fire into every corner of the cottage. The furniture was hand made, of rough-hewn wood. Every piece was perfect except Grandpa's dining table. It leaned and rocked on a short leg. He made it short purposely, as a constant reminder he made mistakes. It made him more patient with everyone around him. I remember him saying to me one day when I was really angry with myself for something or other I did.

"Rog, even Monkey's fall out of trees once in a while. If they learn from it, the Tiger doesn't get them."

I stood thinking of my grandpa, wondering why I hadn't more often. I was very close to him, and realized, I missed his wisdom and his gentle smile. I could almost feel him in the room and see him sitting at the table. He was my best friend. Suddenly, I realized I was angry with him for leaving me when he died. He tried hard to prepare me; I refused to believe it would ever happen. I hadn't been in this cottage since his death. It felt good to be back. It felt good to remember Grandpa in a way he would have liked, with a smile in my heart.

Water had to be pumped by hand at the sink for washing, filling the toilet, or the tub, which set behind a curtain in the corner.

Zeb stopped just inside the door and dropped his bag. He looked around without speaking and I grew nervous. Our Grandpa's tastes were simple. Though he could afford much more, he never cared for modern frills. I was certain Zeb would feel the love in the cottage. Now I wasn't sure at all. He just stood there for several minutes looking around, taking everything in with his eyes. The silence grew enormous.

"You don't like it, do you?" I inquired uneasily.

Zeb didn't answer. He stood silently staring, as heat from the stove took hold. Linda and Timmy wandered over to warm their feet and hands.

"Say something, Zeb." I implored him.

He moved over, encircled me in his arms, and gave me a huge hug. "It's perfect. Thank you." He answered.

I wasn't frightened or even surprised when Zebedia hugged me. It seemed a perfectly natural thing for him to do, and I was elated.

"I'm glad you like it." I answered.

"Remember, I told your friends something would turn up. Well, I never expected anything as beautiful as this. If I built it for myself I couldn't have done better, Roger. I wouldn't change a thing."

I never thought of Grandpa's cottage as beautiful. Now I looked at it in the soft light of dim electric bulbs with shadows dancing on walls cast by flickering flames, and I whispered, "He's right."

It is beautiful. It wasn't small, but all the space was used. It was an easy room, which called out "Welcome."

I tried to lift Zeb's bag and almost fell to the floor. "What do you have in here, Zeb."

"Everything." He answered simply.

Zeb didn't elaborate. I'd already realized it did no good to press him. He took the bag from me, lifting it easily onto a chair. His strength was astonishing, because he wasn't a large man, and he carried this bag seventy-five miles that I knew of. Opening it, he began removing things. There were the dried fruits, along with several other small containers. Setting them on the table, he pointed to the cabinets.

"Are there any cups?" He asked.

I moved to the cabinets, took a few down, washed them at the sink and brought them over.

Zeb opened his containers filled a well-worn kettle at the pump and set it on top of the stove; then drew all of us to the table.

Setting the containers in a row he asked, "What flavor tea would you like? I have orange, herb, mint, cinnamon and apple."

Timmy answered, "I like cinnamon . . . and apples."

Zeb looked at him seriously, but kept his voice light when he answered, "You have to make this difficult, eh? All right, we'll mix the apple and cinnamon, how does that sound for everyone?"

"Sounds great." Timmy replied in a voice much older than his years.

"I like that kind, too." Linda added.

"Ditto." I said.

"Apple and cinnamon it is." Zeb concluded; retrieved the kettle and poured four cups. He set out shortbread and dried fruit on the table and we sat down to eat. Before distributing the bread, Zeb bowed his head. We watched. He waited. Then we followed his example.

After a quiet moment, he raised his head and smiled. "I don't know about you guys, but I wanted to say thank you for such pleasant company and for my obvious good fortune."

He indicated our surroundings with a wave of his hand, then passed the strange meal and we ate. Timmy and Linda tasted it tentatively at first, then dove in. I still wouldn't eat the dried fruit, but nibbled on short bread, and drank my tea, surprised at how good I felt inside. I hadn't eaten supper with Tim and Linda in a while, and was enjoying the time with them. I was at ease, and wasn't interested in racing off anywhere.

Zeb asked us about ourselves; what we liked to do and what we thought. We talked and laughed and he listened, interjecting a thought here, an idea there. Mostly, he just listened, genuinely interested in what we had to say, and enjoying the time with us. We finished dinner, cleaned up together, as if it was something we did every day, and moved over to the stove. A small squirrel found his way into the cottage. Linda jumped, but Zeb gently grabbed her arm and said, "Watch! He is more frightened than you, but he is hungry." He took some nuts from one of his little plastic bags and set them near the squirrel, who grabbed one in his tiny hands, rolled it over twice, nibbled, and then stuck it in his mouth. Turning, he quickly raced to the window. We laughed, because he acted as if he would punch someone if they tried to take his nut away. Just at the window he stopped, looked back, as if to say, "Thanks!" Then he was gone.

"Guess he didn't figure on such a long winter, either?" I said, and it was true.

This winter had been long and brutal, all up and down the Northeast Seaboard. Severe cold and storms were the rule instead of the rarity and everyone was tired of gray skies and gloomy days. Tempers flared easily. People were long passed ready for spring to arrive, with its warmer weather and access to outdoor activities. Everyone awaited its coming with anxious hearts, and I shivered to think what might happen if it failed to arrive.

An hour and ten minutes south of Manhattan, in early March, flowers were normally springing to life. This year, spring lay trapped frozen in the earth and the fire in the stove felt awfully good. We gathered our chairs close around, and Zeb gave us each a little more tea.

This time, he added a few extra drops of honey and Linda said, "This is good. It tastes like Red Hots."

Zeb asked, "What are Red Hots?"

Timmy chimed in, "You don't know what Red Hots are? Are you from, outer space or something?"

"Timmy!" Linda rebuffed him, but Zeb silenced her with a wink.

"Do you know what Babka is, or Black Bean soup, Timmy?"

Our little brother shook his head from side to side, a look of consternation on his face.

"Well then, we have a lot to discuss, don't we?"

Zeb spoke directly to him and Timmy replied, feeling very important, "If you're willing to listen, I will teach you everything I know about candy, Zeb."

Linda and I laughed out loud, but Timmy remained confident, and Zeb replied. "I'm sure you will, sir." He reached out to shake Timmy's hand and held it gently, as if it were a great treasure and I stored this simple gesture in memory. I was quickly coming to a realization. Strength and courage didn't need to be loud and boastful. Zeb was as kind and gentle as he appeared.

We talked of everything and anything that night, until Timmy and Linda were sound asleep in front of the stove. Then, Zeb and I talked some more, in quiet tones. We sat near the stove enjoying its warmth. There came a gentle, barely audible tap at the door. I opened it on Mom and Dad.

"We were getting worried." Mom explained.

I was annoyed at the intrusion and snapped. "Why? You knew where we . . ."

Zeb cut me off, "You were gone for a long while with a stranger, Roger."

Then he added. "I'm sorry, Mrs. Crowley. I enjoy their company enormously. We had something to eat, talked and time just flew. Thank you for letting them stay to keep me company. Would you care for some tea?"

"Perhaps another time. It's a school night and I would like them in bed."

"They are sound asleep already, Mrs. Crowley. Would you like to let them sleep where they are?"

"What do you think, Ben?" She asked my Dad.

Ben turned to me and asked, "Will you stay here with them, Rog?"

"That's not very nice, Dad." I replied before Zeb had a chance to speak, but he cut me off again, and I glared at him. "Your father's concern is natural, Roger. There is no need for you to defend me. Besides, it will give us the chance to finish our conversation."

"All right." I answered still bristling.

"Good, it's settled and the offer of tea still stands."

"I'd love a cup." Mom changed her mind, and Dad added, "I'd like one too, if its not too much trouble.

They were drawn to Zeb, as all of us were. He was easy to talk to. I watched him prepare two more cups of steaming hot tea.

"Roger tells me you were upset with his SAT scores. Are they very important?"

Dad shifted uncomfortably in his chair and gave me a look, wondering why I would tell this to a stranger. I shrugged and sipped my tea, enjoying his discomfort.

Dad answered. "They are, if he wants to get into my Alma Mater. His grades are fine, but SAT test scores carry a lot of weight."

"I know what you mean. I've been questioned by some brilliant scholars over the years." Zeb furrowed his brow in thought and added, "I find there is rarely a question in any discipline, which has only one answer. This is also true of life, don't you think?"

Mom interceded on my behalf, "Roger tries very hard and gets excellent grades, but standardized tests give him trouble."

"Did he start school early?" Zeb asked.

Dad thought back over the years, "As a matter of fact he did. We just moved into town and were anxious for him to make new friends, so we put him in school a half a year early. He was the youngest in his class."

"Not was, Mr. Crowley." Zeb corrected Dad.

Mom asked, "Do you think it affected him."

Zeb smiled, exposing even rows of spotless white teeth. "Who can be certain, Mrs. Crowley. He gets good grades, so it couldn't have hurt him too badly, but it is a struggle for a younger child trying to compete all the time with older children. A half-year makes a difference at an early age. Is it very important he attend your Alma Mater, Mr. Crowley?"

He turned back to Dad.

"It's been a dream of ours since he was a baby."

"Yours and Roger's?"

"No, his and Mom's, Zeb." I interjected, trying to keep the edge out of my voice and failing.

Zeb was easily putting questions we avoided into words. Bathed in the flickering firelight, we were connecting.

More importantly Mom and Dad were remembering good times and I added, "They attended college together."

This time my voice was soft and kind. It felt strange, but in the gentle glow of the fire I didn't see them as my parents. They were people, with faults and fears just like me. I felt a rush of affection towards them. At the same time I was sorry for their trouble with each other.

"Really, is that how you met?" Zeb continued.

I settled to listen, enjoying being here with my family.

Dad answered, "We were members of the cheering squad together. I'd drop my mega-phone, and Beth would dive onto my uplifted hands. She was the best."

He was daydreaming; reminiscing about their youth.

"I wasn't that good." Mom stated, emphatically.

Dad didn't hesitate, "Oh, yes you were that good, and you were the best looking."

He grinned at her. There was a special lilt to his voice and a little twinkle in his eyes.

"You did wonders for that short skirt and white sweater with the large letter on the front. It showed off your great figure."

"Stop it, Ben. You're embarrassing me."

But he wasn't. I could tell she was enjoying his attention. Linda and Timmy woke to the sound of Mom and Dad's laughter, while I sat wondering, "How in God's name. . . ?" and just as the thought entered my head, Zeb turned and smiled at me. I swear he knew exactly what was in my mind. I shivered, shifting uncomfortably.

Mom and Dad went on and on about college, old friends and how happy they were when I was born. They told Zeb stories of their early life together, the good and the bad. Now, looking back, even the bad times take their place in our history and don't seem so bad, though at the time they were monumental. Our family history would be incomplete without some struggle. Grandpa helped us a lot financially, but his emotional support was most important. I don't think any of us realized what a nurturing, calming influence he was. We didn't realize how much we missed him and Grandma, but it all came back in a rush.

Timmy crawled into Mom's lap and Linda snuggled close to my leg. We knew our parents loved us. That was never a question. They lost each other along the way. They needed to find a way back. I remember stroking Linda's hair absently, wondering if this was the beginning of their journey.

By the time we were ready to leave, all of Zeb's apple and cinnamon tea was gone. Timmy and Linda were wide-awake. I didn't say anything else. I was content sitting there, embraced by affection born of years of caring, sacrifice and work. In the course of a couple hours we rehashed our lives together, and I began to acknowledge a very special gift. Our family was more important to me than I realized. I was beginning to understand people were too. I cared what happened, not only to us, but others as well, and it was an excellent feeling. We walked out arm in arm.

Dad stopped at the door and turned to Zeb. "Thank you Mr. Ah . . . sorry, force of habit. Thank you, Zebedia."

"You're welcome, Mr. Crowley."

"Ben, Zebedia. My friends all call me Ben."

"Benjamin is a good name. Thank you, Ben."

Dad started down the path after us, then stopped again. "One other thing, Zeb. About the rent."

Zeb said, "I can pay you out of my first paycheck. Until then, I will do chores."

"I was thinking." Dad cut him off, as if he hadn't heard a word Zeb said. "My Dad helped me financially in the beginning. Wouldn't have made it without that help. This was an awful nice visit. My Pop's cottage hasn't heard laughter since he died a while back. He was a nice man, who loved laughter, and his family."

"I know." Zeb relied in quiet whisper.

"Did you know my father?"

"Not the way you think, but yes, I know him."

We were waiting close by for Dad to finish. Zeb's use of the present tense was lost on him, but I was listening closely for a couple hours and I caught it. It wasn't my imagination when Zeb looked directly at me, smiled and winked, as if we just shared a secret no one else understood. I remember feeling warm inside.

"Your son is a lot like him, don't you think?"

Dad turned and looked at me, as if viewing a mountain of gold then said, "Yes, he is. Perhaps that's why we argue."

Then he smiled and added, "He is a touch more stubborn."

We laughed together, sharing something between father and son that grows without us ever knowing, a bond of hope and aspiration for each other. A bond of knowing each of us is part of the other, forever entwined in characteristics, and emotion. The father knows if he does his job well, the son will be a better human being. He can rest easy. I knew then and there, my Grandpa rested very easy, because my Dad was a special man

Dad looked around the clearing, and waved his hand encompassing the entire yard, "I know my father will like you living here, Zeb. At any rate you don't seem like a stranger anymore, so the chores you do will cover the rent. My Dad was a simple man. You are too."

"Thank you, Ben. That's very kind."

Dad turned, and trotted towards us. There was a spring in his step that hadn't been for a long time. He put his arm around Mom and me, and I reached for the little ones. We started back towards the main house. Mom glanced over her shoulder, back at Zebedia, encased in shadow. I followed her gaze. Zeb's hands were raised towards the sky. He appeared to be speaking to someone she could not see. There was a touch of regret in her eyes. I saw her turn and read the sadness playing about her face. Then she looked up at my Dad, and her faced changed. A small smile appeared, as she rested her head on his shoulder. I raised my eyes towards the stars blinking above straining to see something spiritual. Failing that, but clinging to my little sister and brothers hands tightly, I looked at them and began to hope.

CHAPTER FOUR

Zeb woke as the black night sky faded light gray, then turned pale blue. The sun spewed billows of molten orange liquid gas, just above the horizon like a rocket lurching skyward. He moved about quickly and quietly with an economy of motion, resembling dancing. His comfortable set of clothes needed washing. There was much to do before work.

Reaching into his bag he retrieved several nuts, a container of orange juice, and an old gold leaf book, he'd gotten years before. It was a history of places that, as he read, were familiar to him. It was almost like reading a high school yearbook. Noah, Moses and Ruth were old friends. Their souls were all around him. Matthew, Paul and others discussed and recorded every detail, as nearly perfectly, as any human could. It was a painstaking job, using bare hands and quill pens, but they did it lovingly and well.

He sat on his low bed, feet on the floor, absorbing words his Father wanted passed on. Zeb loved his white plastic copy engraved with gold leaf inscription, which read "Children's Bible." Not a day dawned he didn't read a couple pages. It helped with his human existence, and the trials and temptations that went with it.

I noticed the way he looked at my Mom our first night together, and knew he struggled with his feelings like the rest of us. It heightened his allure.

When he finished reading, he closed his eyes. Breathing deeply, he willed evil out of his body; physically, and mentally draining anger and fear from his heart. He often told me this was a necessary part of everyone's day. He tried to teach me, but at seventeen

I wasn't ready to meditate. At seventeen I was immortal, as are all seventeen-year-olds. Then he rose and stretched towards the sky, as if he would touch the sun. Finally he stretched his legs and was ready. It was good beginning to the day.

He crossed to the stove, stirred the embers to life and added another log. Then he moved to the sink, pumped water for tea and more for a bath. The cold raised small bumps of gooseflesh over his sinewy well-muscled frame, as he washed. Stepping naked from the tub he toweled himself briskly before preparing his tea. While it was brewing, he put on his better set of clothes for work. The shirt was a soft tan color and his pants were navy blue and baggy. They belonged to a rather large man from South Africa who Zeb met on a train. They hit it off immediately. Zeb told me of their lively conversation, because their ideas differed greatly on religion. On kindness and humanity they were united. The man had snow white hair starkly contrasting his blue black skin, wrinkled like soft leather. He told Zeb he was nearly eighty-five years old when he stopped working and started traveling and had been on the go ever since, which was nearly four years. He had given Zeb the trousers and shirt to remember him by. It was the type of simple generosity Zeb appreciated most. He hugged Bradur, knowing he would never forget him, and he would never see him again in this life.

Zeb slipped on his work pants without underclothes, which he did not own. Then, lifted his kettle, laid it on its side, and pressed off his clean shirt and pants. Moving easily, he lifted his jacket, and went into the yard, up the path towards the main house.

The night before, he noticed a rocking chair with a broken leg, and a little wooden bunny that had lost its ears. He lifted both items and returned to the cottage. It took less than a half-hour to carve pegs and drill holes to repair both items. He set them down and walked up the road to a small market, he noticed on his way here the night before. It was just past six A.M. when he came upon the owner carrying the daily papers into the store. Zeb placed one bundle under his arm lifted two more in his hands and set them inside the door, behind the short gray man who could manage only one bundle at a time. Zeb returned outside and brought the remaining bundles in. Jack, the storeowner eyed him suspiciously, and Zeb smiled.

"Thanks a lot for the help, son. What's your name?"

"Zebedia."

"Listen, Zebe . . . Zebe . . ."

"Zebedia."

"Whatever. Listen I don't know what you're selling, but whatever it is can wait for coffee. After we have coffee I can let you down easy, son, because I don't need any more junk."

"Actually, I came to get something." Zeb told him.

Jack became even more animated.

"A customer. Well why didn't you say so? I should have known. No salesman in his right mind gets up at five in the morning. As a matter of fact, no one in their right mind gets up at five in the morning, which doesn't say much for me, cause I been doing it fifty years. So what can I do you out of today, Zebe . . ."

"Zebedia."

"Whatever. Well, I'm waiting son, and I'm going to be dead a long time. So let's get a move on. What do you want?"

"Do you know the Crowley's?"

"Of course I know the Crowley's. I know Benny since he was a baby, and Ben Sr., God rest his soul, went to school with my own son; buried both boys about the same time last year. I know the family since Christ was an altar boy, son. What of it?"

Zebedia couldn't help himself. The laughter came from somewhere deep inside him. This outrageous man, at seventy-nine years, remained a boiling pot of vivacious humanity. Zeb loved everything about him.

Regaining control, Zeb continued. "I am staying in their cottage and have some work to do. I could use some of that wood glue you have over on the shelf, but I can't pay you till the end of the week."

"Can't pay, you say? Do I look like a fool to you, son? I knew you had to be crazy, being up this early in the morning. It figures my first customer of the day can't pay. Probably set the tone for the whole darn week. How long do you think I'd be in business if everyone couldn't pay, son? How do you like your coffee?"

"I'd prefer tea, if you have some."

"This is a take it or leave it proposition, Zebedia. It's uncanny son."

"What is?" Zeb asked.

"My mind, boy. My mind. As soon as you asked me to extend you credit, I remembered your name. Uncanny how that happens. Anyway, what the heck was I talking about?"

"The coffee."

"Oh yes, the coffee. You take coffee; stay and have it with me or you leave without your wood glue. I stopped making tea since Emma is gone."

"I'm sorry. How long ago did your wife pass away."

Jack slammed the counter with the palm of his hand. Zeb instinctively stepped back. Jack roared, laughing until his eyes bulged out of his head and great rumblings and rattling came from his chest. Slowly he straightened up wiping tears of mirth from his face. "Emma was my dog, son, and she left cause I made her tea wrong one day. My mind isn't what it used to be, and I put sugar in it."

Jack laughed again and Zeb let the laughter flow over him like a balm. He recalled situations where laughter alone saved hundreds of lives. He determined to make this his first stop in the morning.

"May I come by tomorrow, Jack."

"This isn't Father Green's offertory mass, Zebedia. Unless people come through that door I don't eat. Besides I have to keep you healthy at least until the weekend."

He handed Zeb a steaming cup of coffee, which he sipped, while looking at Jack perplexed, and Jack laughed again. "So's I can collect for the glue, Zeb. C'mon, boy, you didn't even walk out the door with it and already you're forgetting to come back and pay for it."

Zebedia laughed again in spite of himself. Jack's sense of humor was contagious and Zeb was truly sorry he couldn't stay and listen to the old man talk, because he knew this man, with shirt sleeves rolled up to his elbows, had stories to tell.

"Thanks for the coffee, Jack. Maybe I'll see you later."

"It was nice having someone to talk with so early, Zeb. Is it okay if I call you Zeb?"

"Of course. I'd like that. May I call you Jack."

"Call me anything you like, son, just don't call me late for dinner."

Zebedia took the glue from the shelf and headed for the door.

"Don't forget where you got that glue," Jack called after him.

Zeb turned and answered, "I get the feeling that would be just about impossible."

Jack chuckled, and Zeb pushed open the heavy glass door. Just as he stepped through, a dog appeared from nowhere and hurried inside, as the door settled in its frame.

Zebedia heard Jack's raspy voice saying, "Emma! Emma! Is that you girl?"

Then the door settled and Zeb walked away. He didn't want to embarrass his new friend, but a smile played in his eyes as he walked home. Jack made Emma tea and set it down on the floor alternately rubbing his chin and looking out after the new stranger. Emma slurped her tea contentedly, but how could that be? Emma was a figment of Jack's imagination. A dog he created to keep him company. Now, here she was exactly as he knew her in his head.

"I am getting old." He said, looking at the dog.

"Maybe I did have a dog. Nah."

He determined to question Zeb about it later, now he had work to do. Everyone would be in soon for breakfast and coffee.

CHAPTER FIVE

Zeb hummed a tune that was haunting him for days. He was humming as he moved up the path to his door. Once inside, he made quick work of re-assembling the chair and attaching the bunny's ears. He clamped them and set them by the stove to dry. Stripping off his clothes, he flipped them into the tub and washed them in his bath water, expressly saved for that purpose. Standing, he wrung the excess water out, and also placed them near the stove. Wiping his hands, slipping into clean clothes and hiking shoes he walked out.

The sun hovered just above the trees, as he stepped off the porch and looked around. Neglected bushes and twigs lay strewn everywhere. Small pieces of paper clung to frozen blades of grass. With a little effort, Zeb knew he could put things right. He picked up several small pieces of paper as he walked along. He did this intentionally. When he noticed something to be done he began immediately if possible. Later he told me why.

"Most jobs, begun, get completed, Roger."

Teaching me simply to begin was a most valuable lesson. To this day I begin things as soon as I think of them. People often fail simply because they fear the first step. Zeb paced away hard, swinging his arms. Quickly his cottage was swallowed by the landscape and the main house was receding in the distance behind him. Jack, standing outside his door enjoying the warm sun, saw Zeb and waved. Zeb waved back, but didn't stop. He was anxious to get to work.

Every so often Zeb passed a blue street sign bearing a large white H, posted on the roadside, marking his way. An oversized version of the same sign stood where the main road intersected with the Crowley's street. A man came trotting by, wearing a brightly colored jacket and tight fitting, spandex pants. His bright orange wool hat was pulled down over his ears and steam rose from his body, as he went by.

"Morning," Zeb said, as he approached. The man ignored Zeb, continuing on his way. Zeb didn't mind. He said a silent blessing for him and released the intention into the universe. The large sign pointed right, Zeb turned. A half-hour passed, which left an hour and a half to get to work at nine.

He flagged down a police car to ask the distance to the hospital and the young officer in the car looked him up and down, then answered, "It's about five miles, straight down Providence Road on the left. Can't miss it. You're new around here, aren't you?"

Zeb answered, "Yes, I just got in last night."

The young officer offered, "I live near here. My name is John Sullivan, and my wife's name is Cathy. If you need anything, give a shout."

The young officer had an open friendly face, but Zeb sensed something more. The Hospital was only five miles up the road, which gave Zeb time to spare. He continued the conversation.

"Any children, officer?" He inquired.

"Amy's five and Zack is almost nine." John answered, relaxing a little.

"You don't look old enough to have a nine-year-old son."

"I'm not." The young officer answered, anguish passing briefly on his face, but a smile returned quickly. Zeb could almost feel John's pain. The boy obviously wanted to talk, but his pride wouldn't let him exhibit weakness. He was like a lot of people. We keep hurt feelings hidden until we can't handle the pressure any longer. Some turn to alcohol, or drugs as an escape. Others run away. Others continue as best they can. Zeb hoped the young police officer would work out his problem, whatever it might be.

Zeb felt people's stress, especially when he dealt with many unhappy people at the same time. Negative emotions squeezed him like a sponge, but he enjoyed people and didn't mind listening when they wanted to talk. He never pried and rarely offered advice, as much as a different perspective. Once when a friend was working on a ladder with a power tool he cut himself severely. Zeb listened to him complain for about fifteen minutes about how these things always happened to him. Zeb pointed out how fortunate he was the tool hadn't broken his arm or knocked him off the ladder.

The friend laughed and said, "You always do that, Zeb."

Zeb asked what he meant and he answered, "You always find the good in the bad."

Zeb knew negative thoughts had a cumulative affect on people who harbored them. Gripe piled upon gripe, until the burden becomes too great to bear. He taught me to remain positive as much as possible, realizing the bad flows into good. He also said an extraordinary thing, which is engraved, on my conscious. He told me to be careful of what I say. I asked him what he meant.

He laughed and said he called it the, "I am Syndrome." I am ugly, I am fat, I am useless; things of a negative nature.

I asked him why it was important and he said, "Roger, it is important because in this dimension perception becomes reality. More importantly, we are the sum total of our expectations. What we expect to happen becomes manifest in our reality."

I thought about it a long time. I didn't fully understand and am still working on it to this day. I know it is true. I have faith in it.

The extent or power of opposites are defined by each other. People's thoughts affect their success or destruction. Situations arise when we fail to believe things can get better, and help is only a whispered prayer away or a silent expectation of good things coming. Zebedia lost a lot in his reality. He watched friends put to death, their families ostracized, because of new religious beliefs. They maintained their faith, and it sustained them through terrible times. I became aware that no matter what happens in my brief lifetime, my soul is destined to continue. I began to enjoy good times and triumphs much more, knowing my effort, no matter how small, was worthwhile. I am the caretaker of an eternal life. Zebedia planted these seeds in my heart. It took ten years for them to flower.

John Sullivan's radio squawked, "Mrs. Abernathy can't find the door to her house . . . for the third time this week, Sulli."

John's face lit up.

"She can't find the door, officer?" Zeb asked.

John's voice lifted. "She's one-hundred-four-years-old. One of her neighbors called the station. Grace, that's her name, knows I'm on duty and wants to talk; won't let anyone else help her back into the house. She has Alzheimer's."

"That's too bad, officer."

"Call me John? We're going to be neighbors. What's your name?"

"Zebedia."

"No last name?"

"Just Zebedia."

John thought it a little odd.

"Mrs. Abernathy's house is on the way to the hospital, Zebedia. I'd be happy to give you a lift."

"Perhaps another morning. I promised I would walk. Besides, I want to find out how long it takes me to walk it."

"Are you a therapist or something?"

"No, I'm a maintenance man."

"C'mon, Zeb. What do you really do?"

Zeb thought for a moment. "I clean floors, fix doors, wash out toilets and try to make people smile."

John frowned. His sixth sense told him there was more to this man. "Well, it's been nice taking to you, Zeb."

"I think so too, and I'd like to tell you something if you don't mind?"

"What's that?" John asked defensively expecting a derogatory remark about police officers.

"Being a good cop is one of the hardest things on God's earth. It requires a lot of innate wisdom and patience."

John was surprised and delighted. His face lit up in a huge grin.

"That was a nice thing to say. I needed that more than you know this morning."

"I'm sorry your friend has Alzheimer's, and perhaps one day we can talk about your oldest child."

John was astonished. Anguish flashed in his eyes, but he ignored the last statement. He changed the subject quickly back to Grace Abernathy covering his own problems with thoughts of hers.

His face lightened, "Not as sorry as her neighbors, Zeb. One time she showed up on their porch dressed for the prom, looking for her date. Claire's husband, Harry, danced with her until I got there. Mrs. A kept telling him her dance card wasn't full yet. She kept him dancing with no music for a full hour."

"Good thing you were on duty, huh?" Zebedia asked, sensing something, feeling his way, drawing John out into the sunlight.

"I wasn't, and my wife, is getting tired of me going over there to help at all hours of the day and night. I have to go, Zeb. Good luck at work."

"Thanks. As to the thing I would like you to do."

"What is it?"

"Just put it down when it gets to heavy, John. Put it down and take a breath."

"Put what down, Zebedia?" Sulli asked

Zeb replied, "The past, Sulli. Put it down by the side of the road and leave it for the trash."

John was astonished once more.

"I've got to go, Zeb, but I'll think about what you said."

"I can't ask more than that," Zeb said to himself as John drove away. Zeb slowly raised his hands, palms up, stretching towards the sky. He stood there alone in the morning sun for a few minutes. A smile played on his face. Lowering his hands, he opened his eyes and shivered at the simple, sensual feeling of the sun's warmth on a cold day. It was one of his Father's great gifts to men. He moved along easily, taking in and talking to his surroundings, as if getting acquainted.

A car passed and the driver slowed to stare at Zeb, talking to the trees, and street signs. The driver shook his head from side to side in pity, misunderstanding completely. Zeb saw him, waved, moved towards the car and the driver sped away. Zeb laughed, wondering how anyone could be frightened of him, but then he considered the times. Fear resulted from man's inhumanity. Hiding behind differences in class, race and religion adds to our ignorance.

Unfortunately ten years have passed and, with the benefit of hindsight I know many fears are well founded. Rogue individuals roam the earth, abducting, abusing and murdering, often for no reason at all. Fear is everywhere, and it isn't getting better.

Zeb wanted us to understand that possessing anything only leads to jealousy. He wanted us to wonder what kind of world would it be if no one shared anything; if no one sacrificed anything for another's good? It's taken me ten years, but I am beginning to understand the unlimited possibilities to love, that exist each and everyday, when we refuse to judge anyone.

Zeb stopped to watch a horse walking in a field. Then he spoke to a rabbit darting from place to place in search of food. All at once he began to whistle the same tune as before. A thought crept into his head. It was a memory, of one of the nicest men he ever knew. He hadn't really met him, but he had listened to him and walked miles with him. He recalled a favorite quote.

"I have been to the mountaintop."

Wonderful people existed and nature created colorful shows everyday to lift our spirits. Martin understood the power of people coming together. He also liked the ladies and Zeb understood that too. He could feel it in his own gut. Zeb liked the ladies more than he should. He was attracted to my mom, but he wasn't guilty. Zeb whispered a silent, "Thanks," for this rich gift of raw emotion. Emotions helped him understand the troubles people dealt with each day. These lusty thoughts made him vulnerable. They made him human. He explained this to me later. He allowed me to know his thoughts and the thoughts of others. This ability scared the hell out of me at first. I didn't know I would need it to write this down.

At seventeen, I already knew it was easy to fall in love. I fell in love once a week. I was very surprised I wasn't offended that Zeb loved my mom. It helped that he explained it early on instead of hiding it from me. Zeb explained things simply. He couldn't stop thoughts popping in and out of his head or control his attractions anymore than a young child. He took time with me to explain our ability to reason makes all the difference. We can wonder how things might turn out. We dream and fantasize without consequence as long as we don't hurt anyone. He never acted on his attraction and wouldn't risk damaging our family, further. He loved my mom in a special way. He loved the rest of us, too, and wouldn't disturb our newly re-discovered harmony. It made sense. I think about it, now, sometimes. I know I wouldn't have exercised the same restraint.

Zeb told me my mom was special, which wasn't a huge revelation. He said she had an old soul, which I didn't understand. The former was something I took for granted and shouldn't have. I vowed never to forget this lesson, but I did. I transgressed on friends over the years many times. Each time I did I felt worse. Each time I did I renewed my original vow. Someday soon I know I will be true to it. For now, I keep trying.

I remember feeling awful darn good to be alive on that cold morning in March, and I told God as much with a wink and a nod. You would have thought I knew Him personally. It strikes me funny now that ten years have past, and I realize I resisted knowing God at all, let alone personally. I was afraid to give up that little piece of myself, and most of us are. I was afraid to be hurt.

CHAPTER SIX

Officer Sullivan arrived at Grace Abernathy's house. She was sitting on her porch, wrapped in a blanket, sipping a steaming cup of coffee. The pot was within arms reach, on an electric hot plate, just inside the window next to her rocker.

"Hello, Johnny. What kept you?"

He smiled at the gentle rebuke, and put on his cap. Sulli was handsome in his dark brown uniform. Grace loved him, as she had her own sons, who were all gone. She out lived them all and began to wonder if her last husband was right about her out living everything on the planet. He used to tell her she was older than dirt.

"Hi, Grace," he called. "How are you?"

"Fine, fine. Come sit a minute."

At that moment John believed she was fine. She had some lucid moments, but this was different.

Her condition deteriorated rapidly over the last few months and he came by often, to avoid putting her in a home. A week ago they talked about it on a good day, and Grace tried to be brave, but cried anyway. John left her very upset. Cathy, his wife, didn't understand his time with Grace helped him as much as her. These visits helped balance all the bad he witnessed day by day on patrol.

Only a week ago he arrested a drug dealer on Central Avenue. The suspect turned out to be a sixteen-year-old, carrying two hundred thousand dollars in cash. He offered it all to Sulli, and more each week to let him go. For a cop, who had to tell his daughter she couldn't attend gymnastics with her friends, the bribe was tough to turn down. Knowing the boy would be back on the street in less than three hours didn't make it easier. Zeb was right about it being hard to be a good cop, and visiting Grace helped him. He talked to her about everything. Her stories of struggles growing up as a young black woman made his troubles pale by comparison. Through all her pain and triumphs she maintained a wicked sense of humor.

Born to former slaves, she became an accomplished author, and spent her later years promoting education as the cure for racism and hatred in America. Grace clung to the belief a person could never be truly free until his or her mind was open. She was widely criticized by white and black leaders alike for her views, and retired here, just after her eighty-eighth birthday. She had been a candidate for a Nobel Prize and often joked about which of three husbands she wanted to spend eternity with. She maintained if God had any mercy, eternity would be in a warmer climate than this, with a man a good deal younger than her. Sulli enjoyed her stories.

"You're enough to drive a body to drink, boy. Caused you a hell of a time these last few months haven't I? Couldn't have been much fun bringing a crazy woman home all the time, and Cathy can't be overjoyed with you."

"Cathy doesn't mind, Grace."

"Oh, pooh, boy. Don't lie to me. If it were me and I was home waiting for you, while you were over here, I'd be really pissed off."

Sulli smiled. "Some of the things you did were pretty funny."

"I imagine they were. I was a wild thing in my youth. Of course my youth lasted seventy years."

She laughed, reached for the coffeepot and poured him a cup. Then she added a drop of cream and one sugar. John eyed her suspiciously.

"I know how you like your coffee, even when I'm off my rocker."

She settled back tugging her quilt closer around her legs, as a cold gust of wind chased the dust off her porch. Her face became serious, almost urgent.

"There are things we need to discuss, Johnny. Unless you have an important call, tell them you don't wish to be bothered, and turn down the radio. There isn't much time."

John shifted uncomfortably.

"Don't say that, Grace. You might live fifty more years."

"Are you crazy, son?" She smiled. "You think I want to be all wrinkled and knarly for fifty more years?"

They chuckled together, and John answered, "No, I guess not."

"Johnny, I'm one-hundred-and-four years old. I had Alzheimer's, and . . ."

"Wait a minute Grace. What do you mean had? There is no cure."

"No cure doctors know of."

"What makes you think you're cured?"

"My mind healed, Johnny. I was standing on Mrs. Olgilvy's porch. A kinder woman there never was than Clare Olgilvy, John. You remember that when I'm gone, will you? She is the only one who greeted me warmly when I first moved here. We've had differences over the years, but the woman never speaks a harsh word about anyone.

"The night I made her Harry dance with me must have been very trying. I had him dancing for two hours, before they located you, and another half-hour before you arrived, had to soak his sore feet for hours. Harry and Clare never complained to anyone. I know they told you it was only an hour, now you know better. I never heard of anyone they told either. Tell me another couple who would have kept a juicy story like that to themselves. 'Nobel Laureate loses her mind.' A true friend, Clare Olgilvy; you remember to tell her often how much I cared for her.

"I want her to have all my furniture and the original bound copies of my writings. They're all signed. She and Harry should get a small fortune for them when they retire in a few years, which brings me to my present situation. I accumulated a sizable fortune over the years, Johnny. I want you, Cathy and the children to have most of it. My family is dead and I don't want to wait until the end. I want to see smiles on some faces before I go, especially your

Cathy. Don't be angry with her for guarding her time with you. She loves you, and you are hiding from her affection over here."

"You're talking like you're dying, Grace."

"We're all dying, silly boy. I am fortunate enough to know when."

"You know when you're going to die?"

"Two weeks, give or take. It's unimportant. I'm fine now, and that matters. A little while ago I stood on Clare's porch trying to sell her a fifty-pound bag of cat litter. Everyone knows Clare is allergic to cats, but she patiently explained, for, I think, the tenth time that she has no use for it, when, all of a sudden, my mind clears. I apologized to her, gave her a hug and left. You should have seen the relief on her face. I made some coffee and bundled up to wait for you, feeling better than I have in months."

"When did your mind clear?" Sulli asked, skepticism clearly in his voice.

"I told you while I was standing on Clare's porch.

"What time was that?"

"I guess about twenty minutes before you showed up."

"It has to be. There must be a connection." John said more to himself than to Grace.

"What has to be?"

"I was talking to a stranger about you around the time you say your mind cleared. He told me you would be all right. I didn't think anything of it."

"What does he look like?"

"A little older than me with a kind face and smiling eyes. His clothes are old, but immaculate. Everything about him is quiet, unassuming, yet magnetic. He claims he's a maintenance man, but his hands are much to clean for that type of work. He knew I had trouble with Zack, and said you will be all right, though we were miles away. It's strange, Grace. He has a job at the Holistic Hospital."

"Perhaps he is a Psychic."

"Its more than that, Grace."

"Your cop head is working overtime. It's a coincidence, Johnny. He said I would be all right. Did he also tell you I'm about to die?"

"No."

"Look, I have a couple weeks. I feel blessed, Johnny. Listen to me, boy. Everything is in my will, including instructions for my burial. For now, I want you to have this."

She reached under her quilt, withdrew a shopping bag and handed it to him.

Grace startled him with her enthusiasm. "You're acting as if you're happy to die."

"I am, son." He looked sad and she continued, "C'mon, John. My family is gone and I've lived an exceptional life. To have my mind returned, my greatest gift is a special blessing. Be happy for me. You are my best friend. Look in the bag."

He did and his eyes widened to the size of baseballs.

"That's only a small part of it." Grace said chuckling.

"I can't take this, Grace. I didn't visit to get your money. I came because I wanted to, because we are friends."

"I know that silly. You didn't know there was any money. Now drop this false pride and do what I'd do."

"What's that?" He asked and she was absolutely beaming.

"Have a party. Go have some fun with your family, and don't worry about what other people think. You are the only family I have left on this earth."

John gazed at her, unbelieving, wondering if he could trust this miracle, or if it was another stage of her disease. Grace hadn't stopped speaking.

"And I want you to help people in town, who deserve it, all right? Are you listening?"

He shook his head enthusiastically. "What? Yes of course I will, but how?"

"Later today I will transfer all my assets, about five million, I think, into a trust account in your name. I need an account number to move certificates and to close my own accounts."

Now John was certain this was only another stage of Grace's disease. A bag of money was one thing; five million was something else. Grace was as loony as ever.

"You have five million dollars, Grace?"

She knew he didn't believe her, but it didn't matter.

"Just come back this afternoon, Johnny."

"Yes ma'am."

He rose and kissed her cheek. Confident she was no better mentally. He had no intention of spending the money in the bag. They would need it for her care. Grace didn't fight him, she was tired and wanted to rest. Knowing her time was near, was a wonderful thing. She was experiencing the joy of a child first learning to understand things. Her curiosity was new and limitless, and she understood she was correct her whole life. Knowledge and understanding were the cure to hatred.

John walked to his car, turned, waved and Grace nodded without waving back. He would remember thinking it strange, when questioned later about her behavior, because Grace always waved. Then he got in and drove to town.

Passing Community Hospital, John noticed Zeb crossing the parking lot and glanced at his watch. It was twenty minutes to nine. He stopped the car and watched Zeb for a moment. A gang of tough kids from a bad section of town appeared. They crossed in front of Zeb. He stopped, spoke to them for a moment, then continued on without an angry word exchanged, disappearing inside the hospital. John turned into the lot, stopping near where the gang of kids was still standing.

A short curly haired Mexican boy approached the car. "Why are you guys here this early, man?" John asked.

Raphael answered, "One of the brothers was stabbed last night."

"Who was the guy you spoke to a couple of moments ago?"

"I don't know Sulli, but he's weird, man."

"How do you mean?"

"I figure the guys are going to initiate him, rough him up a little for kicks, you know?"

"What happened?"

He smiles and says he will be glad to meet all of us later and will enjoy speaking to us, but is late to work. He goes inside, and nobody moves. He's either the bravest or the dumbest man I ever met."

"You think someone spotted me, and that's why they let him go, Raph?"

"I doubt it. Pat me down will you, so they don't get suspicious."

John stepped out of his car, spun the undercover detective around, kicking his legs apart. "Why didn't they roust him, Raph?"

"I don't know, Sulli. They all froze when he spoke. They were actually listening."

John pushed Raphael away, roughly and said, "I'll see you later. Be careful."

"Always, brother." Raphael swaggered back over to the group pointing tauntingly at John, who returned to his patrol car, wondering about Zeb. Then he thought of Grace and decided to check Zeb out.

CHAPTER SEVEN

Zeb strolled past nurses' stations greeting everyone briefly, heading for the maintenance office. The hospital, set in a park, surrounded by homes with manicured lawns and white picket fences, was the first of its kind. It was gaining popularity and credibility. On the wall of the main entrance behind the reception desk, hung a bronze plaque with a motto:

This institution and its staff is dedicated to the art of healing in any form. We exist to alleviate human misery in any way possible, and to find the causes which break down our immune system and disrupt life. To this end, we resolve to view each case individually, leaving no stone unturned in our effort to expand the knowledge of all parts of the healing community, without prejudice. In the spirit of cooperation, we put aside our differences in order to explore our limitless potential for the betterment of mankind.

Zebedia read the inscription, then passed to the tablet next to it listing various doctors who worked here. There were impressive credentials across the board. There were traditional medical doctors, chiropractors, nutritionists and homeopaths. Several well-known psychics were also listed.

Holistic medicine was finding its way back into the forefront of healing, as it had been before the advent of the AMA and drug cartels in the late eighteenth century. More and more people believed the strength of a person's faith elevates the power of the mind, directly increasing the incidence of self-healing.

God was getting almost equal credit with medical doctors. He created the human machinery and the medical community was starting to recognize His hand in all repair work. Zebedia's mind wandered, back over centuries, to a time when the human body was free of all ailments. Excessive abuse, toxification, acidosis, anger, and greed, allowed disease to enter; first in the mind, causing a subtle shift in information passed between fifty trillion cells, manifesting as minor ailments, like colds, and major diseases, like cancer. Stress, whether emotional or physical eventually manifests itself in some structural damage, or neurological impairment. In a quiet conversation Zeb told me, it was extremely gratifying to see people valuing their gift of a whole body and sound mind, again.

Zeb noticed a clock on the wall. He had fifteen minutes until his appointment. Heading downstairs into the bowels of the building, he reached the basement floor and turned left at a sign, which read maintenance to the right, operating room to the left. Looking into the operating room, he saw a team gathered around a tiny figure draped with a single cover lying semi-conscious on the table. They were alternately discussing and pointing, as the small child lay there patiently waiting. Her profile appeared normal. Then she turned to look at Zeb, sensing him watching. The far side of her face was deformed by tumors and her right eye resembled a large blue marble. Zeb didn't shy from the terrible sight, as one might expect. There was something innately beautiful about the child. Except for her deformity, she was exquisite.

He began making faces at her, screwing up his features in all sorts of amazing distortions, until finally a glimmer of a smile came to her lips. He waved and her small hand opened slowly twice. He put his hands together in a sign he was cheering and praying for her and she half-waved again. Moving away from the door, he stretched his hands towards the ceiling, closed his eyes and remained motionless. Several people passed without comment. After a few moments he lowered his hands and his face darkened. The answer was not what he'd hoped, but tomorrow was another day and he would ask again. The greatest thing Zeb taught me about prayer was I could ask for anything and expect to get it. There was never a time Zeb remembered being disappointed. Even when the answer was, "No," he continued to ask again and again, wanting to understand the answer, which took time to crystallize in his mind. He didn't get everything he wanted, and tried not to pester.

"God is a loving and benevolent parent, but never weak, or interfering." Zeb told me. "He never intended to spoil us."

I know Zeb didn't like being told no and struggled with his pride when it happened. Backing away from the O.R., he turned and glided down the hall to the maintenance office. Opening the door at a minute past nine, he entered a small cluttered room, with pages of blueprints and diagrams tacked to walls everywhere. He got the sense of being in a construction trailer. Some prints were fairly new, but most were brown with age and wrinkled, a reflection of the main inhabitant of the room, who sat hunched behind his desk. File cabinets with pages sticking out drawers, lined the walls. Boxes stuffed to overflowing stood everywhere.

All of this belied a keen sense of awareness on the face of the burly sixty-year-old black man leaning back in his old wooden chair. His eyes were fixed in a permanent squint, from equal parts of bad lighting and smiles. He exuded confidence and a sense, that if the world came crashing down around him, he would merely sigh and say we'll fix it as soon as we can. His office was in stark contrast to the immaculate surroundings above, where this man of average height, with slack skin and strong arms, was responsible for the entire maintenance operation. He glanced up at Zeb.

Easing back in his chair, wrapping his hands behind his head he inquired, "What have we here?"

"Good morning." Zeb answered, "I'm the new person you hired."

"New person? New person?" He said, as Zeb waited patiently. "Have a seat, will you. I know I have a new person here somewhere."

He was moving things around on his desk, searching for Zeb's paperwork, but couldn't find it. Then he rose, walked to the wall and looked through some papers tacked together raising them one at a time. He turned with half a grin on his face and said, "Your name isn't Ms. Lilly is it?"

Zeb shook his head and Frank returned to his search.

"Had to ask. You can never be sure these days."

Zeb smiled behind him. At last he raised his hands, removed a piece of paper from the wall and said, "Zebedia. Should have asked you your name in the first place. I don't often get Z's, and a new person with one initial Z. Well, I would have found it straight away. You would have thought I was the most efficient janitor, excuse me, maintenance engineer, on the planet."

Zeb let Frank ramble on and didn't interrupt. He was obviously enjoying himself and Zeb was content to wait. Frank returned to his desk.

"You don't look like a maintenance man, Zeb. Your clothes say you could be, but your hands and your posture; well, they say something different, son."

"I'm a hard worker, Mr. Johnson. I won't disappoint you."

"Frank's my name, son, and I'm not saying you will. All I'm saying is you don't look like a janitor. I not saying you have to look like a janitor to be one, just like you don't have to look like a rocket scientist to be one."

"What is a janitor suppose to look like, maybe tomorrow, I can do better."

Frank laughed, "A sense of humor, good. I like that. You need a sense of humor just to get up in the morning with what's going on in this world. Only this morning, I read they're disciplining kids in school for saying Grace before eating lunch. Can you imagine that, Zeb?"

Sadness clouded Zeb's eyes for a second, then he answered, "I'm not surprised."

"I'm not surprised either. I'm angry. I'm no Holy Roller, but I sure as heck respect any family that teaches their young ones to be thankful for their food. If that's wrong, we're in deeper trouble than I thought."

Frank was getting himself all worked up and Zeb was amused.

"As long as there are people who care about being thankful as passionately as you, the world has a fighting chance, Frank."

"I hope you're right, son. But, enough of that, let's walk around and I'll introduce you to some of the staff. There are only eight of us in maintenance, and this is a big job for eight people. I also organize the maid service and laundry crew."

"That's a lot of responsibility for one man, Frank."

"You can say that again, but this hospital has to survive, Zeb."

"Is it in trouble."

"Things were touch and go in the beginning. The Chief-of-Staff, Mary Savage, used to help me make the beds. She's a hell of a woman, a hell of a woman. If I were ten years younger I'd take a shot at that one, I can tell you that. She's a keeper, works harder than any two men I know. A hell of a woman, son, and kind, sweet Jesus, the woman is kind."

"Will I get to meet her."

"Sooner or later. Most people arrive here with bad troubles, Zeb. We try to make them all comfortable. It isn't always possible."

"Aren't most terminal."

"That word doesn't exist here."

Zeb was taken by surprise at the force of Frank's response.

"Dr. Savage teaches living, Zeb. And living begins with outlook. Everyone is living until they draw their last breath. No one here is dying, son. Some aren't living as long or as well as others, but they're living."

"Dr. Savage sounds interesting. She sure has convinced you."

"No doubt about that, son. She spent a lot of time in Honduras and other Central American countries. Did you know the average life expectancy there is only fifty years. Those places are only sixteen hundred miles from where we stand."

"Really! That's depressing."

"Think how I feel, Zeb. If I lived in Central America I'd be dead ten years already."

"Very funny, Frank."

"And you'd be approaching old age," Frank started to chuckle.

He was cantankerous, bubbly, loved people, and showed it. They moved through the halls saying hello to everyone. Frank stuck his head into some of the patient's rooms. His enthusiasm was contagious, and he was earthy with a raucous sense of humor, openly enjoying flirting with the ladies. As they past an older woman's room on the third floor, she appeared in the doorway.

Frank stopped, covered his heart, and leaned back against the wall, as if he needed support and exclaimed, "My God I didn't know Greta Garbo was in the hospital."

He turned to the nurse's station and called, "Nurse why wasn't I informed this beautiful woman was in the hospital."

Mrs. Greenberg blushed and told him to stop it, but he kept right on. Seymour Greenberg appeared behind her, and said, "You've lost your mind again, Frank."

Zeb told me, Frank didn't miss a beat, carrying on with exaggerated bravado. "Excuse me, Mr. Grant. I had no idea you were visiting Miss Garbo. Pardon me for interrupting, sir."

He bowed and pulled Zeb along, as the older man bowed back and took his wife's arm. They strolled down the hall in the opposite direction whispering together like teenagers. Frank touched Zeb's arm to stop him and looked back at the Greenberg's, waiting. They moved a couple steps further and joined hands. It was what Frank waited for. He raised his arms and clasps his hands over his head as if he had just won the heavyweight championship of the world. Then he hurried Zeb on their way, as if nothing happened.

He introduced Zeb to Jim Conklin, Sarah Perkins, and Terry Smith, all members of his staff. Terry would work a double today and Jim tomorrow. Zeb knew then it was important he get started as soon as possible to lighten their load a little. Frank's name came over the paging system for the third time and he excused himself to answer it, while Zeb continued getting orientated. He peeked into a room at the middle of the hall. It was brightly lit by sunshine streaming in a large window, and the perfume of fresh flowers filled his nostrils. Roses, daisies, and carnations were everywhere. At the center of the room, a young woman lay in bed, eyes closed with an intravenous tube taped to the back of her hand. A picture of two small children, this lady, and a large yellow dog stood on a table in the corner. As Zeb moved closer he noticed small sores on the sides of her calves and shoulders, and she appeared much older then her picture indicated she was. He touched the sores lightly, then lifted her lifeless hand and raised his eyes to the ceiling, standing quietly, saying nothing concentrating deeply on the woman's life force and adding his own to it.

Frank appeared in the door behind him and whispered, "Zeb."

Zeb didn't move until Frank came in and touched his arm. Then he nodded and raised one finger indicating he needed a moment longer. Later, Frank would be hard pressed to explain why he didn't insist Zeb leave the room immediately.

Zeb turned back to the woman and laid her hand back down on the bed touched her forehead and whispered, "I'll see you tomorrow."

The woman didn't stir, but in the brilliant light of the room the eyes played no tricks and Frank saw her smiling. Zeb walked passed him into the hall without saying a word and Frank stared at the young woman a moment longer before following him.

"What do you think you were doing in there?"

"Holding the young woman's hand and speaking to her."

"She is in a coma, Zeb. She can't hear anything."

"Is she deaf?" Zeb asked calmly.

"I don't think so."

"Then perhaps she hears me, Frank."

"She looked like she was smiling when you left."

"Maybe she enjoyed what I had to say."

Zeb winked at him and Frank had to laugh. "Yeah, you're loony enough to work here."

"I'm glad you feel that way, because I like you too."

"We can't pay what the large hospitals do. You'll work harder and longer for less money."

"I live alone, and have simple tastes."

"You can eat most meals at the hospital to save money."

"That is kind. I've been here less then a day and I have a place to live and food to eat. Compared to yesterday, I am a very rich man."

Frank thought to himself. "And interesting, too."

Frank explained Zeb's duties while they walked. As they passed, people turned for a second look at the slightly built, handsome stranger. Something about him was different. It wasn't physical beauty. He had ruddy good looks at best, but an unhurried grace surrounded him. It was an intangible magnetism, something akin to charisma, but beyond it.

When Frank left him on the second floor, working with a waxing machine, it was difficult to concentrate. He felt a little empty, like something was missing. Realizing Zeb made him comfortable, he glanced back at him. Zeb was consumed in his simple job. He intended to wax this floor better than it had ever been done, and didn't notice Frank scratching his head staring at him. He began humming the tune Zeb was whistling, as the elevator door closed. It was a nice unforgettable tune.

Zeb worked straight through the day. A number of people stopped to welcome him. He was happy to be working, and put all his effort into it. Consequently, he was tired, when he took the little orange card out of its holder and punched his time out. Then he returned to the third floor and finished cleaning one more bathroom. A silent gift to Frank Johnson. Finishing up, he closed his eyes, thanked his Father for a good day, and was ready to leave.

Once outside, Zeb looked at the sky. The sun was still bright and the air warmer than the day before. A combination, which felt good, as he started home. A couple staff members slowed and ask if he wanted a ride, and he thanked each kindly, but refused. He strolled along, getting acquainted with his semi-rural surroundings. Leaving the hospital grounds, heading west he walked directly into the sun, which loomed, like a large glowing orange ball pasted onto a pale blue background. Shoots of red-orange spikes, like colored ice cycles spread out and melted into the blue.

At five-thirty he turned left into the Crowley's street. John Sullivan was out on his lawn dressed in jeans, work boots, and a heavy sweatshirt. He was puttering around his garden, but Zeb wasn't fooled. As he walked up the street he saw John glancing in his direction every few minutes. It was obvious he was waiting for someone. John put down the nippers he was using to trim the dead twigs off his bushes and strolled to the curb as Zeb approached.

"Hi, Zeb. Long time no see. How was your first day?"

"It was good, very good, John. How about yours?"

"Mine was kind of strange after I left you. By the way what did you say to those kids in front of the hospital this morning?"

"You mean the gang-bangers?" Zeb asked slightly amused.

"Yes."

"Nothing much. I said good morning and they let me pass. I imagine they could be very dangerous."

"So you know about gangs."

"I've had a few problems with mobs in the past."

John missed the subtle distinction between mob and gang. It was in another lifetime, but Zeb still shivered at the memory.

"It's kind of sad, John. We've created a society where some children only feel familial love in the presence of a group of thugs. These kids are lost and looking for something, anything to hold on to. They're desperate to fit in and are easily controlled.

"I remember that little misguided man in Germany, who wanted to rule the world in the early part of this century. The one in the wheel chair, at the same time, in this country wasn't much better."

"You mean Hitler and Roosevelt?" John asked.

"Yes. Hitler was consumed with hate. These street gangs remind me a lot of him and his thugs. I've got to get going. I'll see you in the morning."

He moved up the street evenly.

John Sullivan got the impression Zeb spoke from personal experience, but that was impossible. World War II ended fifty years ago and Zeb appeared to be his early thirties. John watched him fade into the twilight without moving, and felt a twinge in his gut. He was filled with a sense of loss, a foreboding, and almost started to run after Zeb to warn him, but didn't know what from. He returned to his lawn, but the feeling persisted and he kept looking over his shoulder at the spot he and Zeb stood speaking, feeling a little lost himself. He put his things away and hurried inside, where the kids were playing a game with friends from next door.

Cathy was stirring spaghetti sauce at the stove and the table was set for dinner. John stood quietly watching all the things around him and raised his eyes as he'd seen Zeb do. The feeling of loss disappeared, replaced by a sense of wonder at all he had. He went to Cathy at the stove and gently massaged her neck.

She leaned back and said, "That feels good. Where have you been? I was starting to miss you."

John smiled and answered, "Thanks. That smells good. Do you need a hand?"

Cathy turned her head, trying to hide the startled look on her face before smiling. She dropped her wooden spoon, and turned to put her arms around his neck.

She kissed him deeply, momentarily taking his breath away. "That would be very nice," she answered, and turned back to her sauce while John went about setting the table. Cathy kept glancing over her shoulder. It had been too long, but . . .

CHAPTER EIGHT

The sun was sinking fast, Zeb wanted to fix the bunny before dinner. Dusk descended, casting a pale gray curtain on the entire landscape. The path to the cottage was still easily visible in the fading light, and the sight of my mom waiting on his steps startled Zeb. She was wrapped in a shawl, pulled tightly around her shoulders.

Zeb's breath caught in his lungs and his heart fluttered. Her hair was pulled back, secured by one of those little cloth fasteners, the kids called scrunches, in a ponytail to the side. She was a whisper of beauty, sitting on his stoop, and he felt his loins stir. He stopped quickly to collect and control this raw emotion. He felt his legs shaking, but understood his attraction could go no further than his own thoughts.

As he approached, a light whiff of her perfume filled the air. Her understated loveliness was overwhelming, but there was also sadness, a vulnerability not to be abused. It was a line Zeb feared and relished.

He taught me not to be afraid of my own emotions, as he was not of his. They kept him vital, alive and aware of the life force inside him. He recognized the damage they could do to others if left unleashed. He kept a tight rein, but never denied having them.

He remained in awe of this exciting side to his personality. Mary made him feel much the same years ago. It was difficult to separate strong physical attraction from the deep emotional bonds of love. Momentary affection, we label, "instant gratification" was replacing the hard work of staying together, and supporting each other through a lifetime.

My mom rose as he approached. “Hello, Zebedia. How was your first day at work?”

“It went well, Mrs. Crowley, thank you.”

“Please, call me Elizabeth. What did you do?”

“I finished waxing two entire hallways and cleaned out a storage area, before the day was over.”

His pride in doing a good job swelled the volume of his voice. My mom nearly laughed at the importance he obviously placed on these simple tasks, and immediately felt shallow.

“Zeb, perhaps we could find you some more suitable employment.”

“Mrs. Crowley . . .”

“Elizabeth, “she corrected him.

Zeb hesitated a moment. Tapping his upper lip with his index finger, he gathered what he might say.

“Elizabeth, without maintenance hospitals can’t function. It is an important job.”

“I understand that, but the pay.”

“The pay is more than sufficient. I am a single person and look at what I have been paid in two days. Your son’s friendship led you and your husband to giving me the opportunity to stay in this beautiful little cottage. I have a job working around people, who desperately need help and encouragement. There are many different forms of compensation, and abundance, Elizabeth. Perhaps I am less interested in physical rewards as emotional ones.”

“I understand that, but money is important too.”

Zeb smiled at my mom, “Has it made you happy?”

She thought a moment. “Not really, but that’s my fault, not the money. It is easier to be happy if we are comfortable.”

“Elizabeth, I have a friend Paul, who spent most of his time chasing after money and was miserable. It wasn’t until he recognized the needs of his soul, that he found some sense of himself.”

“Did he change?”

“A little. He saw things in a little different light. It made it easier for him to part with things in this life that he wouldn't need in the next."

"Did he continue to work hard."

Zeb laughed at the question remembering Paul.

"He worked until he was bone weary, for very little money, Elizabeth. Still, he invested wisely, and had more than he needed."

"You have done other things! I knew it." She said it almost triumphantly and Zeb chuckled. She shivered adjusting her shawl.

Zeb noticed and said, "You're cold. Come inside, and I'll make some tea."

"I really should go back up to the house."

"The children will be here in a few minutes. I told them I would be back around now, and they are stopping to say hello. You are cold, and lonely. Come in and sit by the fire."

It was an observation not an invitation and Mom was touched by his simple declaration of the truth as it presented itself. His voice was compassionate without condescension, and when he took her arm she felt a rush of affection, missing from her heart for a long time. She sat near the fire, warming herself, as Zeb added wood. He left the lights off, stoking the fire back to life.

Mom watched him closely, wondering what sort of man he was, and what drew her here. She wanted to talk. He was an attractive man in a rugged sense, lean and wiry. He had the body of a gymnast, a balance of flexibility and strength. She watched him move about, saying nothing, knowing he was attracted to her, which was physically obvious. He said nothing, and was not embarrassed. She was nervous and excited at the same time, wondering what might happen, not wanting to get in over her head. She needed someone to talk to. More than anything she wanted a friend, and didn't know if it was possible for a man and a woman to be friends. Sex always seemed to get in the way. Sitting quietly in the firelight, as flames licked the wood in the stove, crackling and dancing up and down, casting her face in an amber hue, Elizabeth, was stunning to look at, and terribly confused.

Sensing her anxiety, Zebedia moved to the stove and took her hands.

"Elizabeth, I want to be your friend, even though I know how difficult it will be to be that and nothing more. I need your help."

Mom smiled and the tension seemed to ebb out of the room. She allowed herself to relax. As the tension left her eyes and face, years fell away.

"I would like that." Came her quiet reply. She reached and touched the side of his face. Zeb nodded and moved away. He wouldn't add to her troubles. He knew it would be difficult not to, because he was half in love with her already. Lifting his battered teapot off the stove, he poured her a mint tea, which she took with a smile; it made his heart stir.

"You are exquisitely beautiful, and have a wonderful family. Both of us are lonely, and need a trusted friend." The truth stated simply removed any remaining tension like air rushing from a deflating balloon.

My mother smiled. She felt safe unthreatened, and she didn't know why. She had heard similar words from different men, but somehow Zeb was different. She told me later she marveled at his ability to remain at ease. He didn't hide his feelings. He acknowledged them and decided what was right. An image of him covered in wet filth came immediately to mind while she related this incident and I laughed.

My mother was then, and remains, to this day unaware of her looks. Zeb liked that. Back then she wore less make-up, just a hint of perfume, and casual clothes. Yet, the effect was overwhelmingly sensual, and this gave Zeb an idea. As he scurried about his business, Mom sat sipping her tea, engulfed in warmth, deep in thought.

She didn't stir, enjoying the closeness and the quiet. Feeling safe wasn't easy. She hardly knew Zeb, yet there was something about him. "A maintenance man who acts more like a philosopher." She laughed, as images of all the discarded hippie philosophers of her youth came to mind in torn jeans and tie-dye tee shirts. She remembered Benny's brightly painted Volkswagen van, and suffering through his Vietnam tour. If only he would take time to see they were losing each other, but there was never enough time. Visions of their life together filled her mind like a newsreel.

After speaking to Zeb, her life didn't seem as drab. The things she accomplished everyday took on the importance they deserved, and she felt something stir inside her. It was a good feeling to be proud of herself, and what she accomplished. Her eyelids grew heavy and her head lay to one side. She fought to stay awake, failed and fell asleep, purring softly, a little drop of spittle hovering at the corner of her mouth. Her mind filled with hopeful dreams.

Zeb brought an old blanket out of his duffel bag, added it to her shawl, and watched her face lit by the firelight. He stood very still watching her, wanting her, and feeling each breath she took filling his lungs, tasting her tongue, knowing it was never to be. A smile played about her lips.

Zeb moved away shaking his head. "Right is not so easy," he thought. "Falling in love is easy, staying in love is extremely hard work. Lust and loneliness are powerful." All these thoughts poured through his mind in an instant.

He understood why people failed against them everyday. He busied himself around the table with the food. That task completed, he switched to repairing the bunny. Her nearness was intoxicating. Putting the finishing touches on the bunny he lifted it and surveyed his handy work.

"Good as new," he thought to himself, and took it outside to place it back in the garden.

There was no time for the rocker today, because he had more important things to do. God was changing His plans on the run, and he needed to adapt. He remembered someone telling him, "The measure of intelligence is the ability to adapt to changing environment."

He felt completely exhilarated. Gazing skyward smiling broadly as he joked, "You could have made her a little less attractive, Father." Then he waited quietly for an answer, like most of us when we pray, except Zeb looked as if someone was speaking to him directly out of thin air.

I arrived first and motioned the little ones not to interrupt, even though I still considered it a little strange. Timmy ignored me and hurried up to Zeb grabbing at his legs. Zeb, far from being angry, scooped my little brother up and hugged him. Quickly, he explained his idea. We nodded, agreeing enthusiastically.

The sound of children's laughter rose through the branches, and Zeb slowed behind us to listen. He loved the sound of joy, as much as he loved the sound of music. Both raised the level of energy in any surrounding. Linda and I hurried about gathering sprigs of frozen flowers giggling in the darkness, while Timmy kept watch for Dad's arrival from work.

His warning pierced the air, "Dad's home!"

Dad pulled into the driveway. Stopping the car, he got out, and asked, "Timmy, what are you doing out here? It's dark, son. Get in the house."

Linda appeared out of the shadows with the flowers, placed them in his hand and grabbed the other.

"C'mon Daddy, we have a surprise." She said pulling him towards the cottage.

"What's going on kids? I have work to do."

I relieved him of his briefcase, leaving only the flowers. I must have looked determined, because Dad didn't protest.

I told him. "No work tonight, Dad. There is something you need to do."

Dad became intrigued, and animated. Linda held his hand tightly as we strolled down the path to Grandpa's cottage.

Ben noticed the repaired lawn animal, and asked, "Who fixed Mr. Cottontail?"

I pointed to Zeb standing off to one side of the lawn. He waved to Dad, who returned the wave with a smile. "I know you have something to do with all this, Zebedia. I'll speak to you later."

Dad's voice was light and airy. He was openly enjoying the

attention. Raising his hands feigning his innocence, Zeb pretended no involvement. I opened the cottage door and Dad entered. Seeing Mom sleeping, her face aglow in the firelight hit him like the first time he ever laid eyes on her, nearly twenty years before. He was seeing her with much the same eyes as Zeb, but with the added affection of one that's loved her for a long time, and the attraction he felt then, still blazed inside him.

Night after night he missed this. Hurrying here, making a deal there, for what? Beth asleep in the firelight was breath taking. He had pushed her away. Dad knew why she went to lunch with someone else. Beth hadn't changed. He had. She wanted a simple life with simple things; Dad insisted we have more. As more became a reality, it was never enough. Dad never intentionally excluded her; just failed to include her when possible. Two candles burned brightly on the table. Their flames created two individual stars reflected in two glasses filled with deep red wine. A loaf of thin French bread lay on a white towel next to a plate of hard cheese slices and a bowl of salad greens. Normally Zeb would have washed and boiled beans, but there simply wasn't time. In the center of the table lay a small card, which read: "Take this time together as our gift," signed by me. "We will be good," signed by Timmy. "Mom you look like a sleeping princess," by Linda.

Dad sank into a chair by the table. The table rocked towards him on Grandpa's short leg. Dad lay his head down and started to cry. We retreated quietly outside to wait, wonder and hope. His sobbing was loud enough to disturb Mom. She opened her eyes, adjusting to the flickering light.

She heard dad and asked, "What's the matter, Benny?"

He rose slowly, and walked into the firelight smiling broadly through shimmering tears, and answered. "Absolutely nothing."

She noticed the arrangements for the first time.

"The kids," Dad whispered, "Go read the cards."

She did, and covered her mouth as tears glistened in her eyes.

"The kids plus a new friend, Benny. What do you think?"

He winked, "I think we've been letting this cottage go to waste."

"We might forget again?"

"Let's not think about it now, Elizabeth. Remind me to thank Roger tomorrow."

"What for?"

"Having the good sense to bring a romantic home with him."

"I think its more than that, Benny. Zeb is kind of . . . kind of . . ."

"Kind of what, Beth?"

"I want to say holy, but that's not even it, Benny. He just seems to good to be true, you know. He is awfully wise for his age. He doesn't even mind being a janitor."

"He likes working, Beth." It was a statement.

Elizabeth nodded agreement.

"He made me think about the things I have, which I take for granted. He considers what I do special. He considers everyone special. I do want to say holy, because it is right. Zebedia is holy and kind and considerate."

"Okay."

"Okay what, Benny?"

"Okay, you convinced me, Elizabeth. I'll thank Zeb in the morning too."

Mom laughed and Dad extended his hand saying, "Hold me for the rest of my life, Beth, and forgive me as often as you can." She moved into his arms and they stood entwined, creating one dancing shadow on the wall.

We three children and a grown man crept away from the cottage window, down the path towards the main house, amidst giggles, and stifled laughter. Our hearts began to believe, and our hopes soared.

CHAPTER NINE

Zeb passed Jack's early the next morning. Cathy Sullivan was just slamming John's car door, when Zeb came within ear-shot. He whistled softly to himself, as storm clouds gathered above, whipped into a frenzy by high March winds. Growing thicker and darker by the second, like a crowd at a rock concert waiting for the show to begin. Cathy yelled at John once, raised her head and noticed Zeb. He raised his hand in greeting, and she raced back into the house, embarrassed by her out burst. Her angry voice swirled away in the whipping wind. Zeb barely heard her.

"Good morning, Cathy."

Zeb chuckled to himself knowing in his heart, she wasn't as angry as she pretended to be.

"We are all actors, playing on life's stage for each other," he thought.

John sat sullenly in his car, also playing his part, torn between staying home and going to visit Grace. It really didn't matter what he chose. He felt guilty anyway, so he started the car and began to back out without ever noticing Cathy lifting the corner of a curtain on the kitchen window.

Zeb was still looking at the house. He saw the curtain move, and decided what he might do. He looked up and prayed for the right words before taking a deep breath. The clouds echoed Cathy's sentiments pushing and shoving jostling for position, trying to find their way and suddenly they burst forth with tears. Zeb was looking skyward, when the first drops fell. He blinked the warm raindrops out of his eyes over his face, thinking, "Warm water, for once," and he laughed at his own private joke.

John wasn't scheduled at work until late in the morning, and figured to spend a couple hours with Grace. Cathy was furious, because John forgot to tell her, and she planned the morning together. Zeb came alongside the car as sprinkles, became droplets beating against the windshield. The warm rain, unusual for March, didn't protect him from blasts of cooler air making him shiver. John signaled him in out of the rain, so Zeb skipped to the passenger door and climbed in. He liked the young police officer and wanted to reassure him everything was going to turn out for the best, but wanted to avoid raising the policeman's natural suspicions. It wasn't time, yet.

"John needs to be supported, not overwhelmed," Zeb reminded himself.

Zebedia learned very early to teach in a way that was interesting and uplifting to the person learning. He never approached a subject with the attitude, "I know it all, and I will prove." His method was to offer what he knew and let the student use what was relevant. This was teaching by listening to pupils needs.

Zeb told me his mentor explained that, "One cannot teach if we never hear more than the sound of our own voice."

Zebedia had confronted men more interested in displaying their knowledge than sharing it when he was only a boy. His mother was angry with him, thinking he was being disrespectful. Zeb obeyed his mother and left, but did not apologize to the faculty. He found them arrogant, condescending and lacking in gentle wisdom. The men he chastened couldn't believe the breadth of his knowledge. At twelve, it was easier to dismiss him as an impudent young man, than to deal with his needs. Looking back, Zeb told me it was important to learn humility, early.

He said, "It serves no purpose to argue unless wisdom is gained. If argument cements only a wall between two egos the wall eventually becomes insurmountable. Humility keeps things in perspective, and possibility alive. Listening to our inner voice helps us teach from the heart, rather than the ego."

I know he used these lessons when he spoke to Sulli.

"Morning, John."

"Hey, Zeb, how ya doing?"

John pretended nothing was wrong.

"Slightly better than you, from the sound of it."

"You heard?"

"Yes, I did. I gather Cathy isn't happy about your going to see Grace this morning."

"She's right, Zeb. I should stay here."

"She isn't right, John."

"What did you say?"

"I said she isn't right."

"So you agree with me."

"Part of the reason Cathy loves you is you're willingness to give of yourself. Grace needs your friendship right now; she has no one else, so you must go. Your mistake is not including Cathy. You are being selfish keeping Grace all to yourself."

"You think it's a treat going to see Grace?" John asked, astonished.

"Yes, I do. Grace makes you a little crazy, but she also fills a bare spot in your heart. She is an extraordinary person. Cathy could use some of Grace's affection, too. What are you afraid of, John? The spotlight is big enough for both of you."

"I hadn't thought of it that way, Zeb. All this time, I only saw what I was doing for Grace. I didn't think about what I was getting in return. I don't think Cathy will come. She's pretty angry."

"Have you asked her? Have you explained to her why you go?"

"Not really."

"Give it shot. What the heck, it's raining anyway. I'll wait for you."

"You want a ride to work?" John asked incredulously.

"Yes. I'd like to meet Cathy and your kids if you don't mind."

John laughed, "You're pretty sure of yourself. What do you want to bet she doesn't come?"

"I'll bet you a new shirt."

"That's a little strange isn't it, Zeb."

"Not when you need a new shirt, it isn't."

John laughed at the earnest look on Zeb's face, and said, "You're on. A new shirt says she's too angry to discuss going"

He stepped into the swirling rain and fought his way up the walk into the house. He returned alone five minutes later. He opened and slammed the door behind him, quickly, as the wind and rain tried to follow him in. He sat for a moment, catching his breath, brushing the droplets from his face, then pulled a new denim shirt with the tags still in place, from under his coat.

"She'll be out in five minutes. She's getting the kids ready. Here's your shirt."

He smiled broadly and tossed the shirt on Zeb's lap. Less than five minutes later, out the door they came. Rain fell steadily, but the wind subsided for a few moments and Cathy breezed down the walk, bristling with excitement. Their two sleepy children were an obvious mix of parents. Neither Cathy nor John could ever deny either of them.

As they piled into the rear seat, Zeb said hello and John made introductions. Cathy reached across the front seat to shake Zeb's hand, and he held it for an instant longer then most people would. Her grip was firm, and her smile warm. The wind returned whipping the rain into a frenzied dance across the car. They pulled away, and Zeb's walking route went by in a blur of telephone wires and parked cars. Kevin and Kimberly, now wide awake, filled the car with laughter, asking all sorts of wild imaginative children's questions. Zeb listened to Cathy interact with them. She was patient and kind and never patronizing. Little Kimberly, who was barely two, already spoke clearly.

Cathy carried a plain canvas beach bag, decorated by hand with great care. It was covered with pastel pictures of animals and small children. Near the top edge, "Magic Story Bag" was embroidered in colorful letters of all different sizes, and Zeb asked, "Do you read to the children a lot, Cathy."

"Yes, I do. I enjoy it as much as they do."

Cathy was bubbly and animated. Her obvious joy at being

with them, moved Zeb. He experienced a spiritual lift, just being close to her.

"Kevin is already reading on his own, and he just turned four. He reads to Kim a lot. Now, if I could just interest their father in a few books. The only thing he reads is the box scores from Yankee games." Cathy joked.

Zeb stared at her blankly, and John noticed.

"Don't tell me you don't know the Yankees? C'mon, Zeb. It's a professional baseball team. The most famous sports franchise in the world."

"You mean the guys that hit the ball with the stick and run around in a circle?" Zeb asked.

Cathy laughed, "That's a pretty good description, Johnny." She baited her husband. "Nice going, Zeb."

John shook his head in mock frustration, "To answer your question, yes, those guys, and it's a diamond, not a circle. I can't believe you don't know the Yankees."

"Don't you like sports, Zeb." Cathy asked.

"Yes, I do. I just learned a new game where you throw the ball at a net hanging from a pole. Some kids were playing it in the park."

Cathy laughed again and John eyed Zeb strangely to see if he was putting them on, but he was serious.

"That's basketball, Zeb. Everyone knows basketball."

"Not everyone, John. I didn't until a few weeks ago." Zeb answered.

"What sports do you like?" John asked as they reached the entrance to the hospital.

"Track and field. The decathlon is my favorite event, because it is a diverse test."

"I meant, spectator sports."

"Many people like to watch track and field, where I come from."

"Where is that? John asked.

"A little town in the Middle East, but I traveled quite a bit. I'm comfortable, as long as I am near people."

John began his turn into the hospital lot, but Zeb stopped him.

"Drop me here please, John. I'm early and have some time to use, as I wish."

"Do you want to come with us?"

"Another time. Give Grace my love."

"Do you know Grace too." Cathy asked.

"I feel I do after John described her, but even though I don't I still send her my love. It's a habit I got into a long time ago."

John stopped the car, "That ain't a bad habit for everyone to get into, Zeb. You sure you want to walk from here? You're going to be soaked."

"I am well prepared, today." Zeb said mischievously.

It was John's turn to be puzzled and Zeb pulled his brand new shirt off the seat. "I have this nice new dry shirt to change into."

John laughed. "Isn't that the shirt you got from your mother for your birthday?" Cathy asked.

"Yup."

"The one with the silver buttons, you hated? She continued.

"You got it."

"Zeb, I don't know if you want to wear that shirt. He hated those buttons."

"The buttons are fine." Zeb answered.

He stepped into the rain, tapped on the rear window, waved to the children, and then slammed the door. John pulled slowly back into traffic. Both children climbed up to stare out the back window. They watched him standing, staring up at the sky with his hands raised, while the warm rain poured over his face and dripped onto his chest. The children stared at him quietly until they couldn't see him anymore and Cathy watched too.

Finally she turned to John and said, "Johnny I can't explain this and I know it is going to sound crazy, but . . ."

"You feel an emptiness."

He finished her statement and continued, "You feel like you want to go back and stay with, Zeb. It's like you miss him already and we only just left him. I know."

Her eyes grew wide as John described exactly how she was feeling.

"How do you know?"

He smiled, took her hand and raised it to his lips, "Because I feel the same way. It's happen to me each time I leave him. I thought maybe I was getting weird, so I didn't say anything."

"You? Weird? How could you ever think that?" she questioned sarcastically.

John chuckled at her distorted face in the mirror, as she leaned up near him from the rear seat. Her warm breath on his neck, combined with her scent raised goose flesh on his arms. Both children continued to stare out the rear window without making a sound.

CHAPTER TEN

Zeb stood in the rain, for nearly five minutes.

Frank Johnson pulled up, rolled down the window and screamed over the wind. "If you're trying to get pneumonia to call in sick, forget it. You work in a hospital, remember? This is where they bring you when you get sick."

He rolled up his window without allowing Zeb to answer and pulled into the lot. Zeb lowered his hands; breathed deeply a couple times and brushed his longish ringlets straight back with his fingers. He now resembled a drowned rat. Pushing his way through the door near the maintenance department at the side of the building, he headed for work. The ground fell away from the building on this side towards a fairly large wood. The hospital foundation was designed to meld into a hill, utilizing the natural grade to avoid disturbing the natural serenity of the setting. The lower floor was exposed, which allowed for the entrance Zeb used at basement level. Blue shale boulders, excavated and blasted from the ground, were kept to landscape and decorate the park-like surroundings. Near the tree line, Zeb noticed a path and made mental note to go exploring the next sunny day.

Frank met him with a towel, "Figured you might need this, you dummy." He kidded Zeb, and Zeb thanked him for his thoughtfulness.

"What in blazes were you doing standing out there in the rain?"

"I was talking to my Father."

"I didn't see him standing anywhere near you, so I wouldn't

be spreading that story around if I was you. We do have a psycho ward here."

"Is that so?"

"Yes, and its full of people who stand in the rain talking to the air."

"I wasn't taking to the air, Frank. I was talking to our Father."

"My father died a long time ago, son, and don't waste no prayers on me." he snapped. All of a sudden there was an edge in his voice bordering on rage.

"Oh, I wouldn't think of wasting any prayers on you, Frank."

"You wouldn't?"

"Nope."

Frank eyed Zeb suspiciously, then swallowed the bait whole. "Why not?"

"Because you don't need them."

Zeb answered quite seriously and Frank was momentarily lost for words, then asked, "Don't you mind all the pain and suffering you see around you, Zeb?"

"Of course I do, but I don't dwell on it. Something happened to put you in this frame of mind. You were so positive yesterday. You made me feel good just to be here. What happened?"

Frank sagged, "A little girl was brought in last night. She probably won't live more than a week."

He held his head in his hands rubbing his face hard enough to remove the skin. "She can't be more than four years old, Zeb. Her mom and dad are just kids themselves. How can your benevolent God allow this."

Zeb listened without comment. Frank continued, speaking of things he normally kept bottled up inside; things he never allowed out, things he refused to think. Putting his fear into words, in hopes of reaching a conclusion, knowing he wouldn't, he couldn't.

"We keep trying," Zeb whispered to himself.

Frank dropped into a chair near the entrance staring out at the rain drumming against the building, sweeping in sheets across the ground. Branches strained back and forth, many snapped off and tumbled to earth while miniature rivers ran along the gutters everywhere.

"Don't ever remember March weather this bad."

"You're changing the subject."

Frank sighed, "I guess I am. She has a tiny scarf around her head; can't weigh more than twenty or thirty pounds. Mary came down last night and we had a shot of Jack Daniel's together. She only does that every so often you know? I knew she'd seen the child. She didn't have to tell me. I knew. We sat here without speaking nearly an hour, then she got up, said, 'Thanks' and left, as if I'd done her some enormous favor. She never shows her grief. That woman is strong, Zeb. Strongest woman I ever knew, and she acts like I did her a favor just sitting with her, ya know."

"You did, Frank. You gave her a quiet hour. Not many people are capable of that gift."

Frank continued as if he hadn't heard. "I know the little O'Brian girl is only one of many, but she is here, now. I wish we could save her."

"Perhaps she isn't as far gone as you think. Yesterday's attitude will do her a lot more good than this. The atmosphere in this hospital is as important as the medical staff."

"You're right. I know it, but I'm having a tough time with this one, Zeb."

"Where is the little girl, Frank?"

"Up in isolation. Go change will you. You're dripping all over my floor and I just waxed it."

Franks mood lightened visibly. He was glad to get it all out, to be able to verbalize the pain he felt.

"I will gladly dry off, if you show me where."

Frank pointed behind Zeb, "The locker room is over there. There's a washer and dryer. I meant it, when I said you couldn't get sick. Rose and Bill both called in and I've been here all night. I went out for coffee and a paper when I passed you standing, praying in the rain."

"Is anyone else working this morning?"

"No, I asked everyone else to come in this afternoon and stay the night. The place is all yours today. I'm glad you came early, you must be psychic." Zeb chuckled at Frank's remark.

Frank lumbered away towards his office and some much-needed sleep. Zeb hurried into the locker room, stripped off all his wet clothes and stood naked close to the dryer, to keep warm, while his clothes dried. He found some towels, took one and dried himself, rubbing briskly. The combination of cold locker room and warm dryer raised goose flesh all over him. Laying the towel across the top of the dryer and draping another around his waist, he pushed himself up and sat, waiting.

Closing his eyes he settled into a self induced trance concentrating wholly and only on all the positive emotions around him, collecting them like a magnet. He felt his life force, or Chi, increase, almost as if a powerful generator had come on line at the electric company transferring all its energy into his body. Sitting in the stillness of the hospital basement waiting for his clothes to dry, Zeb concentrated on little Margaret O'Brian, reversing the process emptying all his stored energy into her desperately ill body.

A buzzer sounded signaling his clothes were dry, breaking his concentration. Quickly he slipped off, opened the door, and retrieved his warm fluffy pile. They felt fresh, soft, and comfortable. Rainwater always made them softer. It also softened and enlivened his hair making him look like a wild man. It flowed all around his head in waves and curls. Zeb grabbed a mop and pail and headed for the fourth floor. It had taken twenty minutes to dry his clothes, but was still before nine o'clock when he approached the Pedi-Intensive Care Unit or PIC-U as the nurses referred to it. He waved to the nurse on duty who promptly put her pen down and asked him who he was.

Zeb moved over and said in low tones, "My name is Zebedia, I started work yesterday with the maintenance department."

His tone was friendly. Patty Kelly looked him up and down. She noticed everything, a trait picked up from her detective father, who died the year before, after eighty wonderful years in this world.

He was a cop for forty-five of those years and Patty was a cop's daughter. Something about Zeb set her gut spinning, but it wasn't a bad or dangerous feeling. Zeb was dressed in neat, clean clothes, but his hair.

"My God," she thought to herself, "His head looks like he's been plugged into a wall socket."

Zeb noticed her stare and smiled. "I got caught in the rain this morning, and my hair took on a life of its own."

"Son, that's the understatement of the century. As my dad used to say, you look like you've been rode hard and put away wet."

They laughed together, as another nurse came around the corner of the desk.

"Zebedia, this is Nancy. Nancy; Zebedia."

Nancy said hello, but couldn't take her eyes off of Zeb's hair.

He chuckled and said, "I had it styled this way, do you like it."

Patty chuckled and Nancy recovered extending her hand, "Hi. I'm sorry. It's just that . . . well . . . your hair . . . it's so . . . so . . . big."

"Thank God it isn't heavy." Patty added and all three of them laughed, then Patty grew serious, "How is she, Nan?"

"She's comfortable and her parents finally fell asleep in the chairs we brought in. Have the doctors decided what they're going to try yet."

Patty took a moment, looked at her orders and said, "Mary feels the little girl is beyond anything conventional. She's much to weak. She called Kevin Richards and he came in early this morning. He promised a course of action as soon as he could finish going over her entire history. He took everything downstairs."

Zeb interrupted, "Is it all right if I start work. Frank is in his office sleeping, if you'd like to check." Patty waved him away, "Go get started, Zebedia and welcome, I hope you like it here."

"Thanks. That's nice of you. I'll see you later."

Zeb moved down the hall towards Margaret O'Brian's room.

The two nurses resumed work. The halls were deserted, except for a few food service personnel. Zeb didn't hesitate. Setting his mop aside, he moved quietly into the room. The child's parents didn't stir, but Zeb noticed a rosary dangling from the young mother's hand.

He stopped, reflecting a moment on all-different faiths and beliefs grown up through the centuries. Organizations created to bring people together only served to drive wedges between them, as everyone claimed theirs was the one true way home. If only everyone could meet Mary. She made it very simple for anyone to come to her, being the epitome of Jewish motherhood.

She told everyone, "Come to me and find rest."

It was nice to see a young mother honoring Mary. Ghandi's wife had a nature similar to Mary. He had met her only once when he visited Mother Teresa before she became famous.

Zeb moved to the bedside and lifted the child's frail hand. His other he held extended just above her tiny form hidden amongst the blankets. Ever so slowly he traced her entire length, down one side and up the other. He emptied every positive feeling he had into the child, drawing on all the life force in the universe, he willed her to become stronger attempting to draw her disease out into his own flesh. After working in her aura, which was pale green, extending barely and inch beyond her frame, he turned his attention to the battle raging within. He imagined her clearly, as the eventual victor. Any thought of failure was abhorrent. The child could not afford a single negative vibration, and Zeb was perfectly prepared. From the basement below, sitting half naked he had sent waves of energy here before him.

Eyes closed standing quietly by her bedside, he mentally joined himself to her battle. Silently he took her side in the struggle. Each time he did this, he was a little afraid. His fear was well founded. Confronting and transferring portions of deadly organisms to his own body and trusting his own immune system, was like playing Russian roulette with a fully loaded gun. It wasn't smart.

He sensed her joy, as her hand warmed in his own. He could feel her letting him in, allowing him entrance into her pain, and sadness. With a child's trust, she placed her life in his hands and, all at once, the tide turned. Zeb felt all the strength of life he could muster flowing into the tiny body and some small portion of her disease flowing out.

Her eyes fluttered, but she was much too weak to open them. Zeb opened his, and looked around, as if expecting to see the armies that battled inside their minds, walking around her room. He was struck by the all-encompassing silence. The child-mother stirred to his right. The air in the room was positively electric, whizzing and stirring like some mad scientists laboratory.

It was time to leave. Placing Margaret's hand back on the bed, he reached under the oxygen tent and held her tiny forehead. If anyone saw him invade this sterile field he would be fired immediately. They wouldn't understand; it was something he needed to do. He and the child were one in spirit. She needed the additional strength.

Conventional wisdom held she needed a miracle and Zeb didn't intend to disappoint. Medical doctors, homeopaths and psychics could argue why she was getting better. This was one they would never understand or explain. Faith, medicine, and imagination, none equaled the natural healing mechanisms our Creator placed in the human machine. This was part of Zeb's message.

Little Margaret had taken her first step back by force of her own will to live. Zeb had joined her will much like one man helping another lift a boulder. It was that simple. Staff members would poke, prod and run tests. None would have an explanation for Margaret's turn around. The knowledge Zeb used was still decades ahead of us. He had me following him around in my mind whenever he wanted and most times I thought I was dreaming. He allowed me just enough presence to make my own decisions and I was afraid. To this day I don't know why he trusted me with this story.

Mary Savage would become cemented in her belief about a

synergy in the healing community immediately. My doubts would linger for years. Everyone would come a little closer to understanding his or her own spiritual connection to the universe, because Margaret O'Brian would live. Zeb hinted at numerous mysteries to unravel about life, death and living together. He pointed to wondrous new inventions and tremendous advances in humanity. I don't know why I resisted. His presence kind of floated into me and scared me more than I can describe. I was a frightened teenager is the best I can figure even now. I wish I could go back, but I can't, except in my mind and on these pages. Zeb wanted to touch her face. He needed to touch her face. She was close to the surface, close to coming back and he wanted to reassure her. He rested his hand there only a moment; then replaced everything as it had been, and left her room as quietly as he had come.

Returning to the hall he started to mop much more slowly than his normal work pace. He was drained. He required the sun's warmth and people nearby to reinforce and restore his energy. He looked out the window, but the sun still hid behind clouds. Driving rain still splattered the window and fell into the puddles below. Zeb closed his eyes imaging the sun's warmth through the window, and felt a little better.

Entering Margaret's world, so near death, was strange. Though he traveled there before, each journey was different. Children were always most difficult to let go, because they leave so much sorrow behind. Margaret was fighting to survive before Zeb joined her. Deep inside, she wanted to live and her place was still in the world. Now she was on her way back to her parents. This morning she won a battle, and her aura shined brighter. The pale green had spread fully a foot by the time Zeb left her. There were more battles to fight in the long and lovely life she would lead. Many lives would change, because of this miracle. Margaret would never forget it, and neither would her parents. They were the new messengers for an apostolate of spirituality and love. They are some of the people who I mentioned. They have been extolling the events in Springfield for ten years, while I kept silent.

As Zeb worked, he sensed Margaret's future accomplishments and smiled, knowing the joy to come. Placing his mop in the wringer attached to the edge of his bucket, he squeezed excess water from it and continued wiping floors methodically, whistling a familiar tune. He hadn't healed her, as much as helped her find the way to healing.

Zeb hadn't accepted the burden of this gift easily and he still trembled thinking of its awesome implications. His Father truly blessed him, and Zeb didn't know why. He had broken every commandment there was at least twice. He admired women to the point of distraction, only recently coming to terms with passion. Now he was able to separate wants from needs. Now he considered how his actions might hurt those around him before going forward. Such was the case with Elizabeth. He would love to take her in his arms and tell her everything would be all right. He could do it. He'd done it before, but it was wrong. His most difficult lesson was accepting his role as conduit. We don't reach our spiritual potential until we stop taking credit. With Elizabeth, an act of love was to ignore lust, concentrating on helping her to see the goodness in her life and the value of her effort. It was extremely difficult to control his desire.

Zeb explained this when I asked him about Mom. "We choose to hurt or help in almost every situation," he stated, then continued, "I can't choose the items that pop in and out of my awareness, Roger. I can't stop the physical effect your mother creates in my body, nor would I want to. We can reason or react on pure instinct. Reason separates us from the animals. We can choose each new course of action or merely react to stimulus."

Our family would stay together, because Zeb reasoned it better to be honorable. He continued working, thinking of Margaret's innocence. Raising his eyes to the ceiling, he whispered his thanks, but shook his head smiling when an image of Elizabeth came to him sitting by the fire in his cottage. It was good he wouldn't be here too long. He wouldn't want to offend her, or any of us. He hoped his reason could control emotion for a while longer.

CHAPTER ELEVEN

Patty Kelly came rushing down the hall, met at the door by Margaret's mother. She hurried into the room and emerged a moment later again at a full run back to the nurse's station. She leaned over and spoke to Nancy in low tones, who then raced to the elevator. The whole event resembled a Pony Express mail transfer. Zeb mopped closer to Margaret's room. Five minutes later, Kevin Richards arrived. Zeb knew Margaret must have been improving rapidly. He asked Nancy what was happening, as Mary Savage tore by. Nancy confirmed Margaret was awake. In her enthusiasm, she didn't notice, he wasn't surprised.

Mary and Kevin emerged, engaged in half conversation and half debate.

"We can't start feeding poison into her, just because she is showing signs of improvement, without knowing why she is improving. It could be because they stopped her chemo days ago and she is just recovering," Kevin offered.

"Then the possibility exists her treatment was working," Mary said, trying hard to convince herself. "Or she is recovering from the treatment itself."

"What do you suggest we do, Mare?"

"I wish I was certain. Did you glean anything important from her history?"

"Every possibility was examined and every accepted method tried. The result was what we saw yesterday. They treated the child as if she was an adult, Mary, and no one can fault them for that, but she is a child and children are more open. You convinced me of that last year with the Kemp's little boy, Brian."

"Brian was quite a kid." Mary answered lovingly, remembering the exuberant little twelve-year-old. "He spent most of his last three years here, because it made him feel better to be cheering people up. I couldn't tell you how many mothers and fathers he made smile."

Mary stopped a moment and Kevin touched her shoulder. She took his hand and grinned. "We learned a lot from Brian. Do you know there were over a thousand people at Brian's funeral? Everyone was laughing and joking. Everyone had their own story about him. It was like a giant party."

"He lived a lot longer, because he met you, Mary."

"It was his faith, Kevin. I taught him to use his mind against pain and despair, but faith, in God and himself, kept him alive."

"Whatever it was, worked, and Brian went through treatment similar to Margaret's before you took him off everything. If you examine their histories side by side, they are almost identical except for the ages."

"So you're saying we should take the same course."

"All I know is something we don't understand is at work and I don't think we should interfere. Her immune system seems to be kicking in again. Why chance screwing it up."

Mary smiled, "You know, it frightens me when I agree with you Kevin. You always say my healing methods will be the death of me."

Kevin chuckled, "Well let me astound you some more, while I have you reeling."

"Shoot."

"The good Father and his friend Rabbi Shulman were in to see this little girl twice already. I think they should continue, and we should monitor results."

"You're saying we should sit back and do nothing, but watch them pray for a miracle."

"Mare, yesterday, hardly twelve hours ago, we were both ready to bury that little girl. Something brought her a long way back in a very short time. I don't know what, and I don't care. I want it to continue."

"You have a point. A miracle would be nice this week. It's been a while. I'll talk to Joe Tomlavich, and let them know what's happening."

They stopped at the nurse's station, and Mary addressed Nancy.

"Nance, would you call Father Tomlavich. I think he's in his office downstairs." Joe was in the Chapel reading when the phone next to his kneeler rang.

"Should I give him any information over the phone."

"Tell him we need God's 800 number badly, and I'd like to see him as soon as possible."

"You want me to say that, Dr. Savage."

"Yes, I want you to say exactly that."

Zeb moved passed and Mary noticed him for the second time, remembering him from the maintenance office the day before.

Today, she stopped him and extended her hand, "Hello, I'm Mary Savage. I'm sorry I didn't introduce myself yesterday, but I was in a bit of a funk over the little girl in this room."

"I'm Zebedia, Dr. Savage. I heard you talking. Is she better?"

"Much better, Zeb. May I call you that?"

"Please do, and please excuse me, Dr. Savage, but Frank is short handed and I have a lot of work to get done."

"Of course." Zeb moved away and Mary watched him go. He didn't seem the least surprised the little girl was better. Mary puzzled to herself. "Why would he? He didn't know her condition to begin with. Then why would he want to know if she was better."

She felt euphoric talking to him and noticed a further lift in her spirits like a shot of adrenaline, just as Sam and Joe arrived and she mistakenly attributed it to their presence.

"Your boss has been working overtime," she kidded the rabbi and priest. The two men were close friends. Traveling through vastly different religious backgrounds, they arrived at similar conclusions. Mary heard them argue philosophy to the boiling point. Anyone who didn't know them would swear they were going to have a knock down, drag out fistfight, but they never did. The arguments always ended with a glass of wine, a hug and no clear resolution. Neither man would give ground.

As I look back on that time. I think of them as two prizefighters fighting continually for the world title, always to a draw. They would sit with desperate families for hours on end with no relief, except each other. Both of them men of God, both with confidence in faith, reduced to its simplest form: "Help when you are able, whenever possible, for as long as you are able." Brilliant men, who had come to the conclusion God was not this vast unreachable entity created by various men running organized religions. God was and remains a simple act of charity or kindness. God is a quiet spontaneous message of hope. God resides in each of us. They argued philosophy for hours, but their faith was simple.

Mary asked them once to express their beliefs, and Joe deferred to Sam who answered, "Open your hand and your heart and let your love flow out. Never look back." Joe nodded in agreement. Mary adored the passion Sam and Joe brought to their work. They made living feel good, just being around them. They explained their job, like medicine, was an imperfect science.

Sam Shulman answered Mary's barb about their boss lightly. "Everyone should have such a generous employer, although he doesn't pay that well."

"I think, Joe does a little better than you, Sam." Mary came back.

"I'm with the new regime, Mary. He's stuck in the past."

"Don't you start that again, meshuginah priest. The boss is still the boss. Am I right?"

"Of course you're right, but . . ."

"But, but, but! Most humans only have one. You have more than most. What is it this time?"

"Oh calm down, Sam."

"Okay. So, I'm calm already. What are you butting about."

"I was going to say, we all rely heavily on the past. God is for all time, therefore He is always current."

"You're saying we shouldn't worship an ancient God, when our God exists today. Tradition entangles religion to the point of strangulation."

"That is precisely what I am saying. We get bogged down in tradition and forget God lives in each of us a full measure. God is, while tradition passes away. We don't create God. We create rituals to honor Him, which all to often end up replacing the spirit of God in us. You don't think Christ would arrive on a donkey today, do you Sam. And Christ would most certainly involve more women in His ministry, simply because it is a different period in our history. The men have made a mess of things quite nicely for long enough, don't you think?"

"What you say is true, Joseph, but removing all tradition allows too much rationalization. God is not to be trifled about on our whims of behavior. There must be some guide of morality, or we are lost."

"We argue much to much on a moot point, my friend. I do not wish to see my Savior trifled with. Your point about rationalization is well stated and I concur."

He turned to Mary "It doesn't take much to get us going, does it, girl."

Mary chuckled, knowing she succeeded in baiting them. "I think you two were placed on earth to argue until you drop."

"And beyond when we drop." Sam responded.

"To God's ears, Sammy. I would hate to think we're doing this for nothing."

"That would be a fine mess especially with all these lovely women floating around. There is something to be said for the old ways, eh, Joseph?"

"One of his pet projects is to get me married. He even offered to intercede on my behalf with the Pope."

"It must be very lonely at times, Joe." Mary interjected, turning serious for a moment.

"It is. But, I am also free of entanglements. I agree, though, celibacy should be a matter of choice." Mary quickly steered the conversation back to the little girl's improvement. Celibacy was not her favorite subject. She had been celibate too long and not by choice.

Good news at County Memorial traveled fast. A savvy journalist had been hanging around the hospital off and on since its inception. You never knew when a sensational break through would come, or a miracle cure would occur. The hospital was a source of juicy stories from the beginning and today was to be a bonanza.

The halls were buzzing with news of two cures. A child admitted only the day before at the edge of death was doing well. A young woman, in a coma for months, opened her eyes and spoke to her husband. Speculation was rampant allowing Rodney to embellish when he wrote his column. He began, what would become the most talked about series of articles of the decade, with a small piece: a teaser to wet the appetite. He never suspected how large the appetite for good news would be. The little girl continued to improve, as did the Caverly woman. He'd already interviewed Mrs. Caverly. Not only was she awake, but preliminary examinations indicated she was perfectly well and able to leave the hospital at any time. She agreed to stay and submit to a battery of tests, which she didn't need. Mary convinced her it was important. They might help others back from the death sleep by learning from Mrs. Caverly's experience.

Rodney Fisher, freelance writer, had hit the mother load. He was smiling from ear to ear as Sam and Joe came around the corner.

"Good morning, Rabbi," he nodded and added, "Father."

Both greeted him warmly and were about to continue when Rodney had a thought and stopped them. "Rabbi, were you in to see a woman on the second floor recently?"

Sam Shulman smiled, "Which woman on the second floor. There are quite a few."

"I'm sorry. Lucinda Caverly."

"The young woman in a coma. We saw her a week ago, but not since then. Why?"

"Just hoping."

Father Joe interrupted, "Is she better?"

"Better, Father? You mean you haven't heard."

"Heard what, Rod?"

"She is going home in three or four days. Go see for yourself. Something is happening around here. It must be in the water, or the holy water if you prefer, Father."

"Very funny, Rod. We'll stop in to see her in a little while. Would you like to join us for coffee?"

"I sure would. I need a couple hours to organize my material." They moved down the hall in quiet conversation. Everyone was talking about the same things. Even the patients were aware, and the atmosphere was almost festive. The nurses stepped livelier and the aids were joking around. When a patient got released with a clean bill of health from this hospital, it was an event.

Lucinda Caverly had not come out of her coma alone. She touched everyone, who worked here. News of Margaret O'Brian's reversal followed quickly, reinforcing everyone's joy.

Rain filled the parking lot with puddles the size of small lakes. Wind howled, bending trees almost to the ground, but inside, the sun was shinning. Zeb spent the day, rushing from job to job as best he could, whistling the little tune stuck in his head for days. He remembered all the notes, but couldn't come up with the words or title. When he finally stopped cleaning to take a break, it was nearly time to go home. Even in a depleted condition, Zeb completed the work of a three-man crew, while Frank slept through the day in his office. When Zeb handed him the list of things he accomplished Frank couldn't believe it.

"Did you hire someone to help you?" He joked.

"I'll take that as a compliment, and I did have help. Today is a special day. That's why I came to wake you."

"What do you mean?"

"The little girl you were worried about will be fine and Lucinda Caverly, too."

"I heard about Mrs. Caverly yesterday, but the child, are you certain about the child?"

Frank dropped Zeb's list becoming animated.

"Go see for yourself."

Frank stood up pulled up his pants zipper and buckled his belt. Hurrying towards the elevator, he called over his shoulder. "I'll see you in the morning, Zeb. Thank you."

Zeb waved and went to put his tools away. It had been a hard day, yet the soreness in his arms felt pleasant. His Father's plan continued to unfold before his eyes. Events were falling into place rapidly, now. Healings — emotional, physical and spiritual — were occurring all around him, soon, someone would make a connection. Joy spread rapidly. Zeb looked towards the heavens.

Much too tired to raise his arms, he whispered, "Thanks."

A light drizzle still fell, as he sloshed through puddles soaking his feet, and a television truck splashed water and mud all over him. The truck driver stopped and apologized.

"I must have a target on my shirt." He thought, looking himself over, as the driver offered a towel. Zeb thanked him for stopping, then hurried on his way. He continued wiping himself as he walked.

Raphael Santiaga stepped out the door of Nuzzio's Pizzeria, his gang's usual hang out, as Zeb passed by wiping himself off. Jimmy Rivera noticed Zeb walking along the street. He moved, blocked his path and was joined by several members of the gang. Raphael swore silently to himself, took a last gulp of soda, flicked his cigarette and jogged over to join the others wondering what to do. He signaled for a patrol car before reaching the group with a little radio transmitter concealed in the cross around his neck.

Jimmy was taunting Zeb, "Hey, brother, your clothes are filthy. How come you dress like a pig, Miho? You work in a hospital, man. Don't you have no self respect?"

Knowing he was in for a rough time, Zeb took a deep breath,

glanced skyward, and answered, "A truck splashed me after work. I have clean clothes right here." Indicating the package he carried. He was tired. His reserves were very low. He felt his patience deserting him.

Jimmy went to snatch the clothes from Zeb's hands, but Zeb anticipated the move and reacted quickly. Jimmy fell flat on his face on the wet pavement. Zeb dropped his clothes, reached to help Jimmy, and was punched for his trouble. The group circled him, as Jimmy stood up stepping on Zeb's discarded package, grinding dirt into the fabric.

"You're a wise ass, Miho, and one thing I don't like is no wise ass on my turf."

Zeb bent to retrieve his soiled clothes without comment, and Jimmy hit him in the face. Zeb fell back and Jimmy hit him again. Zeb's knee buckled this time, and he collapsed to the ground, while Jimmy acknowledged cheers from his friends. A small crowd of onlookers gathered and a siren could be heard in the distance.

Raphael jumped in and said, "Leave him, Jimmy. The cops are coming."

"I just want to give him one more," Jimmy answered and danced in on Zeb to the rousing approval of his friends.

He reeled back and swung as hard as he could at Zeb's exposed ribs, was startled when his fist stopped in mid-flight and Zeb held it fast in his left hand. He squeezed, twisted slightly and Jimmy fell to the ground. Zeb didn't let go. He gathered his clothes with his free hand and spoke to the gang members.

"Why do you take orders from a bully?" Zeb's eye was swollen closed and his cheek was split, but he was calm, his voice even.

"I have little patience with bullies. All of you better leave now, except him. He stays with me."

The siren was very close.

"Cut him, Raphael." Jimmy screamed.

Raphael answered, "Later, Miho. The heat will be here any minute."

All the members hurried away and Zeb released Jimmy's hand.

"You can go, too. They all know you are a coward."

"You're not giving me up to the cops?"

"For hitting me? No, I have suffered worse, and I let you make me angry."

"What is wrong with you, man?"

"What would your grandfather say if he were here to see you, son. Would he be proud of what you're doing."

"You knew my, pop, pop?"

"Yes, I do." Zeb's use of the present tense fell on deaf ears.

"Who are you?"

"I am a cold, wet and tired man who is going home."

A black and white patrol car pulled up and Jimmy turned to run, but Zeb stopped him.

In the gathering dusk Zeb's face didn't look too bad, and the officer asked, "What's the problem, fellas."

Jimmy noticed the cut on Zeb's face was gone and his eye was no longer swollen. He whispered quietly to himself, "Sweet Mary, Mother of God."

Zeb turned and smiled at him, and Jimmy knew Zeb was aware of his thoughts.

Zeb turned back to the officer. "We had an argument, officer, but its over now. I guess we were a little loud."

The officer looked at Zeb curiously and asked for identification. Zeb reached into his pocket and took out his small leather folder full of papers. He unfolded it carefully and removed an old yellow certificate in a language the officer didn't recognize, and he asked, "Don't you have anything in English, I can't read this."

Zeb smiled indicating the paper was all he had and the officer looked frustrated.

"Wait here," he said and returned to his car, not knowing what to do.

Santiaga radioed for help, saying this guy was in danger, but he wasn't.

John Sullivan also answered the call and arrived just as officer Falcone was getting the I.D.

He showed Zeb's paper to John, who wasn't surprised. Accepting it from Bob, he told him Zeb was a neighbor, and he would handle it. Falcone started to protest, but Sulli insisted.

"I'll bet this paper is written in Hebrew, Bob. I'll make a copy and you can check it out later, if that will make you feel better."

Bob Falcone knew when to quit. He got back in his patrol car and started the motor. Pulling away, he felt a sense of loss. He stopped the car and rubbed his stomach.

"Must have been something I ate." He thought and continued on his way. John noticed the confused look on his face and chuckled as he moved over towards Zeb.

"You weren't so lucky this time, Zebedia."

"I guess you could say that, Sulli."

"Your face is bruised."

"Is that still there? I thought it would have healed by now."

Jimmy blessed himself, when Zeb said this. The look on the boy's face wasn't fear or desperation; it was different, one of reverence.

"What happened?"

"We had a fight, Sulli, but its over now."

"Is that true, Jimmy?" The boy nodded.

"You can go, but don't let me catch you harassing anyone else."

Jimmy nodded, "Mister, can I speak to you some time?"

"Anytime you wish, son."

"Is it okay if I stop over tonight?"

"I'll see you then." Jimmy walked away repeatedly looking back over his shoulder.

"You better tell the Crowley's he's coming, Zeb"

"Why is that?"

"They might call us and have him arrested."

"He's not that bad, and his grandparents are wonderful people."

"His grandparents are dead, Zeb. Who are you?"

"I am your tired friend. It has been a long day."

"Jump in. I'll run you home."

CHAPTER TWELVE

Zeb didn't argue. He was bone weary, sore, and angry with himself for losing his temper, and hurting the boy. Jimmy deserved a beating, which Zeb could have given him. Humiliating him in front of his friends was far worse. Zeb looked skyward out of the safety of the patrol car. Streetlights flashed his features in and out of shadow, like an old black and white movie. Sulli glanced sideways, seeing the anguish contorting Zeb's face.

"That boy could have killed you, Zeb."

"I know, Sulli, and I appreciate your concern, but that doesn't excuse what I did."

Sulli noticed Zeb's bruise was gone.

"You defended yourself."

"I humiliated the boy in front of his friends. I was letting him know I was better than he, making him feel small."

"Maybe he'll think twice before picking on someone else."

"I hope your right, John. It would be nice if some good came of my mistake."

"I think I am."

Zeb didn't answer. He knew John was trying to make him feel better. Boiling anger was hard to control. Each day Zeb meditated in the morning and at night for five minutes just to drain the day's anger. It built on itself, like a forest fire smoldering for hours before erupting in blazing, uncontrollable fury. His human failings increased his compassion for those around him.

Anger, greed, and fear, he thought to himself are the most powerful emotions. The only emotion which rivals fear in intensity is lust. The neutralizing agent for all is love.

He smiled, thinking of Elizabeth, and his thoughts turned gentle. He and Sulli glided along darkening streets in silence. He lusted, but he loved too and the feeling in his stomach quickened when John stopped in front of the big house and Elizabeth was seated on the front porch. Zeb stared at her bathed in satin, silver moonlight slipping through opaque clouds, caressing her translucent skin. His heart pounded inside his chest hard enough to be heard, and he glanced at John, who put the car in neutral.

"If you have time tomorrow, I'd like to talk about Grace."

"Is it important? We can talk now if it is." Zeb replied.

"It will keep until morning, Zeb." He had noticed Zeb gazing, starry eyed, at my mom.

"She is a beautiful woman, isn't she?"

Zeb shook his head slowly up and down. My mother waved, rising to approach the car.

"Breath taking," Zeb answered quietly with a slow sigh, as she glided smoothly over the wet grass.

"Hi, Zeb. Hi, John. How are Cathy and the kids?"

"Fine, Elizabeth. The kids are growing up fast." I came out the door, as he answered and Mom looked over her shoulder, "They grow up in the blink of an eye, Sulli." She winked at me. It was the first time she called him Sulli in months, and her features were soft and untroubled. She didn't appear sad or worried, and John glanced at Zeb, who sat quietly listening to her speak like a puppy with its mother. John didn't have to be a cop to know that look. Zeb was infatuated with her. Sulli wasn't surprised. Most men were enthralled by her looks when they met Elizabeth and she threatened women, for no reason. Elizabeth would never hurt anyone intentionally. Sulli knew that. In fact most everyone who knew her well experienced her kindness. Mom was out going and pleasant, unaware of her physical beauty. Men had trouble being her friend and women wouldn't risk it.

In that instant I suddenly understood loneliness. It became crystal clear to me, though people surrounded her, Mom was still all alone. This person, who taught me to walk, talk, and smile, hid a secret pain. She was without good friends, because she was extraordinary. It didn't seem fair, but life isn't always. I watched her with renewed affection.

"Are you and Ben coming to the dance Friday?" John asked breaking the growing silence.

"I'll mention it to him, again." She smiled. "Maybe Zeb will come too." She reached for Zeb's arm and brushed it lightly. He blushed slightly, but recovered, covering her hand with his free one.

"That would be wonderful. I love to dance, though I never get much practice." He popped the door open and hopped out. Casually he draped his arm around Mom's waist and held her close in an affectionate way. She looked up at him, a silent message passing, and he reached for me. I moved closer and relaxed.

John laughed, "When you're dancing with Elizabeth, no one notices you."

Zeb looked Elizabeth up and down, as if she were the only woman alive. "You're right, John."

"Both of you stop it, you're embarrassing me."

She loved the attention and I was happy for her deep in my heart. Her smile and easy way as they spoke to her with true affection made every cell in my body smile. She was happy. It was such a small thing and yet meant everything.

"Then its set. We'll pick the three of you up around seven."

John started the car and Zeb slammed the door. John drove away thinking Elizabeth finally had a friend, yet I knew it was much more. Zeb would move a mountain for our mother.

I chuckled inwardly at the image, thinking, "Zeb probably could move a mountain."

As Sulli drove away, he looked back at us and waved. He was already thinking of Grace, beginning to understand his possessive feelings. Cathy was involved now and it was easier. Zebedia came into their lives and it just happened. Zeb didn't say much. He listened, observed, but never seemed to judge. I guess I would say he was and is the least judgmental person I ever knew.

Our lives were changing. Sulli noticed, and I noticed it too, not only in myself, but Mom especially. The corners of her mouth were curled upward and there was a spring to her step that had been missing. Timmy flew out the door and she scooped him up, as we headed up the walk. Love was infectious, breeding by-products of joy, trust and hope. Zeb loved openly. He explained I should too, and was amused when I made a face. He told me loving is essential and must be exercised, or it goes dormant and eventually dies.

"Will you join us for dinner, Zeb?" Mom asked, and a voice behind him answered, "Of course he will. He must let us return some of his generosity."

Dad was home from work, and I instinctively looked at my watch. It was hours before his usual arrival time, and Mom raced into his arms. "Hi, Benny." He hugged her close, and I wondered what Zeb might be feeling. Searching his face in the shadows I saw tears brimming. A smile played there too. He loved Mom. I know he did, but there was something more. He loved me, Dad, and the kids, too. Not the same way as he loved Mom, but because of her, and John was right. Mom would never know how much Zeb loved her. That was part of his gift to us as a family. I speak of this now as if I understood it then, I didn't. I am still learning to love unselfishly without expecting a return or a pat on the back.

"Zebedia would you honor us with your presence, sir?" Dad asked grandly and Zeb taking his cue, bowed to Dad with exaggerated grandeur of his own answering, "I would be delighted, sir."

Everyone strolled towards the main house, but I hung back. Zeb was carrying Timmy; Mom and Dad were holding hands. I remember this scene distinctly, because in only forty-eight hours our lives changed forever. It was hard to imagine ever wanting to run away from Springfield. Or our family splitting up, yet two days before, that was exactly where we were. Zeb hadn't done anything specific to heal our wounds, yet I couldn't help wondering at how he altered my outlook. And we all experienced this sense of well being.

Dad stopped and waited for me. The others stopped too, but he urged them to continue. He waited and put his arm around me. I could feel the warmth of his affection, as I hadn't in a long while.

"Whatever you decide about school is fine with me, Rog."

"You mean it, Dad?"

He nodded, and we headed back to his car. There was enough food in plastic containers to feed three families. Containers full of home made baked ziti, eggplant parmesan, and angel-hair pasta covered with seafood sauce. Everything smelled wonderful. He looked at me and said, "I slaved over a hot stove for hours to prepare this food."

I looked at him cross-eyed, "Sure you did. You want me to call Alfredo's?"

He laughed, "Caught. It's tough when your son grows up smarter than you."

"That will be the day."

"I mean it, Roger. I know I don't say it enough, but I am extremely proud of you."

All I remember squeezing past the tremendous lump in my throat was, "Thanks, Dad."

We ate, talked and laughed until well past midnight. Zeb excused himself early, because he was tired and I watched him go, feeling immensely grateful. I had never experienced a true sense of thankfulness in my eighteen years and I felt a stab of fear. I didn't want anything to change this. Somehow I knew people wouldn't let Zeb be. He turned just before disappearing in the darkness. In the half-light spread by our spotlights, reaching the edge of the wooded area, I saw Zeb wave. I couldn't see his face, but I knew he was smiling. I knew he understood my thoughts. I heard him in my heart. Then, he was gone.

I returned to the dining room, where Dad finished clearing dishes and serving ice cream. Normally, I would be out in search of my friends by this point of any family meal. Tonight, I sat down to enjoy the musical laughter and bask in the smiles of loved ones rediscovering each other. I am telling this part with the perfect vision of hindsight, because I didn't know it then. At the time, all I knew was I felt awful good.

It was no coincidence this metamorphosis began when I splashed mud all over Zeb. If I didn't live that time, and see it with my own eyes I would swear it was all a dream. Zeb's kindness and simple approach to life were a Godsend in the most literal sense. And I think dreams are made of little pieces of hope, and hope is all we really need to continue. My family had lost perspective and suddenly a simple man setting a simple example brought it back into focus. Nothing earth shattering; that was yet to come.

People all over town were beginning to talk about him. Most importantly they were discussing his simple ways, his rich sense of humor and his openness. There was a genuine effort afoot to emulate him. Even now, ten years later I marvel at his gentle strength, and try to copy it. He was never judgmental. He didn't put anyone down. He continually tried to raise people up. My mom was a great example. He let her see her value again. Something she lost along the way. Her beauty was enhanced by the peace she found within. That was true of each of us. It wasn't that anyone changed drastically. This was a path of self-discovery and realization. I will never forget Zeb explaining maintenance being as important as surgery to the hospital's existence. I never considered it until that day and I never would have known he was right unless I considered it.

CHAPTER THIRTEEN

Zeb wandered up the path towards his cottage. A sudden chilly breeze touched his neck and he drew his coat closer. He still had several things to do. The shutters needed straightening and a couple windows were cracked or missing. There was no urgency, but Zeb intended to keep his word about doing chores, until he could pay his rent. He wasn't embarrassed to accept our help, but wouldn't take advantage of our generosity. Zeb seemed to approach each day intent on giving everything he had and receiving everything he could. I couldn't comprehend either notion.

Reaching the cottage, he lifted tools in tired hands and went to work. We heard him hammering above the cool March wind, and Dad started towards the door.

Mom stopped him. "Leave him be, Ben. It's a matter of friendship to him. He made a promise and intends to keep it."

"I suppose you're right, Beth, but it doesn't seem right, with all that's happened, all he's done for us so quickly."

She came up behind Dad and slid her arms around his waist. "I know, Benny. We are fortunate he accepted our help and he is grateful for it. Stay here with us. We are happy to have you home. Zeb knows he is part of us. Let him be."

Dad slid around to face her. His eyes were glistening. He pushed a stray hair gently back over Mom's ear and let his hand continue back over her shoulder behind her neck. He drew her in and kissed her deeply while his heart pounded inside him almost as loud as Zeb's hammer.

Mom backed away breathless and whispered, "Welcome home, Ben."

He kissed her again, longer than before.

CHAPTER FOURTEEN

Zeb made short work of the shutters, most were merely loose, needing fastening. One set was split with several slats missing. He removed them, and brought them inside. He placed them near the counter, where he wouldn't forget them. Then he knelt by a chair in front of the stove.

It had been an extraordinary day, as he recounted the events in his mind. People around here adapted quickly. They were already accepting simple things. Many were drawn to a slower way of life, longing for things of a spiritual nature. Friendship, kindness, and patience had been lost somewhere between hurry up, and succeed at any cost.

Zeb placed his face in his hands and thanked God for the blessings of the day. He asked forgiveness, for nearly striking the young boy, knowing he wanted to, and still would like to. Zeb shuddered at the temptation. He acknowledged his anger and let it fade away. The little O'Brian girl would live, as would Lucinda Caverly. He achieved a balance today and though his anger nearly got the best of him, Zeb felt good. As thoughts of healing and hope swirled in his head he fell fast asleep on the floor in front of the stove.

The sound of wind whipping through the treetops woke Zeb just before first light. He sat up stretched, then went to find his Bible. After reading a while, he began washing his clothes, generally cleaning up and preparing breakfast. As he finished he heard a noise outside followed by a light tapping on the door. He opened it, as the sky was beginning to lighten to gray-blue, exposing the trees hiding in the mist. Dew mixed with the frost on the ground and two squirrels moved passed the porch searching for food. Raphael stood in front of Zeb with bruises up and down his arms and the side of his face was bleeding. He stared at Zeb without speaking.

"I've been wandering around for hours wondering what to do. They want to hurt you real bad."

"I thought they might."

"We had a fight with a rival gang last night and Jimmy stopped it. He came and found us after you left, and he's changed. I want to know who you are. I've worked around these street gangs a long time. Kids like Jimmy don't change. He should have come back to us screaming for your head and he didn't. Why?"

Zeb shrugged.

Raphael continued as if Zeb had answered him. "You let Jimmy beat you and didn't turn him in. I know you were angry. It was in your eyes. You could have whipped his ass. You didn't. I'm confused."

"I was too. I was tired from work and I let my anger get the best of me."

"John Sullivan asked me why the gang let you past two days ago at the hospital."

Zeb stopped him. "We can talk, while I clean you up."

Zeb went to his bag and removed some cloth and a few leaves. He got some water and mashed the leaves into a paste, adding warm water from his teapot.

"Take your shirt off and sit down." Zeb didn't ask what happened to Raphael's jacket.

"You must be freezing."

"Not really, I drove over."

"You have a car?"

Raphael laughed, "Yes, I do. Does that surprise you?"

"I suppose it does." Zeb answered dipping the cloth into the warm water and dabbing the laceration on Raphael's cheek. It wasn't as bad as it appeared and Zeb took the paste he had made, rubbing it gently into the cut.

"What's that?"

"Antibiotics." Zeb answered, laughing.

"What are you, some sort of Indian medicine man, Zeb? You've got the whole town wondering."

"Do they wonder about you too, Raphael? You aren't what you appear to be either."

"I was. I belonged to these gangs growing up."

"I learned from medicine men growing up and I read a lot now, but I enjoy working with my hands."

"That's why you work maintenance."

"Is that bad?"

"People don't think it's enough for you."

"Okay Raphael, what do you think?"

"I don't know what to think. I know you could be a philosopher or a doctor or some kind of healer. That isn't a normal hospital."

"You have answered your own question."

"What do you mean?" Zeb smiled.

"I am all those things you mentioned. I get paid for cleaning. I choose to heal and council and so do you, or at least you try to. You get paid to enforce law."

Raphael looked perplexed and Zeb continued. "Who summoned the police yesterday, Raphael?"

"How did you know?"

"I didn't until now, but your secret is safe. You are paid to protect and serve, but you feel best when you save. We aren't so different."

Raphael Santiaga, product of the streets of South Philadelphia, survivor of abuse, continual witness to rape and murder softened. It really didn't matter to Zeb what people thought, and Raphael lived his life the same way. His life depended on secrecy, existing on the streets among thugs, drug dealers and pimps. The job he was paid for wasn't the job he loved. His job was more than being a cop. He'd saved dozens of children's lives over the past five years.

Zeb finished dressing his wound. The sun pushed half its mass above the treetops, rising slowly, like a bright orange ball. It slid silently skyward, gaining distance, lighting the new day along the way, and Raphael watched in awe through the window. Zeb whistled softly, as he began pressing his clothes. Raphael hadn't noticed Zeb's nakedness, until now. He chuckled, imagining what his wife would say if she could see this scene.

Zeb slipped on his pants and shirt. "I'm going over to Jack's before work. Do you want to come along?"

"I have to get home Zeb. My wife is sick and she needs help with Latitia today."

"What's wrong with her."

"She has the flu or something. It started yesterday and I suppose she will be sick for a few days. It's too bad, because we were suppose to go to a dance on Friday night."

"I wouldn't worry." Zeb answered and though Raphael thought it was an odd comment, he didn't respond.

"Thanks for cleaning me up, Zeb. I'll see you later."

"Your welcome and I'll see you Friday night."

Raphael didn't answer. As the door closed behind him, he felt a little sad. He would have liked to stay and talk longer, but Zeb had to work and he wanted to get home. Reaching his car, he sat for a minute thinking about their conversation and was comfortable he had the answer he came for. He felt a whole lot better thinking to himself, "We are all much more than we believe. We touch so many other people and affect so many other lives, which we never consider."

He headed home, looking forward to seeing Latitia, his little girl, and Sarah his wife. Checking his rear view mirror caused him to swerve, making his tires squeal. He touched the razor slash in his cheek softly. It appeared as if it happened days ago instead of hours. There was hardly a scab. What he knew was a severe wound now appeared to be only a scratch. He settled back in his seat, considering turning around, but changed his mind. Zeb answered all his questions. What he believed, after all, was up to him. It was years later I realized what Zeb meant one night when we were alone.

He said to me, "Roger there are things about me I can not tell you. There are things you will decide on your own. Others will tell you things and some of them you may not believe." I didn't know what he meant. Back then, I was to close to the situation and I was so young, but I know now. He wanted me to begin to understand faith, because sometimes it is all we have.

Raphael started to whistle a tune as he drove away. He didn't realize it was the same tune Zeb had been whistling for days. I saw him leave and hurried back to the cottage. I was worried about Zeb. Not knowing Raphael was a cop, at the time, I thought he was here to make trouble. When I reached the edge of the clearing I noticed the shutters and a few loose shingles were already repaired. With only a little work the cottage was starting to resemble my grandfather's home again. Only one set of missing shutters remained to be fixed. Zeb walked towards me.

"Good morning."

"That it is," Zeb answered. Then he said something strange. "Thank you for caring about me, but you needn't worry. Raphael is a friend."

"How did you know what I was thinking?" I asked him.

He smiled. "I'm sure you and your friends have run into him on several occasions." The look on your face was a little bleak.

"He hangs with the toughest crowd around here, Zeb, a bunch of losers. He is dangerous."

"Perhaps, and perhaps not."

"Those kids aren't like me and my friends, Zeb. They don't care about anybody. They'd kill you as soon as look at you. It's not something to take lightly."

"You're right about the group as a whole, and your concern is warranted, but maybe one or two could change."

"You're talking about a miracle."

"Don't you believe in miracles, Rog?"

"I don't know."

"You're spending a lot of time with your little brother and sister aren't you."

"What does that have to do with miracles?"

"Your mom and Dad surely consider it a miracle."

He was kidding me.

"Okay, I'll bite. What if a miracle occurs and you do save one or two of them."

"That's two less you and your friends have to worry about."

"You know you're right. Let's try to save three."

"Three it is." Zeb said laughing at my joke. "Can you come to Jacks with me?"

"Nah, I'd like to, but I promised Mom I'd walk Linda and Timmy to school."

"Another miracle."

"Actually the miracle is she and Dad are going to an art exhibit in the city."

A shadow appeared in Zeb's eyes, but he recovered quickly. "That is great news."

He made the statement with conviction, then turned towards the driveway and hurried down the street. I followed my emotions swirling inside me. He opened doors for us to reach each other and struggled mightily with his own emotions. He wasn't flashy and didn't try to hide things. I knew where I stood with Zeb. I knew he was a little envious of Dad. I knew how he felt and why he felt, because he allowed me to know. I am telling you this with a mixture of what I felt then and know now. These things popped into my head. I knew what others were thinking and feeling; things I couldn't know, but I did. It scared me then, but it doesn't any longer. My only regret is I wasn't strong enough then to be more help.

Zeb placed our needs before his own. It took me years to get comfortable with that single facet of his personality.

I had found a friend. At seventeen, I owned something others searched for their entire lives. Zeb was my friend and I trusted him. I would never betray that trust. I promised myself before Almighty God, I wouldn't. I was very naive.

CHAPTER FIFTEEN

Zeb walked up the street, happy for our family and frustrated. He didn't like being jealous and wouldn't interfere, but he couldn't control the way he felt about Elizabeth.

He looked skyward and whispered, "Some help here, Maestro. My heart is pounding like a teenager, and I am feeling things for that woman which are beyond my control."

He stopped a minute to collect his thoughts, then added, "Please help me, Father. I am grateful Elizabeth and Ben found the good in each other again, but I'll be darned if I can hide my feelings."

He closed his eyes and his face became radiant. He was aware of my presence; I could feel him drawing me in. As I watched I got a good feeling throughout my body. I felt as if every dream I ever dreamed would come true.

Zeb opened his eyes and said, "Thanks."

I asked him, "For what?" and he said he wasn't speaking to me.

I told him how I felt and he laughed saying. "Trust those feelings."

I asked him what he saw and he said the strangest thing. "He said he was speaking to his mother about my family's future."

He patted me on the shoulder and told me his mother liked my dad a whole lot. I remember thinking he might be a little off his rocker, because I didn't see anybody and then he stopped me cold in my tracks.

"She made you feel good, Roger and still you doubt. Trust me, she is very near by. I told you I have a very special Guardian Angel."

I stood there watching Zeb go. He was at peace again, his emotions intact, his ego in control, and his humor at the ready. I never met anyone like him before, haven't since and I doubt I ever will again. He walked away whistling his tune, turned, waved and turned again.

"Who the heck are you, Zebedia?" I asked the morning breeze, but I really didn't need to ask.

Then I hurried back to the house. Mom and Dad were waiting with the kids dressed and ready. I grabbed my lunch, took Linda's hand and headed for her school. Timmy was going to class with me for the day. He held onto her. We waved, as Mom rested her head on Dad's shoulder and smiled. I could almost hear Zeb saying, "she gave you the good feeling, and she is very near" because the feeling surged all through my body. I couldn't have frowned if I wanted to and I didn't want to. I felt like laughing, singing and dancing all at the same time. Yet, I still couldn't let that last little doubt go. It was my security blanket against being hurt, against the possibility that this wasn't real. My heart knew it was. I could sense it, and the kids felt it too, but my head wouldn't allow it. Linda and Timmy giggled with delight, holding hands and walking along. We were living moment by moment and each moment was better than the previous one.

CHAPTER SIXTEEN

Jack was holding court when Zeb entered. He was perched on a stool clutching his coffee cup like a glass. A few local people sat at the counter listening to him pontificate on the ills of the country. He was hard at explaining the last good President was Harry Truman, when he saw Zeb walk in and turned, "What do you think of this bum in Washington, Zeb."

Zeb refused to be baited and answered, "Which bum are we talking about? There are several to consider."

Jack slapped the counter and laughed, "Ain't that the truth boy."

Several customers laughed too and Jack introduced Zeb all around. The Walker brothers owned a plumbing contracting business and Viola Johnson, the beauty store. Mary Kennedy delivered mail and was the town celebrity. She had nearly qualified for the summer Olympics in the marathon. She was widowed, raising two small children on her own. Everyone was certain she would make it next try. Henry Runningwater ran the drug store. He was strong and quiet. He taught reading in the back room of his store four nights a week and presented quite a sight on Saturday morning entering the Synagogue. His long, blue black hair flowed out in every direction under his Yamulkah. Jack kidded him about being the only Jewish, Sioux Chief in America.

"He's thinking about changing his name to Runningwaterberg."

"You talk to much, old man." Henry rose from his stool like a tree growing in front of your eyes. He was nearly seven feet tall, with broad shoulders and huge hands, which he extended to Zeb. Gazing at him out of deep gentle black pools, which seemed to go on forever. Zeb reached with his right and Henry grasped his wrist in a traditional clasp. "Jack says you work at the hospital. Welcome to Springfield."

"Is it true you are an Israeli Indian?" Zeb asked.

"That sounds like the name of a baseball team." Henry joked, then continued. "Yes, it's true, and Jack is going easy on me this morning.

"Normally he calls me one of the few Sioux Jews in America; not that there is an abundance anywhere else." Zeb was surprised and showed it.

"Relax, Zeb. The old fart can say anything he wants to me."

He said it loud enough for Jack to hear.

"Your damn right I can. Fought three wars for the privilege. And who do you think you're calling an old fart, prince Standingwater."

The others at the counter turned to hear the two play verbal volleyball. It was obvious they liked each other. They had known each other since Henry was a boy. Henry helped care for Jack's wife when she was ill. Jack lent him the money to open his store, which was true of a lot of businesses in town. When the bank turned you down you went to Jack. If Jack turned you down, you were one of two things, a pervert or a liar. Other than that, if you lived in Springfield, you got your loan.

Jack taught Henry to read and write Hebrew. He was amazed at the boys' thirst for knowledge. Henry was the only Indian boy in town when Jack was the only Jewish male. Jack's position changed rapidly, over recent years and a synagogue stood in evidence, but Henry's family was still the sole Indians. Henry's grandmother worked at the same hospital as Zeb. Mary Savage recruited her as soon as it opened.

Jack's bluster didn't hide his great pleasure when Henry started to study Hebrew. Henry explained to Zeb later, he believed Jews, Mexicans, and Orientals all had ties to Indian culture. There were similarities in some words and symbols from the different languages. This discussion was ongoing with Zeb offering insights far beyond Jack's wildest imaginings, but all that would come later. Now was happening at a rapid pace.

"Why don't you get the man a cup of coffee, Jack," Henry suggested.

"He don't drink coffee, son, and I don't have to wait on the bugger either. He knows where the coffee is and he knows he's welcome to a cup. How long do you think these old bones will last jumping up and down serving you buggers coffee? Bad enough I have to make it."

Henry turned to Zeb and said, "I'd forgotten we come here for the shear pleasure of the old goat's company."

"Old goat, eh, I wonder if your grandmother will agree with you Friday night, speaking of old goats."

The ancient brass bell hanging from a spring wire on the front door tinkled signaling another arrival. Everyone glanced over. A striking woman, about six feet tall, her back and shoulders straight as a board, stood there glaring. She had hair the color of new snow, flowing to her waist, and coal black eyes, like stones polished until you can see deep into the mineral. Smooth, soft light brown skin belied her age. Everything about her was long, lean, delicate, yet strong.

"Did I hear you mention me, Jack? Or was that some other old goat."

"L . . . L . . . Lea," he finally stammered. "We were kidding around about the dance."

"Just remember you're not the only single old goat in this town. It's lucky for you, you can dance." She kidded him, then turned serious, walked up to Zeb and stood quietly in front of him. She whispered something to him in a language no one else understood except her grandson, and to everyone's, except Lea's surprise, Zeb answered. She softened and took his hand, as if he were an old friend. Henry introduced her.

"Lea Tenfingers Runningwater, this is Zebedia."

"I know who he is, Grandson. Everyone at the hospital is whispering about him."

Her beauty was exquisite; her melodic voice enchanting and Zeb was not immune. He asked how many years she had. The room grew silent. This closely guarded secret was the subject of much speculation in Springfield. Everyone wondered, but didn't dare ask Lea the question. She answered easily.

"I will be eighty-seven some time in June. I'm not sure of the exact date."

Just like that, one of the great town mysteries dissolved. I learned something about Zeb I didn't realize before. He didn't consider chronology. He used his time well, but wasn't concerned with the quantity, as much as the quality. It was a lesson I would carry the rest of my days.

Zeb took Lea's hand and caressed it with his thumb.

"You look much younger."

She laughed. "I feel thirty-five and want to be twenty like everyone else."

Her voice was light, and lyrical, melding with and floating on the air, bouncy, with a trace of humor. She loved life, fondling her world much like an artist molds clay to form, or places paint to canvas. Creating her life was her art.

"I know at least one younger man, who would love to dance with you Friday night." Zeb added.

She glanced over his shoulder and spoke to Jack. "Did you hear that, Jack. If you're not careful I'm going to fill my dance card with young stallions."

Jack laughed, "He'll have to go some to keep up with us, Lea, but he's welcome to try."

Lea returned her gaze to Zeb. "You're in for quite a contest young man, because one thing that old Jew can do is dance." The entire group laughed as one.

Everyone joined in then, with chatter and stories. It seemed they all wanted to tell a story about Jack from years past. The old Jewish shopkeeper was much loved and respected. Jack moved to Lea, placed a cup on the counter in front of her and she leaned close, kissing him lightly on the cheek, while he patted her hand in silent show of affection. Zeb took note of them and his eyes seemed as if he were sending a message.

I could have imagined it, but at that same moment, as I sat in school, I felt something inside me change. It wasn't physical, but it was real. Deep inside I knew Lea and Jack were special, not that we all aren't in some way, but they were just a little more so. They were people you didn't ignore and never forget. They were two people, who made deep impressions on everyone around them, though they made no effort to. I sensed Zeb spreading a net around them to protect them. To this day I don't know why he included me. Perhaps in time I will understand.

Then Zeb looked back at the others and joined in the conversation. The good feeling inside me persisted and grew. I felt at peace. I felt I could accept anything. I wish I could tell you I kept that feeling always, but it takes work, and I fail a lot. That feeling is something I strive for everyday and always will. Even at seventeen I knew how good it felt knowing I am loved and accepted beyond recrimination simply because I am here and I am me.

"Old goat, huh. We'll see about that after the dance." Lea whispered and Jack looked around quickly to see if anyone heard, but they were all engrossed in the adventures of Jack Fein, bouncing one story after another off Zebedia, who listened to all of them, while Jack and Lea spoke in low tones to each other. Zeb heard it all.

"You better watch what you say, woman. I don't want it to get out that I'm consorting with a female witch-doctor."

"Medicine woman."

She corrected him for the thousandth time. "And that young man is a powerful medicine man."

Zeb glanced over at her sipping coffee. She was taller and her eyes were slightly darker, but she could have been his mother's twin sister. As the stories continued, Lea examined him with those piercing black orbs, getting an urgent feeling. She could see a pale blue aura surrounding him, describing it later as translucent. She didn't mention the disruption, or excited state it was in. She sensed the hospital was going to see cures as it never had before, and wondered if Zeb would survive the notoriety. Lea hoped enough people were ready to believe, knowing she could never protect him from curiosity. People would pull, poke and test him trying to find the source of his power.

"A source available to all of us." She mused then, and would write later.

Jack asked, "Did you say something?"

She shook her head, concentrating on Zeb, adding her energy to his, much as he'd done for Margaret. He glanced over and a silent thank you passed between them. Lea felt her chi surge. Years fell away inside her. It took her breath away. Zeb smiled at the expression on her face. Jack took her hand concerned.

"What is it, Lea?"

She gathered herself, knowing she had just taped into a life force far advanced of her own. It was a completely exhilarating experience. She felt warm and young inside. She reached beyond mortality to touch eternity. It was intoxicating and comforting at the same time.

CHAPTER SEVENTEEN

Grace was baking cookies when Cathy arrived, with her children. Several metal racks covered in chocolate chip and oatmeal raisin cooled by an open window. Cathy walked in, keeping her coat on.

"You can take it off, Cathy. I'm not afraid to be closed in anymore. The rest of the windows are closed and the heat is on, girl."

"That's wonderful, Grace," her voice skeptical.

"You think I'm still a little nuts. That's okay. I'd like to get to know you better, anyway."

"About the money you gave Sulli, Grace."

"He went to the bank?"

"Yes, he has."

"Good. When is he quitting his job?"

"He isn't."

"Why? For God's sake, girl, there is money enough to last two lifetimes."

"He and Raphael Santiaga want to start a school. He doesn't want you to be angry, but he doesn't want all the money."

"Girl you listen to me and you listen good. He can start any damn school he wants, but I don't want him wasting time and effort on hooligans."

Cathy was surprised at the vehemence in Grace's voice. She expected the old woman to be pleased, instead, she was incensed.

"How did he know you might be angry?"

"He's read a lot of my work, and knows how I feel. Black folk won't be equal until we all stop being separate. Young black folk need to learn about their ancestors and take pride in those who fought a biased system. We need to be comfortable with who we are. Johnny knows I feel this way. All of us of every background should be thankful we reached America. It doesn't matter how, for any ethnic group. History is ripe with atrocities. It is time to get over it and sort things out.

"We are an integral part of this great experiment, have suffered much for freedom and deserve our place in this country's and the world's heart. What would we be able to accomplish if we were all still stuck in Africa? Where would the Irish and Italians be if they stayed home? Child, I'm an old woman; almost old enough to date God Himself." She chuckled, "If I hadn't gotten so darn ugly."

Now Cathy smiled, but didn't interrupt. "Education is important, but literacy is paramount. When people can read, they have access to what is possible and aren't frightened by new ideas.

"Johnny and Raphael worry too much about a few big-mouthed bad apples. They need to focus on the good kids. Stepping on each other's toes is normal and healthy if we acknowledge the fact we are all prejudice to some degree. That is how we learn about each other. Few of us are saints, honey.

"I don't like everyone I meet. God forgive me, I didn't like my youngest boy a whole heck of a lot. You think I don't know people in this town don't like me because of my color. Shoot, child, sure I do, but I refuse let hate orchestrate my life. There are many others to love, like John, and you, Cathy; Frank Johnson, at the hospital; Claire and Harry next door; Raphael and Sarah Santiaga. We all represent a brighter future, child."

Cathy interrupted. "I don't understand. Everything you are saying is exactly what Johnny says."

Grace laughed, "You were annoyed at Sulli for spending so much time with me, but you stuck it out. You didn't hate me or resent Sulli."

"He needed you, Grace. I didn't want to take that away. I wanted to be part of it."

"I know, child. That's the point. Sulli can't waste time on angry people, who think the world owes them something, no matter who they are, what color, or what particular ax they feel the necessity to grind. Special interests keep us divided. Many are open and willing to learn about each other, Cathy. People will learn much from you."

"From me, Grace. What can anyone learn from me?"

"To be color blind, child; not to be jealous, but most of all just to be compassionate. There is an Indian prayer I love if I can remember the words. Lea Runningwater taught it to me years ago. I want you to remember it for me, because it best describes how to approach life, and will help you when you are troubled with your family. Will you memorize it, girl?"

Cathy nodded her head enthusiastically; the children played happily outside. Cathy noticed the rack of cookies were gone, as Grace took her arm and led her out onto the porch. A glaring sun raced up through billowy white clouds past eight-thirty and the breeze freshened, but the air didn't bite with cold. A gentle warm breeze flowed into a cool March wind, caressing the porch swing in a loving embrace. Grace handed Cathy a cup of coffee from her ready pot and sat down in her rocker wrapping her blanket around her legs. Cathy sat by her feet on the stairs watching the children running, jumping on the lawn.

Grace was silent for a moment, thinking, trying to remember the precise words Lea gave her. "I don't want to screw this up, child."

Grace began in her earthy style, and Cathy chuckled laying her head on the older woman's knee. Grace stroked her hair lovingly.

"I've thought about writing it down, but it's the type of message to convey personally, the Indian way. It's part of Indian tradition, Cathy and you must never forget the words. You promise?"

Cathy was startled at Grace's intensity, lifted her head and looked directly into Grace's eyes.

"I promise." She answered and Grace began.

"It goes like this.

O Great Spirit,
Whose voice I hear in the winds,
And whose breath gives life to all the world,
Hear me. I am small and weak,
I need your strength and wisdom.
Let me walk in beauty,
And make my eyes ever behold the red and purple sunset.
Make my hands respect the things you have made,
And my ears sharp to hear your voice.
Make me wise so that I may understand the things you have taught my people.
Let me learn the Lessons you have hidden in every rock.
I seek strength, not to be greater than my brother, but to fight my greatest enemy, Myself.
Make me always ready to come to you with clean hands and straight eyes.
So when life fades, as the fading sunset.
My spirit may come to you without shame.

When Grace finished, she settled back in her rocker and closed her eyes. "Not bad for an old broad who thought her high school prom was only a couple days ago." She mumbled, but Cathy was consumed with the simplicity, and enormity of the prayer.

"What?" she questioned.

Grace laughed. "It doesn't matter."

She looked over at the children. Cathy followed her gaze. The silence grew comfortably around them. Each began to speak at the same time and laughed.

Grace said, "You first."

Cathy was about to say "No, you first," but thought better of it. Instead, she straightened her dress and raised her head. Joyful tears filled her eyes.

"You're glad it's nearly over aren't you?"

"Of course I am, child. I fought a good fight, raised a solid, productive family and left a small mark on the world by example and with my words. When people read my work, they don't automatically see a black woman. They see a woman writer, a spinner of yarns, and I can say, in all honesty, I enjoyed my life. I am a good storyteller. The world's a better place, because I was here. It's time to turn the page."

Cathy shifted and leaned her head against Grace's knee once more. Grace stroked her hair again gently.

"We never want to be alone in this world, Grace. We're all a little selfish that way with those we love. That's why we don't want to let you go."

Struck by the simple wisdom in such a young woman, Grace answered.

"It's funny. I might have wandered around for another year annoying people, making John and you crazy. Now, I have a couple weeks with a clear head to enjoy you and the kids. That's a healing in the best sense, Cathy. To have my mind, the greatest physical gift of my life, returned at the end is my miracle."

Cathy looked up at her and whispered, "Zebedia."

"What did you say, child?"

A bird landed on the railing of the porch, its wings pushed and bristled by the March wind. As the sun passed nine o'clock Cathy answered. "Zebedia. He's new in town and he's a little strange, but . . ."

"But what, child. Spit it out."

"I just realized, you got better, and John brought me over here when Zeb arrived. He suggested John share you with us and here I am, a lot happier than I've been in a long time, Grace. Does that make sense."

"It makes sense, Cathy, but it seems a coincidence."

Cathy didn't press, but the thought nagged her, finally disappearing into the back of her conscious, as they chatted and laughed while the children played nicely on the first warm spring day.

CHAPTER EIGHTEEN

Blazing an arching trail the sun skirted past nine-thirty and continued soaring ever upward into an endless blue sky. Grace and Cathy chatted on as Zeb neared work, walking briskly. He stayed too long at Jack's enjoying the easy chatter and meeting Lea Tenfingers Runningwater, and had to hurry. He was late for work. He couldn't get Friday night's dance out of his mind. It was going to be wonderful and he would have a dance with Elizabeth.

As Zeb quick stepped along the road, a car spun out of control and hit a pole in front of him. A young woman driver lay more dead than alive inside, when Zeb and Rod Fisher arrived.

Rod looked in and exclaimed, "Jesus!" Blood was everywhere. "I'll get help."

He was surprised when Zeb answered quietly. "That won't be necessary."

Rod was shocked when Zeb leaned into the car reaching for the young driver's hand. Rod grabbed him and pulled him back.

"Don't move her, man. You could do more damage."

Zeb answered in an even voice. "I won't do any harm. I promise."

Rod would recall later feeling no compulsion to argue. Zeb touched the driver's wounds lightly and she began to stir. Rod helped him get the door open and they lay the girl on the ground. Zeb knelt next to her, feeling each injury again and also touching the rear of her head. Rod was almost positive her cuts grew smaller and her head, which appeared to hang on her shoulders when he first peered into the wreck, now appeared normal. He sat down on the curb when the paramedics arrived and took over. Zeb came over and sat down next to him.

"Well, what do you think?" He asked Rod who had taken a cigarette from his coat pocket.

"About what?"

Zeb looked down the road towards the hospital.

"About the price of apples in Bangkok."

"I would imagine they're pretty high this time of year." Rod answered and offered a cigarette to Zebedia, who smiled and refused.

"Listen, I have to get to work. Do you want to tag along."

"I wouldn't miss it for the world. I've seen some pretty miraculous things since I started covering this hospital. Your little trick ranks up there with the best."

Rod rose to join Zeb in stride and added, "So, are you going to tell me anything?"

"Apples in Bangkok are expensive?"

"I deserve that. What happened here?"

"You saw with your own eyes."

"I know what I saw. I don't know what I believe."

"You've had that problem longer than just today."

"Are you the newest addition to the faith healing crew at the hospital?"

"Actually, I'm part of the janitorial staff."

"My editor is going to love this. Holistic hospital staff heals right down to its mops and pails."

"That's not bad. I like it."

"Thanks. It will be the lead headline in tomorrow's paper."

The sun moved towards ten-thirty. Zeb was late and would spend most of the day trying to catch up anyway. He made a quick decision.

"C'mon, Rod. I'll buy you a cup of coffee at the cafeteria."

"That's a deal."

They walked along in silence. Cars rushed by, and the smell of the ground thawing filled their nostrils. Along the brick wall near the entrance to the hospital parking lot, a few wild flowers had managed to poke their heads out of the frozen earth. Birds winged back and forth searching for building material, while squirrels bobbed up and down along the ground checking out the area. Nearing the hospital staff entrance, Rod touched Zeb's arm.

"That child's neck was broken, Zeb."

"Yes, it was." Zeb replied simply.

"God darnit. How in heck did you do it?"

Zeb smiled, "Look at the squirrels, Rod. What makes them come back? They don't spend a day in a Nursing home. They climb trees until the last day of their life. Why is it different for us? How do squirrels know there will be food? They pop their heads up and down seeing if any humans are around, but after a while they even trust us to leave them alone. The birds too. They wait until they know it is time and then go in search of simple items for their nests and these items are provided."

"What has all that got to do with the girl's neck?"

"If we had the squirrel's faith we would understand better what goes on in this hospital and could release the power within us."

"You healed that girls neck."

"That is what you saw, Rod. A power greater than I healed the child and she helped. So did you. Part of all of us helped heal her. Part of me because I asked for help and have developed my own power by using it. Part of her, because she has more to do in this world and part of you Rod, because you want desperately to believe, yet refuse to acknowledge even what you see. I'm late, but I'll see you for coffee, okay."

Rod made no reply. He was thinking. Zeb obviously felt good about the young reporter. He performed what amounted to a miracle by anyone's standards right before his eyes. He hadn't done that with anyone else, including me. Looking back, I think the time limitation may have forced him to get known faster. Zeb was aware of things we weren't. He knew Rod was introspective. He was willing examine his own weak areas, and keep searching for answers. It was a good honest combination. It was rare in a journalist. Rod was actually interested in writing the truth.

CHAPTER NINETEEN

When Zeb walked into the maintenance office, Frank wasn't there. He found him running a waxing machine on the third floor.

"Sorry, I'm late."

Frank stopped waxing, "Won't be the last time. Take over here, Zeb, so's I can check on the laundry staff."

Zeb took the waxing machine and watched Frank, knowing if the maids were behind on their work, Frank would pitch in and help them too. There would be no tirade, no raised voice, or recrimination. Frank Johnson recruited his staff, knew they worked hard and helped whenever he could.

Zeb decided to work an extra shift tonight if he could convince Frank to go home and get some rest. Frank's hair was disheveled. His beard bore a few days growth, and he hadn't slept away from here in several days. There didn't appear to be any relief in sight. The flu had taken its toll on the staff, and as news of new cures spread across the state, requests for bed space quadrupled. AIDS cases were among those most often requesting space.

Zeb finished waxing the hall, as Mary Savage rounded the corner. She hurried past Zebedia, who said good morning. Mary nodded, preoccupied with the chart in her hand, then raised her head, and stopped.

"Didn't mean to ignore you, Zeb. It's been a little hectic around here these past few days. How are you getting along?"

"I'm doing fine, Dr. Savage. How are you?"

"Very well!" She answered emphatically. "As a matter of fact I would say these have been the two most extraordinary days of my career."

"I'm glad to see you smiling. You are much lovelier when you smile."

"Thank you, Zeb. That's nice to hear."

She entered the elevator thinking Zeb an unusual man and made a mental note to discuss him with Frank Johnson. Zeb moved past the nurse's station to store his waxing machine in the closet at the end of the hall, near the window. Removing a mop from a pail on wheels, he filled the pail with water, added disinfectant soap, dipped the mop in and rolled it towards the visitor's bathrooms inside a glass lounge enclosure. As he entered, he noticed an older gentleman sitting in a chair with his head in his hands sobbing. Zeb looked around checking if anyone was nearby. They were alone.

"What's the problem, old timer?" He inquired.

The old man wiped tears from his eyes without looking up.

"What's it to you?"

"I wondered if I could help. My name is Zebedia."

The old man looked up realizing Zeb wasn't going to be put off.

"Zebedia is an unusual name, son. Why do you care about an old man's tears?"

"I care when anyone is unhappy, Mr. . . . er . . ."

"Just like that?"

"Just like that, Mr. . . . er . . ."

"Warthog. Bill Warthog."

"And you think Zebedia is unusual!"

The old man laughed in spite of himself, wiping his eyes on his sleeve.

"You the janitor in this place, Zeb?"

"One of them."

The older man was avoiding talking about his troubles. His face resembled a prune and his fingers were distinctly purple, swollen and crooked at the knuckles. He appeared to be about eighty years old and must have been a powerful man when he was younger, because he spilled out past the edges of his chair and his legs reached almost to the center of the lounge floor, as he leaned back and stretched out.

"Someone close to you in the hospital?"

"Was. She passed away this morning." He answered quietly.

"I see. Was it your wife."

"Yes, yes it was." Bill barely got the words out before burying his head in his hands again. "I don't know what I'm going to do without her. She was my world."

"Were you married a long time?"

"Forty-nine years last month, son."

"That is a heck of an accomplishment in this day and age."

"You might be right, Zeb, for other people, but being married to Melissa was a joy. Oh, I'm not saying our life was perfect. Hell, nobody's is, but my Lisa had a way of smoothing out the rough spots. Sweet Jesus, she was trying to console me just this morning and she was dying. Zeb." Bill was having trouble controlling the shudders that came over him.

"Your Melissa is a special person." Zeb spoke of her in the present, while Bill gave him a strange look and corrected him.

"She certainly was, young fella."

"Do you have to contact the children."

Bill was astonished. "How do you know we have children?"

"Oh, I couldn't imagine someone as special as your Melissa without them."

Bill accepted Zeb's logic and began to talk about her, their children and grandchildren; a family history spanning five decades. He spoke non-stop for almost an hour and a half, and Zeb never interrupted once. It was a beautiful, semi-sweet story laced with tragedy and magic. Bill enjoyed the telling. It was obviously his favorite subject.

He didn't embellish the death of a son in Vietnam, nor did he hide his pride at accepting the Medal of Honor posthumously for him at the White House. It was the only part of the story, which told of Melissa shedding a tear. The rest painted a picture of a woman who enjoyed her life and family and gave of herself continuously. She made dresses, coached softball, consoled and encouraged everyone around her while being an accomplished painter. Bill told of parties, love, laughter and sadness.

Zebedia was impressed with the joy in Bill's voice as he spoke. He was intrigued by Bill's obvious lack of concern for playing second fiddle to his wife. In the telling, he stood beside Melissa and all their accomplishments were shared, but you knew he looked up to her. He respected her as much as he loved her. It was a rare combination for a man Bill's age, a successful plumber and businessman, but there it was. Bill and Melissa were more together than apart, and Zeb understood a portion of the despair Bill felt at losing her.

He touched Bill's shoulder when he finished and said, "That is an inspirational story. You should tell it often."

Bill suddenly realized he had been speaking for nearly two hours and apologized to Zeb.

"I'm gonna get you fired, son. I shouldn't have taken so much of your time."

"Nonsense, Bill." Zeb replied. "I wish you would tell me more another time."

"That's a deal on one condition."

"Which is?"

"Let me help you clean for a while, till you get caught up."

Zeb was happy to have help and got Bill started mopping floors, while he scrubbed the sink and toilets.

Bill didn't stop talking, as they worked side by side. Story built on story and each one was as good as the one preceding it. They worked hard without a break, stopping only to laugh. They finished bathrooms in no time at all. When they stopped, four hours later, eight halls and thirty bathrooms were clean.

Zeb stood up, looked back down the hall they just completed and clapped Bill on the back grinning from ear to ear. "You are one hard working son of a gun. We darn near cleaned a quarter of the hospital. Frank, my boss, will be pleased. Thank you."

Bill leaned on his mop handle eyeing the young man with a crooked smile on his face. "I'm tired son, and I'm happy. I haven't put in a good hard day in a while. I know I'm going to sleep tonight and I get the feeling you knew that all along."

Zeb started to protest, and Bill held up his hand grinning. "You know what the Bard said, son. Don't protest too much or something like that. Anyway thanks. Going over our lives put things in perspective. I wanted to die, Zeb, and you knew it. Lissy wouldn't like it either. She told me as much this morning. You healed my mind, son."

Now Zeb stopped him and said something Bill would repeat over and over, for many years. "Our Father put the power to heal our bodies inside each of us a long time ago. We all help heal each other and ourselves when we remember we are spiritual beings as well as physical. You healed me a little too, with your history. I needed uplifting, a better mind set and you gave it to me, besides almost working me to death."

Bill asked, "Is there some way I can volunteer to help here? I could spend a couple days a week."

"I'll talk to Frank Johnson about it on one condition."

"Which is?"

"Two days a week you visit people your age, telling your stories and listening to theirs. You have a gift of healing soured spirits."

"I don't know if I can, Zeb. Hard work I'm used to, talking to strangers . . ." He was scratching his chin.

"Nonsense! We were strangers a few hours ago. Are we strangers now? You have a wonderful knack for making the stories come to life. People will identify with many parts of your life. Your humorous slant on things is wonderful."

"You're different, Zeb, easy to talk with. A lot of people don't care."

"You're right. A lot of people don't care, but an awful lot do. Should we abandon them, because we are afraid to confront our own fears of rejection? Is that what your Melissa would do? We choose to act out of love rather than fear. That's the difference and it makes all the difference in the world, Bill."

"You're still different."

"You're saying I'm strange, eh?"

"A little." Bill added with a grin.

"I gave you the conditions, Mr. Warthog. God needs angels as much as janitors. You're going on split shift, my friend."

Zeb grinned and Bill felt better. He understood what Melissa meant when she said they would only be apart for a little while and she would never be far away. It was very much like working on a job out of the country. He always carried her picture with him and counted the days until they would be together again. He didn't think it morbid at all thinking he would see her again very soon. And he would see Jimmy, his son, too. It made sense to him, this ending of life to begin new adventures. This morning he felt as if he would die from the loss and no one should love someone else that much, but he did and always would. Eighty years weren't much when he considered being with Lissy forever.

"Hell what's a couple more years." He whispered to himself.

Zeb interrupted, "Excuse me. What are you whispering?"

Zeb never let on he heard every word.

Bill looked up, a smile firmly in place "Just thinking out loud. I guess we have a deal, Zeb."

"Good. When Frank sees the work we did, I don't think he'll refuse."

Zeb asked Bill to wait then headed downstairs to find Frank, who had settled on his couch less than an hour before. The maids were far behind when Frank left Zeb waxing the floor. Two of them were out with the flu for three days already. Lenore and Consuela were doing their best to cover, but were falling steadily behind. Frank couldn't leave them without helping, so he pitched in. It took most of the day, but they finished every room with time to spare, and Frank sent the two women home. He was grateful to them. They did the work of four people without complaining once.

Zeb knocked, interrupting a pleasant dream, sticking his head in the door.

Frank roused himself slowly, massaged his scalp, stretched and opened his eyes. "What do you want, boy?"

He rubbed his head again and kidded Zeb. "You tell me to get some rest then you wake me up. On top of that I was just having dinner with Lena Horne and Sophia Loren was waiting in the wings, so this better be important."

He didn't give Zeb a chance to answer before rambling on, "God, what a dream, and it was just getting started."

He whined. "What do you want, son? You're standing there like a teenager who just got his first kiss. For God's sake spit it out so I can go back to my dream."

Zeb explained what he and Bill discussed, and was surprised when Frank frowned.

"What's the matter?"

"It's a great idea."

"But?"

"But, we can't do it. We can't hire him."

"Why not?"

"Two reasons. First, the union will complain; second, his age."

"I already thought of that."

"You did?"

"Yes."

"And the answer is behind door number one, or you want me to keep me guessing?"

"I'm not in the union, yet."

"Well there's a startling revelation given you've only been here two days."

"We'll both be part time and you can pay him with my wages."

"That's nice, but I need you full time."

"I didn't mean I would work any less. You just pay me less."

"You are one crazy son-of a . . . sorry. Go on, what about his age?"

"You lie about his age."

"We lie about his age. Isn't that a little out of character."

"I said, you lie about his age." Zeb smiled. "It's perfectly in character. I've seen Consuela, the maid, Frank. I might have believed sixty, but when she told me she was fifty-one with a straight face, I nearly busted a gut."

"She has great-grand children to feed."

"I'm sure Bill will happily add his pay check to hers."

"Oh, all right. You're not going to let me alone until I agree anyway."

Zeb rushed over and hugged Frank right there in bed and was gone before Frank could respond. He lay there thinking what a weird, lovable guy Zeb was. Then punched up his pillows, and laid his head back down. Lena Horne was his for the asking, and Sophia wouldn't wait forever.

CHAPTER TWENTY

Zeb hurried back to the glass-enclosed lounge where he left Bill. He was seated, talking to a woman his age. Zeb stopped to watch, as the woman broke into a huge smile. Her teeth were yellowed appearing soft, but still her own. She wore a linen dress with plain black shoes and must have been very beautiful once. She held herself royally and her eyes were dark blue, almost violet.

She put her hands up to her face and then touched Bill's cheek. Suddenly there were tears in those violet pools, making them appear translucent, reflecting light in a myriad of colors. She whispered her thanks to Bill for helping her with her sadness and she was sorry about his Melissa. Actually she hoped her Harry would join Melissa soon. She rose to return to Harry's room, stopped and kissed Bill softly on the lips.

"You have a real gift, Bill Warthog. You talk a lot about your Melissa, but I'll tell you something I know already. She was a lucky woman."

Bill was flustered by the intimacy of the kiss, and the moment.

Blushing he offered. "I'll see you tomorrow, Evelyn."

"You're coming back tomorrow."

"You're the second person today says I have a gift. The other is a young janitor here who needs my help. Can't keep the place clean without me."

"Is that so?" Zeb interrupted.

"Zebedia. I didn't hear you return." Bill said unaffected.

"Obviously. Has he been troubling you with his stories ma'am? If he has, tell me, I'll have him flogged."

Evelyn knew from his tone, Zeb was joking, and decided to go along.

"The man is a bit long winded, young fella. If I didn't know better I'd say he was flirting with me."

"Evelyn!" Bill interjected. "I never . . ."

She silenced him with an affectionate peck on the cheek. "Thanks again, Bill. See you later young man."

"Yes ma'am," Zeb answered. As she moved away, Zeb raised his hands into the air joyfully. Bill watched, automatically compelled to raise his eyes. When he looked back at Zeb he noticed a faint color surrounding him. It was light blue with pale pink streaks disappearing at the edges, which reached all the way to the walls beyond the enclosure. Zeb smiled, nodded and lowered his hands unembarrassed by joyful tears streaming down his cheeks. "This has been a wonderful day, Bill."

"You aren't angry with me are you?"

"Heck no. You made that woman feel much better and you were telling the truth. If you hadn't helped I would still be cleaning. I must say I didn't expect you to take to counseling so readily." He indicated Evelyn disappearing down the hall.

Bill blushed. "Talking about Lissy and my family comes natural, Zeb. Evelyn shared parts of her life with Harry, which made her smile. I'm glad Lissy kept all her faculties until the end. It must be hard watching someone you've loved for a long time become a stranger before your eyes."

Zeb nodded as they strolled down the hall. "Do you want to know the verdict?"

"About what?"

"About you working with me."

"Oh that. I figured I'd start tomorrow."

"You did, huh?"

"Of course. You don't seem the type to take no for an answer."

"I have to sometimes. Like you, though, it depends on who is saying no to what."

Bill put his hand out and Zeb took it firmly in his own. Bill covered them with his free hand.

"Thank you, Zebedia. I don't know what I would have done without you today."

"You're welcome. I was glad to help."

"I'm taking Lissy to the funeral parlor early tomorrow, but I can come back for a couple hours."

"If you want to."

"It feels right, Zeb. The kids won't be in until the afternoon and it will keep me occupied."

"Good. I'll see you in the morning."

He watched until the older man reached his car and waved. Then he went back to his locker area, found his jacket and headed home. It had been a wonderful day. He hadn't had to stay an extra shift because of his new friend.

Lucinda Caverly was up and walking about the hospital getting stronger by the hour. Everyone at the hospital was bursting to learn how these cures came about. During the next few days Lucinda would undergo tests from every modality of the healing arts. The scientists would probe and the parapsychologists would analyze. The psychics would meditate. Scientists, herbalists, homeopaths, holistic healers, chiropractors, and Shiatsu massage therapists; all of them would accept the simple undeniable fact, Lucinda's recovery was spontaneous, and unexplainable. It was a miracle.

Zeb searched inside himself for some way to describe the great goodness he felt around him, savoring each moment. There were only so many more allotted and he didn't intend to waste them.

CHAPTER TWENTY-ONE

The next few days passed in a whirlwind of activity. National wire services picked up on Rod Fisher's columns; he became an overnight celebrity. I still read his nationally syndicated column today. He and I have remained close over the years. He is a big reason I finally found the courage to write my view of the events.

After Rod's first columns hit the wires, different television news crews arrived daily. Zeb could see portable antenna tower's rising into the sky from atop vans miles away. He was intrigued by all the attention the hospital was receiving. Each and every newsperson hoped to interview someone, anyone who could explain what happened. Everyone hoped another cure would take place and Zeb didn't intend to disappoint them. He also didn't intend for this to become a sideshow. The seeds he was sowing must grow strong roots to survive after he was gone.

Friday morning, the day of the dance, arrived after several uneventful days. All the television crews departed except one when no more miracles occurred. A beautiful young Hispanic reporter, Maria Menendez, refused to go. She convinced her boss to let her stay another few days and was having coffee in the cafeteria when the head of Physical Therapy, Gloria Peret, came hurrying in searching for Mary Savage. She leaned in close to her and whispered something.

"What!" Mary exclaimed loud enough to make everyone look up.

Gloria shook her head.

"Everyone?" Mary questioned.

Gloria shook her head again affirmatively and Mary jumped up from her chair knocking her coffee to the floor. She apologized to the young doctor seated next to her, but didn't wait for a response, and didn't have to. He over heard enough of their conversation and when Mary and Gloria headed off at a trot he was right behind them.

Maria was behind all three followed by most of the occupants of the cafeteria. Zeb was scrubbing the bath across from Physical Therapy, when everyone arrived. He moved off to one side. Mary nodded to him on her way in to the therapy room. Two patients, stroke victims, unable to speak for years, were sitting chatting amiably. Another young woman confined to a wheel chair from Multiple Sclerosis was up at the walking bar supporting herself with only her fingertips.

Mary looked around the room with unbelieving eyes and asked Gloria, "You said there are others?"

Gloria nodded and answered, "Everyone who has walked through the door this morning has made immediate progress. With each success I grew happier and happier until I realized these healings bordered on the . . ."

Mary finished the sentence for her, "Miraculous. Unexplainable. Wonderful."

Mary put her hands together in front of her lips while tears welled deeply in her eyes.

"Yes, Doctor. I've never experienced anything like this. I've wished and prayed for things just like everyone else, but I never really truly believed in miracle cures. Not that I didn't want to, I just . . ."

"It's all right, Gloria, and if it's any consolation. I don't understand the miraculous things I've seen either. That's why we're here, to learn as much as possible and to use any method available, whether it be touch, energy, nutrition, surgery or anything else in order to allow the body time to heal itself. Your specialty didn't exist fifty years ago, or at least it didn't get recognized along with a whole host of others. We know the art of healing belongs along side the science of healing. Thanks to some forward thinking medical doctors, who are in touch with their mortality, we have the opportunity to explore possibility."

"What do you mean?"

Mary smiled and spread her hands before her in the room. "Look at this." Indicating the three patients in the room. "Something healed these people. Call it the collective positive energy of this entire staff, or therapy or surgery or anything you darn well please. I tell you, Gloria, this is medicine. Perhaps, some time soon we will understand, or maybe we never will, but for now a little faith never killed anyone."

Mary was crying, laughing and speaking all at the same time. "This is why I started in medicine. I don't know why these people are better, and it doesn't matter. What matters is they are better."

Mary was euphoric. Her eyes were glowing and her skin was flushed. The raw emotion she radiated was contagious. Gloria giggled and asked, "What should I do, Doctor?"

Mary thought a moment, then brightened. "Come on, Gloria." She answered turning on her heel.

"Where are we going?"

"We're going to fill your room with patients and see what happens."

"But my scheduled sessions . . ."

"Forget them. Come on, woman. Whatever is in this room this morning shouldn't be wasted."

By the time the parade in the therapy room slowed in the early afternoon one thing was certain. Something greater than medical science was operating inside Community Hospital. Every person entering the room brightened and felt better including the staff. Most were emotional healings brought on by the high level of joy and positive energy engulfing the room. There were a few solid miracles, like the stroke patients, and several cancer remissions. One child whose leg was short and deformed was healed completely in full view of staff and media.

Mary described the day enthusiastically and called the healings miraculous when she and the young reporter, Maria Menendez, filmed a segment for the five o'clock news. They taped in the lobby and Mary was disheveled, but happy.

She answered Maria's questions patiently and pointedly without evasion. Mary was not afraid to say she had little direct knowledge or control of the healings, which occurred today. She did say she believed they happened because the medical doctors were becoming more open and willing to accept ancient ways as valuable.

She stopped short of attributing these ways equal billing with modern methods. She had no intention of losing funding by starting a war she couldn't win. It was her place in life to be a bridge builder. Her joy at living mattered more than winning an argument. Arguments engendered strife. Her contribution to the future of medicine was secure in her heart and that is where she intended to keep it. She didn't intend to enrage old-line doctors, who bent enough to support her efforts here. It didn't matter that they secretly hoped she would fail.

Maria faced the camera, as it panned the hallway where a slightly built maintenance attendant came into view. He looked up waved and went back to work. That afternoon the television station was inundated with calls concerning the yellow light surrounding Mary Savage, and the pale blue light emanating from the maintenance man. There was the normal outcry, that the hospital was conducting some weird experiments and filling the area with strange radiation.

There were other callers though, who knew of lights and auras. Science was using auryllic photography to take pictures of energy fields surrounding each of us. Everyone was curious how they could be seen by a television camera. The combination of sensitivity of equipment and the high level of joy in the hospital allowed both Mary and Zeb's energy fields to be photographed was the explanation distributed. "We have no idea." would have been closer to the truth.

Mary watched the recorded tape over and over. It wasn't her own aura that interested her. She'd seen it before, but never anything like Zeb's. The pale blue energy field surrounding him faded into another color at the edges extending far out, and a color barely visible beyond the second. She strained to see and picked a tape measure off the shelf over her kitchen sink. His aura was brighter than hers. In the picture they appeared about the same, but Mary realized she had been standing thirty yards closer to the camera. Her aura was no more visible than Zeb's. His extended out almost ten times the distance hers did; further than the camera could physically record. She sensed something very special.

As she examined him closely, she eased back in her chair; convinced she was looking at the primary source of healing energy in the hospital. Now she must decide what to do about it. She didn't want to frighten him away in case he wasn't aware of his gift, and she didn't want to offend the medical staff. She decided the best way to approach the matter was away from the hospital. She would visit Zeb at home.

Relieved and exhilarated, she flicked off the tape player, and skipped into her room to prepare for the dance. She sang in the shower at the top of her lungs, "Baby, baby, I'd get down on my knees for you. If you would only, tell me, what you want me to doooo."

Then a thought hit her and she streamed soaking wet from the bath leaving a trail of water through her dressing area into her bedroom, where she wrote herself a note reminding herself to show Lea Tenfingers Runningwater the tape.

Naked, dripping water on paper and floor she danced slowly back to her shower, singing, "Barump, Barump, barump ump. Ump Ump Ump berummp bump, Baby baby I'd get down on my knees, gurgle, gurgle, for you . . ." It was a familiar tune, banging around inside her head for days. Zeb began whistling it over a month before.

CHAPTER TWENTY-TWO

Zeb was busy cleaning his clothes. He stopped at a second hand store on his way home to purchase a jacket with two dollars from his paycheck. Though slightly dated the jacket fit well and was almost new. He was ecstatic at the prospect of holding a woman close again. He loved weddings and parties. He loved any occasion full of happy people with exciting thoughts. Mostly, he loved to dance and it didn't matter how. He had danced by fire light with Indian warriors and waltzed at functions of state in European manor homes. He had swiveled and shook to the to the beat of drums in the Congo and rolled his hips to the rhythm of steel drums in the Caribbean.

Zeb loved music because it brought out the best in people. When someone walked and moved well, comments almost always followed like, "He or she must be a dancer." Zeb equated grace, poise and athletic ability with dance. He understood some movements were suggestive, while others were outright statements of sexuality and it didn't phase him in the slightest.

His Father made and tuned this body he wore and nothing about it was dirty or disgusting. It astounded him that women were only recently allowed to nurse their babies in public in America. Some religious thinking had gone terribly wrong over the centuries and it was past time to correct it. Respect was the ingredient Zeb found most lacking. People had little respect for themselves, let alone each other. He found all aspects of the human form pleasing and the manor in which it moved delightful. It was a unique and wonderful machine. He considered the female form much more elegant than the male and more closely in line with what its

Creator originally intended. He laughed, as if comparing an Edsel and a Mercedes. There was no doubt the Mercedes was more attractive.

The dance flew back into his thoughts as he considered this comparison. He couldn't remember when he had last let his hair down and enjoyed himself. Some people were going to get the wrong idea about him. It didn't matter. He was content to risk their ire, knowing he could never please everyone. Zeb needed a night out and wasn't going to let anything spoil it. At the back of his mind a vision of a dance with Elisabeth kept playing. He'd gone over it at least fifty times, and knew it would be gentle, sensual, perfect. He wouldn't allow it to go beyond friendship, but he would thoroughly enjoy it.

When he finished pressing his coat, he realized, he had no dress shoes to wear, so he knocked at our door and I answered.

"Hi Zeb."

"Hi Roger. I was hoping you could do me a favor."

"Anything. Name it."

"I need to borrow a pair of shoes for the dance."

"Is that all? What size do you wear?"

"Eight and a half."

"That could be tough. I haven't worn an eight for a few years now." I said staring down at my size elevens.

Maybe there is a pair in the cellar. Mom saves everything. We hurried towards the cellar entrance, as Dad came around the corner from the kitchen.

Zeb greeted him warmly. "Hi, Ben. Are you ready for the dance?"

Dad laughed, "Thanks to you, I'm going. I've missed it the last five years."

Zeb smiled broadly, "This is wonderful news and I have something for you."

Zeb removed an envelope from his pocket. It contained the amount of rent I told Zeb he would have to pay at our original meeting. Dad went to return some of it to Zeb for the chores he completed and Zeb stopped him.

"Those chores are my gift to a very special man. Your dad's house was getting a little run down, and he understood simplicity."

Dad shook his head in agreement.

"There is one thing I would ask, though if I could."

"Anything, Zebedia." My father answered honestly.

Zeb hesitated only a second, which I noticed and then said, "I would like to dance once with Elizabeth, without guilt."

I waited, not knowing what to expect, because I didn't know my father very well. He looked at Zeb thoughtfully and a silent message passed between them. When Dad spoke, I could feel the affection and respect he had for this simple, beautifully honest human being. He spoke as a man to another, because there was no competition between them. "She is quite easy to fall in love with isn't she?"

Zeb didn't hesitate for a moment, "Extremely."

"I am a most fortunate man, Zebedia. I have found my family and a true friend, in a matter of days when it took years to separate myself from them."

Zeb thought for a moment and then in typical fashion he resorted to humor to lighten the moment.

"I take that as a yes."

Dad laughed and I smiled, putting something of trust and honor in a safe place in my heart to keep for the rest of my days. I loved my father everyday of my life and that night I began to understand why.

I interrupted them, "I want to dance with her too, and if I don't find some shoes in the cellar for Zeb he will be dancing in his work boots."

Dad answered before Zeb could, "I imagine it wouldn't be the first time."

Zeb laid his hand on Dad's shoulder. "Thank you for trusting me, Ben."

Then he and I headed down the stairs. It took less than five minutes to locate a pair of old school shoes I wore and hated. Zeb was happy to have them and thanked me profusely.

We hurried back upstairs and he disappeared out the rear door calling back over his shoulder that he'd see me later. Dad was dressing when I past his room. He glanced away from the mirror and winked at me. I had little compulsion to wink back, not having sunk far enough into the dork abyss, but I was dropping fast. I did manage a smile and stood watching him comb his hair for a minute, thinking he looked different, somehow.

My perception of our entire family had changed in less than a week. Where, normally I couldn't stand to be around them, now I considered my time with all of them precious. Moving away I felt his eyes watching me, sensing his great affection. He began to whistle a tune from the Broadway show *Les Miserable*. It wasn't a sad or happy tune, lying somewhere between the Barney theme song and taps. It was a touching melody. I knew he was whistling, because we talked and things were better between us.

I stopped, turned to face him, and he asked. "What do you think?" I was taken back, because he rarely asked my opinion about things.

"About what?" I asked knowing perfectly well what he was asking and buying time.

"About Zeb dancing with Mom. Are you okay with it?"

I answered out of inexperience, but honestly. "I think you're taking quite a chance."

"Do you trust him, Roger? He's your friend."

I knew he was asking and not dumping on me by his tone. I didn't want to be disloyal to either of them so I asked.

"Do you?"

He laughed. "I don't have to."

I was confused and asked, "Why not?"

"Because I trust your mother."

I nodded and began to turn away when he added. "He's one of

the finest people I've ever met, Roger. You're a good judge of character."

I swelled with pride, blushed, because I remembered how I met Zeb, and hurried off to my room to get ready. We pulled into the hall parking lot just after eight-thirty. It was nearly full. Practically everyone in town was here. The hall was all lit like a Christmas tree. There were huge baskets of fresh flowers around the entrance, and searchlights reaching far up into the night sky.

Mom held Dad's and my hand, as we wandered towards the entrance joking and laughing lightly. We could hear the band playing inside. They started an old Roy Orbeson song and Dad hurried us along, because he was anxious to dance with Mom.

As soon as we got in the door he swept her away onto the floor bowed and took her firmly in his arms. I watched for a minute, as she rested her head on his shoulder. She looked very young and beautiful to me. I laughed, because I could see Dad's lips move as he sang the words to "I'll be crying over you" in her ear.

Jack sat behind a table at the entrance with Lea Tenfingers selling tickets. I returned to ask if they had seen Zeb come in, but they hadn't. The price of admission was intended to cover food and expenses. Anything extra was automatically donated to the hospital charity fund. The amount donated to the hospital increased year after year along with the popularity of the dance.

I told Julie I would be here around eight-thirty and she was standing with a group of her friends in the corner. As I approached I noticed her hair was pulled back away from her face and she wore very little make-up. She looked fantastic and I told her so, as soon as I got close enough to be heard.

"You look great." I said, and she smiled.

"You like it? I think it makes me look kind of young."

"I think it makes you look beautiful."

All the kids around us looked at me like I was crazy, but that was how I felt and Julie appreciated my saying so in front of everyone. I was curious why she decided to change and led her away so she wouldn't be embarrassed.

"What made you decide not to wear all the make-up."

"I didn't feel like trying to act grown-up. I was speaking to Zeb yesterday."

"You spoke to him?"

"Yes. I came by your house hoping to catch you but you had left to take the kids to school, and I saw him coming down the path."

"I walked with him for a while."

"And?"

"He makes me feel good, you know?"

"Yes, I do."

"I found myself talking to him about things, Rog: things I don't talk to anyone about."

"Did he help?"

"He listened mostly. He did say I was never alone, and I believed him. He also said I was much too pretty to be painting a mask on my face and I would only be young for a little longer, so I should enjoy it. He said most people spend so much time trying to pretend they are something else or someone else, they never enjoy who or what they are right then. He said, 'Be as you are, Julie, because you are good enough for anyone.'"

"That makes sense." I interjected.

"I thought so too. When I turned towards school I felt kind of lonely for a few minutes."

"He has a strange affect on people, and I think I'm beginning to understand why," I told her.

"What is it, Rog?"

"He's a strange visitor from another planet."

She folded her arms and tapped her foot, "Be serious, Roger."

"Okay, okay." I answered and she relaxed.

"Well, tell me Roger. You've spent more time with him than anyone."

She was right. I had, but hadn't realized it.

"He looks for the good in people, Julie. He never looks at the bad and he accepts everyone without question. I don't think he judges anyone, and he is comfortable with himself, so we feel comfortable being ourselves with him. Does that make sense to you?"

"Yes it does. It explains almost exactly how I felt talking to him. I could have told him anything. I feel good about myself, and I haven't in a while."

"I'm glad, because you are exquisite."

The band broke into a song by Melissa Ethridge and we headed out onto the dance floor. Jack and Lea were already out there, along with Cathy and John Sullivan. Frank Johnson was busy turning Mary Savage around the floor and Grace Abernathy sat on the bottom row of the bleachers tapping her foot in time to the music. It was her first dance in quite some time. She looked wonderful. Raphael Santiaga came in with his wife, who had gotten well very quickly. No one would ever confuse Santiaga, the undercover cop, with the neatly groomed, well-dressed young man on the dance floor with his gorgeous young wife. They fit together nicely as a couple. Raphael's dark brooding eyes and Hispanic good looks contrasted and accented his wife's flaming red hair and green eyes. They moved as one.

Zeb slipped into the room unnoticed and moved over to the bleachers. He sat at the edge next to Claire and Harry Olgivy watching everyone dance. As soon as there was a break in the music, he came up and asked Julie to dance. I felt a twinge of jealousy, but got over it quickly. I was proud of myself when she looked at me, and I smiled. At any other point in my young life I would have been furious with her for even considering a dance with someone else. Now, that seemed foreign and foolish.

Zeb clapped me on the arm and they hurried out as the band took a break and a disc jockey took over. He put on the tango music from the movie *Dirty Dancing* and Zeb led Julie around the floor as if she was born to dance, and they had been partners for years. Before long everyone stopped to watch them. When the music finished everyone applauded.

Mary Savage moved over and spoke to Zeb; "You are full of surprises."

Then she asked him to dance and it began all over. They moved around the room as if they were made for each other. When they finished Zeb held Mary longer than any of the others. I couldn't help noticing they were both a little breathless. And so it went throughout he night. Zeb danced with everyone and he danced to everything. I noticed he kept returning to Mary Savage.

It didn't matter if the music was for us kids, the young adults, or the older people. He was comfortable with everyone. He joked with Grace for more than an hour. Lea Tenfingers watched him carefully and moved over to Grace when Zeb moved away, "What do you think, Grace?"

"You don't want to know, Lea."

"Tell me."

"There is something very special and powerful about that young man. If I didn't know better I'd say he wasn't of this world."

Lea shocked Grace with her reply. "You're right, Grace. He is here to accomplish something and he possesses very powerful medicine."

"What makes you say that?"

"I can feel it. His soul is ancient."

"Older than mine?" Grace kidded her, but Lea was concentrating and didn't blink when she answered.

"Older than time itself."

Grace didn't answer, following Lea's gaze back out onto the floor. The DJ spun a record and the haunting sweet sound of a clarinet filled the room. The song was instrumental and the DJ announced it was the final song of the evening. It was a slow sensual melody and Zeb hadn't danced with my mom yet. I looked across the room where he approached her and my Dad and she smiled at him with open admiration.

I felt my heart flutter when she took Zeb's face in her hands. She kissed him softly on the lips, then shook her head and looked at my Dad. She took his hand and led him out onto the floor for the last dance. He looked at Zeb and shrugged, as if to say, "What can I do?" And Zeb smiled. He brought his hands together and raised them thoughtfully to his lips.

I could almost feel him willing my mom and dad to do well. There was no jealousy or animosity in his eyes and I watched in wonder. Then Julie grabbed me and when I turned back, he was gone. I couldn't help feeling grateful, knowing he didn't expect it. The one thing he asked for at this dance, he wouldn't have. Thinking about it later changed my mind. Zeb had gotten exactly what he wanted. My mom chose, as he knew she would. That was reality. His fantasy, he held in his heart where it belonged, because he loved our family. It was a lesson, which would serve me well through out my life and one he taught without effort.

CHAPTER TWENTY-THREE

The next few days were crazy. Television crews were everywhere. Miracles occurred several times a day at the hospital and Rodney Fisher became a national celebrity. He told the story honestly without embellishment or false pronouncements of understanding. It wasn't his place to convince anyone. His job was reporting the facts, even when the facts were unbelievable.

Government agencies sent crews to test everything, from the water supply to the nutrients in the soil in the surrounding area. All of these tests came back normal. The AMA, FDA, and large drug companies were inundated with inquiries about the healings occurring in Springfield, and offered no answers.

Their official response was, "We are very interested, but have no comment at this time." Behind the scenes they were scrambling to license and control the institution and staff.

None of the staff members of the hospital tried to explain anything. All of them were grateful for the success and went about their routines; not wanting to disrupt whatever was at work. Mary Savage summed up their attitude in an interview with Maria Menendez for the five o'clock news on the day Lucinda Caverly left for home.

"We are an institution of healing. Whether we understand all of it is irrelevant. That is like asking if I can bottle sunlight. We work in an imprecise world. Call it art, science, or miracle. I call it medicine. It doesn't matter as long as we heal and learn more each day. Our importance, which was raised to the realm of a Deity by over-zealous doctors possessed of their own importance, grew out of a battle we wage with death. It is time to recognize the limits of our own contributions. We, here, are grateful to have won a few skirmishes. There in lies the essence of healing. We are not interested in placing Band-Aids on hemorrhoids. We want to understand what caused them to begin with."

Maria noticed Mrs. Caverly and her husband come through the door behind Mary, heading for the parking lot. She asked Mary whether she expected Lucinda to live.

Mary chuckled answering in her most ingenuous voice, "Of course I expect her to live. Lucinda lives each day like the rest of us. I expect everyone to live. That is part of the magic of this place. No one is dying. We are all living until we take that last breath."

Maria wouldn't let go, "C'mon, doc. That's a stock answer. I want to know what your guts tell you."

Mary thought a moment, and rubbed her chin, "We are limited, only by what we haven't learned yet. It is within the realm of possibility that physical bodies aided by collective knowledge and positive energy generated within them and around them, hastens the healing process. I, as a doctor, provide a frame work for the body to do the work its Creator intended, but the body-mind, especially when surrounded by like thinking intelligence is capable of more than I can fathom."

Maria pounced. "So, you're saying these healings were faith healings?"

Maria was pushing hard, asking a question that was sensational on its face. Mary Savage didn't intend to become part of a media circus. She transferred her hand from chin to tired bloodshot eyes, rubbed them and answered, "No. These were not faith healings. That cheapens what is occurring here. Would I call them miraculous? Yes, I would. These people were healed, because we have worked hard to open every door possible to aid healing, and our patients are open to every possibility.

"Before any procedure I pray. When medical science, psychology, parapsychology and mysticism fail, I pray some more. Prayer works not only on the patient, but also the doctor. And that's about all I have to say."

Maria softened, "What do you pray for, Doctor?"

Mary smiled, exposing a slightly chipped front tooth and answered, "I pray for the strength to continue, the ability to understand a little better, and the humility to accept my blessings without questioning their origin."

Maria stated a fact, "That's faith."

Mary laughed in spite of herself and answered, "I suppose it is after a fashion. Our knowledge is imperfect. Medicine has all the trappings of a modern religion, but I don't subscribe to a set path. If our knowledge were perfect I would be out of a job. All of us would have faith and there would be no reason to heal anything, because everything would be accepted in a natural progression."

Maria embellished Mary's words on camera, as Mary knew she would. News people are interested in ratings. Excitement creates ratings. After seeing her interview aired, Mary expected to be over run with quacks believing they had the singular power of God coursing through their veins. This created an immediate problem. She needed to keep her honest practitioners, separated from the self-serving. There was also a recruiting opportunity here. Mary didn't mind first cousins to God, as long as they understood they were only channels of energy and not cures for humanity. Then she thought of Zeb and chuckled. She realized he might be the closest relative to the Supreme Being she had ever met. But he certainly felt real in her arms on the dance floor. He felt real and strong and warm. She could still smell the fresh washed aroma. Her chuckle covered her uncertainty.

She strolled back towards the hospital feeling a sense of loss. Things were changing rapidly. There would be little time to study the essence of what was occurring, because everyone would expect miracles upon miracles. Most of the important data would be lost in the sensational aspect of everyday healings and she wondered which was more important, gathering information and gaining wisdom or the healings themselves. More than enough idiots would be around claiming the power to provide answers where none existed.

She folded her arms, as if it would protect her from the emotional onslaught ahead. The energy of the entire area was changing. She sensed it, as surely as she knew her heart was beating. It was always her intention to create miracles and now that it was happening everyday she was frightened and didn't know why. She had always taken an Oriental view of healing, not needing explanation as long as something worked. This was a little different. Everything and anything was working. She surmised her feelings might be anxiety over losing the chance to understand what was at work here. It was very difficult to accept all this at face value, which disturbed her deeply. Her philosophy was steeped in oriental tradition, but her formal education was in allopathic western medicine. She was a true measure of yin and yang contained in one spirit.

The weather had taken a distinct turn for the better and she stopped walking, enjoying the smells of new life. Spring rain gave a washed and scrubbed aspect to everything in view, while the sun lingered, glowing high above the trees, creating a glistening macadam mirror on the surface of the parking area. A small boy walked his dog across the parking lot, disappearing into the woods at the edge of hospital property, reappearing moments later. He threw a ball and the dog ran after it. Time and again he threw it and the dog returned it, until at last he lay panting at the boy's feet. The boy knelt down, ruffled his pet's head, and hugged it close. Then they started off again with the dog looking longingly at the ball until the boy laughed and threw it again.

Several other hardy people were out walking in the late afternoon air. It wasn't warm yet. It was teasing weather. The kind of warmth that said, "It won't be long now," but still chilly enough to run goose bumps inside your overcoat. Mary wasn't cold at all, though she only wore her thin lab coat open in the front. Normally, she was bundled up to the maximum. Standing here in a lab coat and open collared shirt, she was comfortable.

"Strange," she thought, dismissing it and thinking about her growth, as a human being and a doctor over the last few years. She recruited the brightest most forward thinking individuals she could find, wherever on the planet she might find them. This was much to the chagrin of her medical colleagues, who didn't think some of these individuals belonged on the planet at all. She persisted, and after several successes, utilizing dual modalities, a coalition of minds and hearts formed. She remained open to new ideas. Very early on, she rejected any credit for the healing process; instead the process itself absorbed her.

Her central belief was, "God and medicine are not mutually exclusive. Anything is possible when occurring along lines of natural selection."

This conviction enabled her to push hard for this institute and the zany wonderful people who staffed it. At times, she was at a loss to follow their discussions of cause, effect and probability. Layers of energy passing in, out and around the body were discussed at length. The search for our center of life force, chi, or soul, was part of an on-going quest for several staff members.

Muscle relaxation, reflexology, and psychic phenomenon were all a part of her medicine. Medicine was intended to help heal the physical body as part of a spiritual entity. I didn't understand any of this until years later. Zeb allowed me to sense his emotions and experience his discoveries, in a healthy way for a seventeen-year-old. He offered a full sense of giving with no need to control. He stayed well within the limitations of his power, always in control and never out to control anyone else. He allowed me to learn, and decide for myself naturally, as he did with everyone.

Looking back I can now trace most of my life interests to that period of several weeks. I was able to draw conclusions about those around me without judging them. I got to know Doctor Savage.

Her first love was and is wellness. She is always searching for root causes of physical problems. She studies diet, cellular nutrition, reflexology, and massage, simply to reach beyond the parameters of conventional science. Delving into Shiatsu and acupuncture led her further into Oriental medicine and the search for "chi" (The life force which energizes the body mechanic). The body-mind is universal, encompassing all energy flowing in each of us throughout the entire universe. We are part of each other. Everything is affected.

The best example I can give is of a pebble thrown into a pool of still water. The ripples spread throughout the entire pool evenly unless another pebble is thrown. It causes disharmony until a balance is found for the two forces. Each flows into and affects the other, eventually becoming part of the whole in harmony. It is called Yin and Yang. Darkness flows into light, strength into weakness, love into hate. Each contains part of the other.

Utilizing the fourteen primary channels and the classic acupuncture points in the body, discovered three millennia ago, she wandered through ancient methods and current practice arriving at a balance, a compromise. There are no absolutes. Right is always part of wrong. Up needs down. Yes needs no.

Holistic medicine attempts to heal before a problem escalates. Allopathy is concerned with treating and is best in crisis situations. It remains her goal in life to create a balance, without tearing apart the good parts of both schools.

Her medical specialty was pediatrics, which furthered her interest in preventative measures. She hated seeing children suffer. Researching causes for breakdowns in the human machinery, while treating symptoms, eventually led to questions about traditional medications. It astounded her when she learned pediatrics had grown ten fold when women stopped breast-feeding and went to work during World War Two. Formula sales were phenomenal supporting all these new doctors nicely and setting the stage for chronic illness decades later. She still placed salves on warts and prescribed radiation for cancer, but she longed for the day when she could treat the cause of disease.

Discussions with her staff, who were always thinking in three dimensions, were exhausting. Some of them went well beyond three dimensions, stretching her own genius intellect beyond limitation. Mary didn't go along with all of them and even chuckled at some of the really off-the-wall ideas in the privacy of her office, but publicly she was a pillar of support for her people. All of them were here because of their brilliance, and a united front was extremely important. The AMA, FDA, and drug companies were always looking for reason to shut the institute down.

Mary knew they were foolish, greedy and misguided, but refused to label them evil. Looking back I would differ on this point. They were evil, greedy, concerned with wealth and power at all cost. Their own self-importance mattered even above the deaths of women and children.

Mary never understood she was in a war. In her mind there was no such thing as medicine and alternative medicine. Those distinctions were creations of cancer research centers, drug companies and the AMA. Mary saw only medicine. Good medicine helped individuals heal. It didn't matter if it came from the skin of a chicken, or the sterile labs at Schering Plough. Whatever the modality, if it induced healing, it was medicine.

She knew in her heart, Hippocrates would tickle an old man's scrotum with an owl feather if it cured his asthma, and so would she. This strict adherence to the spirit of her Hippocratic oath defined Mary Savage and set her apart.

Watching people stroll by in over coats, made her aware of her open lab coat. Then Zebedia appeared in the doorway. He saw her immediately and crossed to her side. She felt a surge of energy inside her, which grew steadily as he approached. Any doubt she harbored fell away. There was no priest or Rabbi around. The source of healing energy was standing right in front of her, and she felt a little lightheaded.

"It is you, isn't it?"

Zeb nodded.

"Are you all right?" Mary continued, "You're doing all of this aren't you?"

Zeb shook his head, insisting he was not.

"What exactly is happening?"

Zeb laughed, "Aren't you looking a gift horse in the mouth?"

Mary chuckled and took his arm lightly turning him towards

her car. "Can we go for a drive, Zeb? I need to get away from here for a little while, and I promised myself a talk with you. I am going a little crazy with all the attention."

The stirring he experienced at her touch surprised Zeb. It grew in the pit of his stomach, warmed him all over. He admired her looks on a casual basis. He hadn't noticed her powerful sensuality, even at the dance. There were so many people and he was expecting a dance with Elizabeth. But out here, alone when she touched him, the affect was enormous. It filled him instantly from head to toe. She was electric with positive energy. Even in her depleted state Zeb sensed and experienced her need to raise the spirits of those around her. Some people would heal faster just by being close to her. She had yet to begin tapping her potential. She had no idea the power she possessed.

Zeb recognized the toll not knowing took on her personally. She rarely left the hospital long enough to get her mail, let alone, replenish her own emotional reserves.

She and Zeb crossed the parking lot towards her car and he noticed she wasn't wearing a jacket.

"Shouldn't you get a coat?" he asked.

"I'm not cold, Zeb. It's the strangest thing, because normally I'm freezing, but I'm quite comfortable now. Maybe its because I'm so close to you." She teased him gently.

Zeb felt himself blush. He could not remember ever feeling this unsettled. Mary watched, thoroughly enjoying his discomfort.

"Relax, Zebedia. I'm not going to bite you, at least not tonight. I want to talk. I need to talk about everything happening at the hospital. I need to laugh. Can you help, Zeb? I hope so."

Zeb stopped and stared directly into her eyes as if searching for something. He hadn't noticed the deep green color before. The dying sunlight enhanced their vibrancy. A light glowed far inside them. They appeared luminescent, possessing a light of their own, but that was impossible.

Zeb laughed to himself.

"What's so funny?" Mary asked defensively.

"I'm not laughing at you, Mary. I'm laughing at myself and the human condition. I just thought something was impossible when I know nothing is."

She reached forward resting her hands on his shoulders and he trembled, "What is it? You look as if you've seen a ghost."

"Perhaps I have. You resemble somebody I knew centuries ago."

She caught her breath, and raised her hand back to her mouth involuntarily. "I knew it. I knew it." She whispered eyes ablaze.

"Now you look like you've seen a ghost. You knew what?"

He questioned lightly, "You said someone you knew centuries ago."

"It is a figure of speech you use, isn't it?" he asked lightly.

Mary relaxed, "You meant you knew someone ages ago?"

Zeb laughed, "I mixed up words again?"

"Yes, you did, and with all that's happening around here I thought you meant you actually knew someone centuries ago whom I resemble."

He studied her face and made a decision, "I did and you do." He answered quietly as the lights surrounding the parking area began to blink on. She squeezed her hands together tightly, looking directly into his eyes. Mary was frightened and ecstatic at the same time.

"You're not kidding, Zeb?"

"No. I'm not. You require answers, a true Capricorn and there is little time. I want to leave something behind."

"What do you mean, leave behind?"

"You are on the right path, and always have been. I came here to show you the potential of your philosophy. You will teach healing much more than even you imagine."

"But, why not tell everyone?" Mary questioned.

"As you have limits, so do I. I don't wish to become the center of attention. I am not the issue. Each person and their dream is important. Caring about each person is important. Caring about others more than you do for yourself is akin to Godliness. You are a godly woman Mary Savage."

Mary stood stock still, staring at him not knowing what to say. Zeb continued.

"There is only so much I am empowered to do and the world is in a sorry state. Let's go for that drive you suggested. I feel like being human. I feel like being held tightly, Mary Savage."

With that she moved into his arms and held him close. She didn't say anything at all. She slid her strong arms around his waist and placed her face close enough to his to feel his breath in her hair. She could feel his heart pounding or maybe it was her own. She really didn't know and when she relayed the story it really didn't matter. They spent a long time there in the parking lot under the fluorescent lamps holding each other closely.

"Another Mary has been warning the world for years. I guess I'm sort of a last messenger. I don't know why anymore than you do."

Zeb finally broke the silence. Mary Savage raised her head from his shoulder and brushed his lips with her own. Zeb smiled and kissed her deeply then, crushing her against his chest and then releasing her without taking his lips from her mouth. When he did they were both a little out of breath and started to laugh simultaneously.

"It must take centuries of practice to learn to kiss like that," Mary joked.

Zeb blushed again. "I've only done that one other time."

Mary tried to hide her surprised look, but Zeb caught it. He told her of another woman long ago and then continued speaking of the other Mary.

"Instead of embracing her, men make rules governing her appearances as if they can control the Chi in the universe. Their time is at an end and yours is just beginning. The earth is moving from a warrior society towards a nurturing society. There is no turning back and earth must become part of the whole or cease to exist. There is no room for more evil in this universe."

Mary hesitated. A slight sense of fear touched her causing her to hesitate.

Zeb smiled. “You wonder why I can’t tell everyone. I’ve told you very little and you shy from me, already. If someone of your nature and intellect is hesitant, can you imagine the problems I could create?”

“Are you . . . are you the. . . ?”

“I am the same as you.”

She told me he said it just that way. I don’t think Mary Savage understood how special that made her. I know I didn’t, not then anyway.

After several moments of silently staring into each other’s eyes, Zeb said, “Lets go for the drive. I will answer as many questions as I can.”

Mary read his face and felt the warmth of his hands on her back. She didn’t want the moment to end. The joy playing here was consistent and infectious. She couldn’t imagine Zeb harming anyone, as she imagined he might only seconds ago. They moved to her car and he hurried around to the passenger’s side

Mary stopped and asked, “Would you prefer to drive?”

Zeb chuckled, “I never learned how.”

“There is no time like the present. Here.”

She threw him the keys and he eyed her strangely, knowing she was testing him. He walked around to the driver’s side and let himself in, settling in the seat behind the wheel. She moved to the passenger seat and slid in just after he settled. Mary began instructing him and he took her hand.

“Please sit back and concentrate on what you would do if you were driving. You want proof. You shall have a small measure.”

Without another word she sat back and relaxed, ticking off the steps she would take in her mind. One by one he performed each task as if it were second nature. He fastened his seat belt, adjusted the mirrors and started the car.

“Amazing.” She thought, without uttering a sound, and received an answer inside her head.

"Extremely." Zeb glanced over and smiled, still holding her hand.

"Is the test over?" he asked aloud.

"Yes, it is," she answered. "But I have a question. Why pretend to be a maintenance man?"

"It is honest work, not a pretense. I enjoy the physical aspect and the contact with people."

"You are much more than a maintenance man."

"And you are much more than a hospital administrator, but neither of us could work without Frank Johnson. Without Frank and his staff your hospital could not function," he answered.

"Point taken," she answered. "I would still like to know why you insist on passing for someone so common, when you might accomplish so much more."

Zeb glanced in the mirror and backed out. He put the car in drive and pulled up towards the hospital, which was a beehive of activity.

"How much more would I like to accomplish?" They laughed together, as they watched television crews and newspaper people rushing about.

"Let's get out of here," Mary ordered.

He responded, "Now, I'm a chauffeur. Is that more or less than a maintenance man? When we get back I might apply for your job."

"Your welcome to it."

"You don't mean that."

"I suppose I don't, but I could use a break."

"You shall have it."

He headed out of the lot. They weaved their way out of town without speaking. Passing buildings, houses, schools, all becoming fewer and fewer until finally fading into open land. They drove along, holding hands, enjoying the silence.

Zeb was certain of his emotions. Over the last few years his control was weakening. He was struck by his deep feelings for Mary. It was different than with my mom. That was a purely physical response. This was different. Something inside him clicked with Mary. He felt like more around her. There was an emotional connection here. His animal instincts lived loudly inside him, too. He felt no guilt. There were no obstacles with Mary, as there were with my mom. No family, no constraint prevented this encounter from reaching a logical conclusion.

Zeb's time was running out. Again he smiled to himself. His frailty and confusion were mounting. His humanness was surging. He wanted this woman the way any man might and was glad to experience feeling sensual love and lust. Zeb knew he had been in the body much too long.

Driving along back roads, they made their way to the Interstate, paid the toll, and then headed North towards Poughkeepsie. Slipping silently by darkening fields, layered like a huge quilt with patches of snow, they remained lost in their own thoughts. Ice clung in towering masses to the cliffs lining the sides of the road. Half-circle linear indentations ran up through the granite walls. These were remnants of deep holes drilled to set charges blasting the highway through the mountains. Shear exposed rock was now covered with chain link fence material guarding against boulders spilling onto the roadway.

Time passed in a vacuum, as night descended around them, filling passing cars with shadows. Still, at the top of the mountain chain, the sky remained bright violet and orange, where the last remnants of sunlight streamed upward indirectly over the horizon. Visibility disappeared quickly along the road, like a translucent shroud falling. Lights of on-coming cars flicked on in a never-ending panorama of approaching fireflies. It was nearly six-o'clock when Mary touched Zeb's arm, pointing to the gas gauge.

He asked. "What is it?"

She was mildly amused, "You really don't know. Do you?"

He shook his head and she pointed to a blue sign reading, "Rest Area, Two Miles." She asked him to pull up to the gas pumps, watching as he did as she instructed. Now, only hours out of Manhattan, they were surrounded by wilderness. Bard College, her

Alma Mater was close by, nestled at the edge of the Hudson River two thirds of the way between Manhattan and Albany.

She envisioned her dad's cabin, not far from here and started rummaging in the glove compartment. She hadn't consciously decided to go there, but here they were. The key was where it always was and she decided without asking Zeb. After filling the gas tank, they stopped at a food store. She bought a bottle of wine, some cheese and several different types of nuts and raisins. She also gathered what vegetables were available, then stopped at the meat counter and decided to pass. She sensed he wouldn't eat meat. She grabbed pretzels and chips, then hurried back to the car.

Hopping back in the car, she poked him in the arm. "That's not fair. Nothing can be a surprise if you know what I am thinking."

He smiled, "You can block me out if you wish, as I can you, but our Chi is so closely in tune, it is difficult."

"Does this happen often?"

He laughed out loud and she frowned. "What is so funny now?"

He stopped laughing and brushed a strand of hair back from her face, instinctively wanting to touch her face.

"Once in two hundred centuries and twice in one week. Do you think my luck is changing."

They both laughed at the joke. Mary slid close to him, laid her head on his shoulder, and wrapped her arms around his waist. She was thinking of her father's cabin and Zeb took the right roads without asking directions.

CHAPTER TWENTY-FOUR

John Sullivan strolled out to his patrol car, waved to his wife and was greeted by an urgent radio message.

"Units 512, 430, and 214 please respond. Shots fired, officer needs assistance. Do you copy?"

Sulli and Morgan Townsend responded immediately, both units were only minutes away. From the general location and specific address Sulli was afraid the officer in trouble could only be Raphael Santiaga.

He threw the car into gear smoking, burning the tires in reverse out into the street. Then he slammed it into drive and sped away leaving Cathy worried and wondering at the door. With lights flashing and tires screeching he wheeled around the corner heading for the playgrounds. Morgan skidded to a halt seconds before Sulli, but they were already too late. Morgan saw the carnage before leaving his car and radioed for ambulances. Sulli jumped out and started towards the scene when Morgan grabbed him.

"Slow down, son. He's my friend too. We need backup and a couple of ambulances."

Sulli knew Morgan was right. The older officer had been working the streets for years, ever since returning from Vietnam. He never grew cynical, though he had reason to be. His little brother died on these playgrounds, while he was off fighting for some other country's right to choose freedom.

Morgan graduated City College night school taking a degree in Philosophy, while minoring in criminal justice. He was the oldest member of the philosophy department and the only black male. Sulli kidded him about being the Socrates of law enforcement.

Morgan refused his first two promotions. He wanted to stay in the streets, feeling he worked best with the kids on a face to face basis. He was right. Finally, the department recognized his talent and gave him his promotions without altering his assignment. It was a smart public relations move. Morgan stopped more bloodshed, saved more lives and sent more kids to trade school and college than any Federal program ever. He also watched children die by each other's hand on a daily basis and today was no exception.

Lying before them were six lifeless lumps of flesh, drenched in puddles of their own blood, scattered about the basketball court. Two more sat moaning against the wall of the youth center and another was draped over a bicycle rack. Four red bandannas and five black ones wrapped securely to each person's head signified their gang affiliation, like team uniforms.

As Morgan and Sulli approached cautiously, Morgan quipped, "I guess the reds won today, huh Sulli?"

Sulli didn't smile, "Yeah, they sure did Morgan. Some victory, huh. Let's call out the cheer leaders."

Morgan heard the horrified sickness in the young officer's voice and didn't say anything further. Sulli wouldn't quit. Morgan was glad to have him here, in the neighborhood. Sulli was a rare one. He didn't blame the kids, knowing all the parts were interchangeable.

He once remarked to Morgan over a beer, when he was more than a little tipsy. "Morgan, if you took every white middle class kid and made them grow up here we would be counting dead white kids and complaining about them. Put the neighborhood kids in the suburbs and they would be attending prep schools and putting golf balls at the club."

Morgan remembered his response, "You figured that out all by yourself?"

Sulli laughed though a drunken haze and answered proudly, "Yeah . . . yeah, I sure did."

Morgan clapped him on the back and said, "I think we'll keep you, blonde hair, blue eyes and all."

Morgan threw him in the back of his car that night and carried him into his home. Cathy had thanked Morgan and given him a huge hug. He was pleasantly surprised and told Sulli the next day he better hold on to Cathy with both hands, because she was a keeper. It was the highest compliment a street cop could pay any wife. It meant she was one hell of a special woman. That sealed a friendship and solidified a good working relationship. Sulli respected Morgan, because Morgan taught by example.

Morgan is the one person in this entire story that I never met; yet I feel a part of him. Everything I know of him came from John Sullivan.

Morgan drew his weapon and started across the deserted lot, with Sulli close behind. The sound of their back-up's sirens screaming grew louder with each passing second.

They rolled the first three kids over on their backs, gently. Two of them couldn't be more than fourteen, and probably wouldn't see fifteen. They were all whimpering, all the fight leaking out the wounds in their young bodies.

Angry tears welled in Morgan's eyes. "Babies, just babies." He whispered to himself.

They quickly checked the others. One was dead already and another was closer to death than life. Sulli threw up in a trashcan by the court, then quickly returned to help. Morgan attended to the three most serious while Sulli rounded up the other four. Five ambulances arrived along with three more squad cars, freeing Sulli and Morgan to take their search into the surrounding tenements.

Sulli had a bad feeling, but kept it to himself. It wasn't like Raphael, to be out of touch for so long, not while a war was going on and they found the reason three feet into the shadow of an alleyway leading to the opposite street. He sat propped against a pole with a pay telephone, ripped from the wall, resting on his shattered kneecaps. His hands were crushed and bleeding. God only knew what else was broken.

Morgan knelt down, touched his neck and Santiaga stirred.

He turned to Sulli and said, "Get them over here, he's still alive."

Raphael opened his left eye, not quite swollen shut, and indicated his left hand. Clutched in it was a blood stained note. Morgan read it and understood immediately.

He called after Sulli, "Get a car over to Santiaga's house right away."

Sulli called back, "I'll go myself."

Raphael smiled up at Morgan with his broken swollen face and dropped the note, which read, "Protect my family, they know about me."

Morgan tried to be cheery; "You don't look so hot, Raph."

The paramedics arrived and one of them slipped, saying, "Sweet mother-of-mercy, why bother?"

Morgan grabbed him by the collar; "He's a cop and a good friend. Is that a good reason?"

The young attendant whispered, "Sorry, officer I didn't know . . ."

Morgan stopped him. "I'm sorry too, son, sorry this happens over and over again. It's gonna be a long night for everybody." He sank down next to Raphael, cradling his broken bleeding head, while the paramedics went to work.

Sulli hustled back to his car and made short work of checking what units were near Santiaga's house. He was the only one. It took him nearly ten minutes weaving through traffic to reach the house. Skidding to a halt on Raphael's front lawn, he heard screams from inside over the sound of his car's dying siren. There was no doubt whoever was in the house knew he was here and there was no time to lose. Sulli didn't wait for backup, as he should have. Bursting through the door, he caught two gang members trying to run out the rear door, while Raphael's wife, Maryann, pulled her dress back down and straightened her torn blouse.

He raised his gun and Maryann screamed to stop him, "No Sulli. We're okay. They're just kids."

"Kids don't threaten three-year-olds, then rape their mothers," he yelled and went after them. One stopped and turned, firing from his hip a short burst from a nine-millimeter semi-automatic weapon. It ripped into Sulli's chest driving him back against the house and he fell stunned to the ground. The child-gunman stood slowly. Grinning from ear to ear, he approached, while the other beckoned him to flee and left disappearing into the darkness.

The shooter walked confidently towards Sulli with the weapon hanging at his side. Through the haze Sulli instinctively raised his gun and fired six rounds, fearing he was going to die. It was enough. Though he missed his assailant by nearly five feet, the sight of the gun muzzle spitting fire at him wiped the grin from the boy's face and sent him racing after his friend. He ran like a wolf was gaining on him.

Sulli struggled to a sitting position. His chest felt as if he had been hit by a falling tree. One bullet glanced off the top of his bulletproof vest and tore a groove through his shoulder, chipping his collarbone. He got to his feet slowly, took a last look after the fleeing kids and went back inside.

"Johnny, you're hurt," Maryann sobbed.

He inspected his shoulder and grimaced. "More my pride than anything else. It was stupid leaving you alone. Where is Latitia?"

She didn't bother to pull her torn blouse around her when she approached him. They were childhood friends. She touched his shoulder and he winced, but repeated his question.

"Where is the baby?"

This time she answered, as she moved into the bath and returned with some bandages and a bottle of peroxide.

"I put her in her room and told her to stay there until I get her. I already checked and she is fine."

"Go get her, Mare. I want to see her. I promised Raph . . . I promised . . ."

"Did something happen to Raphael tonight? Is he. . . ? Is he. . . ?"

"I don't know and that's the truth. He was alive when I left to come here. The paramedics were working on him. Get the baby, Mare. You should get over to the hospital."

"But your shoulder."

"It will keep until you get to the hospital. Get some things together, because you'll be spending the night."

"What about the baby?"

"Cathy and I will see to Latitia. Raphael is going to need you."

When they reached the hospital Morgan was sitting in the lounge sipping coffee, filling out papers, mumbling about the waste of his time. He rose as they approached.

"How is he, Morgan?" Maryann asked, racing up to him.

"He's fighting hard, Mare. You better go to him. He's asking for you."

They raced her upstairs to the Intensive Care Unit, where the nurse dressed her in a surgical gown and rapidly propelled her down the hall. Maryann felt like an observer of a bad movie. She had been beaten and almost raped, and her husband was fighting for his life in the hospital. It was like a bad nightmare. It would be morning soon and all this would be over. She would be home with her husband and baby.

She entered the room and the reality hit her full in the face. Nearly fainting when she saw him covered with bandages like some large broken toy doll; she reached a chair and held on for a moment staring. His face was partially obscured by a large tube taped to his mouth. Bulky plaster casts encased both arms and legs, hanging from pulleys. His head was hidden in bandages and a spiderweb of tubes entered his body, connected to polls or hanging off the bed. She couldn't tell which fluids were going in and which were coming out.

She steadied herself, wiped her tears away, took a deep breath and moved to his bedside. He stirred at her approach and a smile appeared at the corners of his mouth. It was as if he were waiting to see if Morgan reached her in time.

Maryann covered her mouth and tears flowed out the corners of her eyes as she whispered, "Raphael. Raphael . . ."

A steady, irritating beep emanated from his heart monitor, while a machine enclosed in plastic, resembling a squeeze box pushed air into his lungs every five seconds or so. Two tubes drained wounds in his side and two more exited his chest emptying into bags hanging from the side of his bed. She hadn't seen the fourth from across the room.

Maryann surveyed the carnage, which used to be her husband wondering if she would lose him.

It was a small negative thought, insignificant really. She wouldn't even remember it later, but in that delicate state between coming and going, it opened the door for his exit.

I wish I understood all of these things then, but I didn't and I still don't. Raphael's soul was ready to move on, but would have remained. There is a fine line between what is and what must be. Faith and hope determine so many things and our very existence may turn on a mere thought, or whim, because, our existence is so fragile. Zeb showed us our frailty by exposing his own. He lived with us by choice, when his world was much better than ours. I wish I understood then. I wish so many things about that time. I wish I believed, but I didn't. I wouldn't let myself. I didn't want to appear foolish.

The smile on Raphael's face faded. He relaxed and the line on his heart monitor went flat. A steady screaming whine replaced the beep. Almost instantly the room, became a beehive of activity. Nurses and doctors poured in, pushing Maryann to the side. Her head turned this way and that as if she were watching a tennis match. She kept repeating, as she retreated into a corner of the room, forgotten in the onslaught.

"Don't you die on me, Santiaga! Sweet mother of mercy, please . . ."

Again a small positive prayer forgotten in the larger scheme of things, but so very important. It held Raphael just an instant. As he was glimpsing his immortality he turned back and saw her. He hesitated watching her face, feeling her love.

Forgotten in the darkened corner of the room, she watched in horror as they tried to jump-start her husband's heart, much as he jump-started her car in winter. The doctor drove a needle into Raphael's chest while a nurse prepared electric paddles. She handed them to the doctor and Maryann winced when he yelled, "Clear."

CHAPTER TWENTY-FIVE

It was ending, as the most relaxing day of their lives. Zeb worked magic with the salad, vegetables and pasta while Mary watched. They lit candles and feasted by firelight, getting to know each other softly and tenderly. Melding easily together, they searched each other's mind and bodies like kids in a candy store, savoring each morsel, while digging for the next. Zeb slid down on couch beside her and she complained of soreness in her neck. He asked her to lie down, removed her white Reeboks and began massaging her feet.

"I said my neck, Zebedia. You do know the top from the bottom don't you?" She kidded him.

He chuckled, "All good things begins with balance. Be patient. I'll get to your neck."

He pressed into the ball of her foot and she winced. "Geeze!!! I felt that all the way up here." She pointed to her shoulder. "Don't tell me you know Reflexology, too?"

He laughed. " A little. I learned Shiatsu massage from a Zen master . . ."

She cut him off. "Let me guess. It was centuries ago, right?"

Zeb pushed into a tsubo and she winced again, "Actually it was three years ago, in England. Now, please be quiet so I can concentrate. You are completely blocked and you have a problem in your abdomen."

Her face darkened, but he didn't notice and she lay back easily, allowing her mind to drift, while he worked slowly up the kidney, spleen and stomach channels in her legs, manipulating tsubos, and freeing tension at almost every juncture. Zeb searched deep into the tissues and then gently massaged the area before digging in again always maintaining contact, sharing his energy and emotion.

Reaching the top of her thigh he returned down each leg stroking evenly searching for residual blockages. They were much better than when he started a half-hour earlier. He stroked them evenly for an extra few minutes, raw sexuality pulsing inside him. He laid his hand on her Hara just below her navel and took several deep breaths. He was aware of the stiffness and heat radiating from her abdomen and asked how long she had known of the tumor in her intestine.

Mary didn't open her eyes when she answered, "You have an excellent touch for a maintenance man."

Zeb breathed deeply and sighed, "You're evading the question and I need your help here."

Mary frowned. A pained expression creased her brow. She squeezed the bridge of her nose with her right hand, then relaxed. "I've known about four weeks."

"How bad is it?"

"The prognosis is not good. I've decided on a course of treatment beginning next week."

"It is amazing the havoc stress plays in the human body." Zeb spoke matter-of-factly, and she opened one eye surveying his face.

"You don't seem very concerned," she said directly.

"About what?"

"I just told you I will probably die from cancer. That usually elicits a sympathetic response."

Zeb kidded her, "I'm so sorry to hear you have cancer. Is that better?"

She smiled and closed her eyes, "Much better, and just my luck. I take one day off with a weirdo with no feelings."

Zeb grew serious, "Are you afraid of death, Mary Savage?"

"That's a difficult question, Zeb. Until four weeks ago, I never thought much about my own death and I've never faced it within my family. Mom and Dad are both well and I don't think you could kill my brother with a bazooka."

"Mary, you are evading me again. Are you afraid to die?"

"If you put it that way; yes, I am."

"Why?"

"I think it is knowing I haven't accomplished all I set out to do, more than the actual death itself. I am like anyone else when it comes down to hard facts."

"What are the hard facts?"

"I love what I'm doing. I am comfortable with who I am. Death is an uncertainty, Zeb."

"Most would say death is very certain."

"That is a linear explanation, one which is accepted by the masses. The great certainties are death and taxes. I'm not afraid of the physical dying. Being dead concerns me. It is an unknown. I know I can't control it and won't know anything about it until I do it. Not knowing where it leads creates trepidation."

"You just described birth and living, Mary Savage. Death is just one more door; it leads to your future. Our Father created everything in the universe in circular fashion, yet humans fail to see their lives in that light. You have an old soul, and charisma, which extends far out into the universe. Your energy has been growing for thousands of years. It will not end. It is part of creation."

"Now you sound like some of the geeks I hired. I can't follow their thinking half the time. The cosmos, the universe, I only think of them when I am at a loss to explain phenomenon. I work with here and now. I live and breathe in each moment. I let you and the others deal with abstracts."

"The important thing, the pivotal thing about your soul, is you are open to those abstracts. You are aware of circular thought."

"I suppose I am, but that doesn't mean I agree with all of it."

"And it is that discerning wisdom which sets you apart. Your healing potential is enormous, Mary Savage."

"Then why can't I heal the stupid tumor in my own body?"

"Fear is insidious. I wondered why you couldn't heal it yourself. That's why I asked if you were afraid of death."

"So what is the answer, Einstein?"

"He was a brilliant man."

"You knew him too, Zeb?"

"No. But I had you going, didn't I?"

"Be serious. Why can't I heal the tumor?"

"You've used a lot of energy on other people and you've taken on more than a few of their problems. Your immune system is overburdened and your liver is over taxed. I think you are more afraid of failing those in your care, than of your own demise. It's why you run so fast. You never believed what you preached, simply because you cannot fully define it. How silly for someone who deals with death daily. The combination prevents you from restarting your immune system."

"What combination?"

The combinations of healing while you are treating. Because of your education, you chase an elusive magic potion, all the while knowing, the answers are locked inside you. You don't believe you will be here to see the outcome. I assure you that isn't true."

"That's all well and good on the spiritual side. There I am comfortable I will always exist, Zeb, but why trade in this perfectly good body when there is forty more years of usefulness in it."

"Exactly what I was wondering myself. Remember what you tell anyone who uses the word 'terminal' in reference to a patient?"

"I'd forgotten. How many times I've said it to others, but as soon as I was certain of my own prognosis, I was dying."

"Precisely right. Your patients are first and foremost, living — each moment, each day — never dying. Your belief is contagious, Mary. Effort, compassion and kindness are your most important tools. We are living until the instant of death, and death is beginning again."

"How did you know those words." Instantly she realized he had read her memory. "That's from my Doctoral Thesis."

"I know." Zeb replied.

Mary added. "I always objected to doctors guessing how long people will live. Along the way we all lose something of the wonder of youth."

"You don't have any idea what losing youth is all about, Mary Savage."

She laughed. Zeb knew she didn't really believe he was centuries old.

"You're thinking I'm really out there aren't you?"

She softened and kidded him gently. "I suppose you think you are normal."

Zeb didn't laugh. His face darkened and his eyes grew angry. He seemed to grow in front of her and she was startled.

"I am normal, Mary," he whispered.

"Kindness, compassion, caring are normal. Greed, arrogance, lust, hatred are aberrations. All the things you wrote in your thesis are true. You have it within you to heal anything in your body or spirit. Each person can tap the power of the universe. It is a matter of faith only because we haven't discovered all knowledge again. Somewhere along the way we humans lost faith. I am having a hard time with it. I have grown to love life so much, that I also, am a little afraid. My time here is short."

Zeb saw the look on her face and stopped. She would understand soon enough. His mood lightened, "Enough of gloom and doom, Mary Savage. Being alive is precious. This moment with you is wonderful and you are in luck. I am about to expose for your singular edification the secrets of the universe. Ta da!!"

It was that way with Zeb. One minute he was deadly serious and the next seemed like there were no cares in the world. He didn't dwell on problems; he dealt with them and then moved on physically and emotionally. Mary didn't know whether he was serious or not.

"You're nuts, Zebedia."

"Eccentric is a much kinder thought, Mary."

She laughed again knowing he read her thoughts, "I told you that's not fair."

"Oh, but it is dear lady and our closeness in essence will aid us in the task at hand."

"Which is?"

"Healing 304 is our lesson today. Tumors happen to be my forte'. I am very good with this type of thing."

"Oh boy."

"C'mon, Mary. Have a little faith, girl."

He was completely animated like a medicine man selling snake oil off a brightly colored wagon. Zeb bounced around, laughing and beaming, challenging her at the same time.

"What have you got to lose, woman. We can kick that tumor's butt right now. Are you with me?"

He laughed breathlessly and touched her face gently. Lying his head on her thigh he whispered, "There are forty years to gain, sweet woman."

She picked her head up and looked down at him gazing back at her. "Eccentric is a little mild, Zebedia."

"Perhaps. But I am telling you the truth. Our energy combined is beneficial to you."

She surveyed his face, "Are you kidding around?"

He chuckled, "I can afford to be less serious about these problems. Help me with this tumor, Mary. Learn from the experience. It is a request, not a challenge or a demand. Please help me teach you to heal yourself? It is a simple thing. Letting your fear of failure go is not so simple. Success has always come from your openness. Open now, Mary. Accept a gift without the need to return something."

Mary understood exactly what he meant. She relaxed and lay back ready to accept anything, open to everything.

"Good." He replied unbuttoning her blouse and lying his hand at the lower extremity of the tumor.

He breathed evenly and raised one hand toward the ceiling praying quietly. Then he lowered his hand next to the other and asked Mary to breathe in unison with him, to think of the tumor in the shape of something she disliked.

"Mary Savage," he whispered softly. "Allow me to give to you as you have to others. Allow me to love you as you have given love. Give me a portion of your pain. Share with me your fear. Allow me to know you as you do yourself."

She heard his thoughts, though no sound passed between them. She melded her thoughts to his, drifting along collecting energy from all around her. The temperature in the room rose, rapidly.

Mary concentrated and breathed with Zeb. She could feel his breath coming in and out of her nostrils. His life force added strength to hers, flowing in and out of her as his hands grew hotter and hotter over the disease growing inside her and then she felt it start to melt away. His hand drifted. She kept her eyes closed, seeing her tumor as a wart. She had the sensation of his hand sinking into her skin, she felt as if he were inside her. She became frightened and started to pull away back to conscious thought, but he held her with the force of his will and she relaxed again.

She imagined only that part of her body opening and releasing the disease. It was almost complete. She moved slightly and he adjusted his touch. The tumor was reduced to millions of minute electrical impulses, which flowed out of Mary into Zeb's hands and beyond. He accepted them without fear, for his chemical make-up was vastly different from hers and the chance they could combine into a tumor again was minuscule. She fell asleep exhausted.

He relaxed, reached for her hand separated the fingers and worked his way up her arms to her neck. Every tsubo was blocked and her neck was one huge knot. Zeb put pressure on the sides of her head, working her gall bladder channel, then reached under her using her weight on his hands to release the stiffness in her neck, and her bladder meridian. Utilizing her weight in this fashion kept his hands steady and fresh.

She moaned and opened her eyes, staring up into his gentle face lightly beaded with sweat. Reaching up she placed her hands on his biceps and felt the strength as he worked on her neck. He moved behind her and stroked down lightly moving lymph and releasing inflamed facia.

"That was wonderful. I almost felt as if the tumor were disintegrating inside me."

Zeb looked at her and chuckled, "Why do you doubt? Feel your lower abdomen."

Mary did and moved her hand all over quickly. She couldn't find stiffness anywhere. Her breath caught in her throat and tears of relief fell from her eyes.

"How? Who are you, Zeb?"

"You know me and this was always possible. God and medicine were never mutually exclusive. You understood this from the beginning of your life. People learn fear and stop trusting their instincts because of it. The cyclical nature of a woman's body is a distinct advantage, Mary. Your body will always tell you what it needs. Fear is the destroyer of hope. Some call it original sin, but it really doesn't matter what generates the fear. Facing it is paralyzing. The darkness has almost as much power as the light, Mary. The evil one is a great spiritual being. He uses every ounce of his greatness to make people doubt. We did this together, you and I."

"Are you doing all the healing at the hospital?" She asked intensity, clouding and obscuring her delicate features.

"No."

"Then why did it start when you arrived?"

"Because I added my energy to yours, plus the energy of the thousands of angels who have gathered to watch you. The spirit who watches over me happens to be particularly well connected and I have certain privileges."

"Are you human?"

"Very much so, Mary. Look at me. You can readily see how you affect me. This is a totally human characteristic."

She looked at him and became slightly flushed realizing what he was referring to. "I am fascinated at how well we humans perform with all our imperfections, and temptations."

"I can't believe any of this is happening."

"Will you do me a favor?"

"What?"

"Stop thinking and analyzing for little while. Become Oriental for an hour. They have no compulsion to understand why things work. If something works consistently well for a thousand years, there is proof enough. Let me finish your massage. The tension in your cranial passage at the occipital ridge is massive. Let me work it out before you add to it."

"Why can't you just will it away."

"That might be easier." He moved away an inch or so while she waited. Then he massaged her again. "Nah, it wouldn't be any fun," he answered mischievously.

"All right, but answer one more question. Are you allowed to fall in love, Zebedia, whoever you are?"

He smiled and in the firelight, his eyes sparkled like moonlight shimmering on the surface of the ocean.

"I said you reminded me of someone."

Mary nodded, remembering.

"Her name was Mary also. It, literally, was centuries ago. She was the first woman I loved. No one else has ever mattered until someone just recently and she is married."

"Did you just say you love me, Mary also, or someone else." Mary asked eyes aglow, and Zeb replied.

"Very funny. Yes, I guess I did."

"I like it better when you're being human." She whispered. Responding to his touch she reached up drawing his face down to hers. Her lips were warm, full and moist. Her tongue was sweet and Zeb trembled as lightning passed behind his closed eyelids.

He pulled back gently, kissed her eyes and nipped her ear before asking, "May I finish your neck now."

Mary ran her hands up and down his arms, then his legs, and he didn't shy from her touch. She explored at will then answered, "Yes, you can, as long as it doesn't take all night."

Zeb laughed and Mary continued, her voice lilting, and giddy,

"I've never loved a maintenance man, and I've never liked someone as quickly."

"There are first times for everything." He answered, and Mary sensed, Zeb was also speaking of his own sexual experience. Touched by the simple honesty of the admission, she wondered how it might be possible in this day and age, for him to be a virgin.

Deciding not to pry further she lay back reveling in the cranial work he was performing on her. She could feel her brain pulses rising. His hands were strong and his touch instinctive, as he rolled her head from side to side stretching, and releasing points along the large intestine meridian passing through her neck and shoulders. Then he searched behind her ear at the base of her skull for the gall bladder meridian once more. He pressed and released until he felt the blockage free like a damn collapsing in a river. After working all the meridians, he switched to a more conventional relaxation technique. He was gentle as well as strong and the last part of the massage was thoroughly enjoyable, and erotic.

They spoke of many things in the next hour exploring feelings and expressions foreign to both of them and when he finally lay down next to her in front of the fire it seemed they were together for years. Both were gentle, and caring, each intent on pleasing the other. Mary's beeper sounded in her lab coat pocket hanging on a chair near the door. She ignored it; something she never did. It went off again and she ignored it again. The third time Zeb raised his head from her chest and said, "I think you should call." His eyes were set and she knew he sensed something wrong.

"What is it, Zeb?"

"Answer the call, Mary," he said it quietly without any real sense of urgency, but Mary knew something had happened. His normally placid face was drawn in concentration. He couldn't conceal the sadness playing around his eyes. She moved to the phone picked it up and reached the operator. Waiting patiently for the rural Phone Company to connect her call, she watched Zeb move about the room collecting their clothes and cleaning up their mess.

"You have a beautiful body, Zebedia." Mary offered, and he turned to look at her.

"Thank you, very much." Came the simple reply, which made her chuckle. He made no pretense of false humility, accepting the compliment as a natural thing to say. Mary pondered that, finally realizing that it is a natural thing to say to someone you care about. Zeb gathered her clothes together for her and she said, "We barely got started. Are you sure we can't stay?"

"You decide." Zeb answered, as the call went through and Mary covered her free ear to hear better.

"Would you repeat that?" She listened as the person repeated what was said. A great shadow grew across her face, like a cloud suddenly blocking out sunlight. She slumped in the chair next to the table and buried her face in her free hand.

"Yes, I understand. It will take a couple hours, but I'll be there as soon as I can. Yes, thanks."

She rubbed her eyes and Zeb lifted her chin. He kissed her softly on the mouth and said the oddest thing. "I will miss you, forever." Then he smiled into her eyes, "This was the easiest night of my life and you are the most exquisite creature I've ever known."

She tried to laugh, but couldn't quite manage. Zeb lifted her into his arms holding her close.

She squeezed him hard. "There was a gang fight, Zeb. Four children are dead, one, only thirteen. Raphael Santiaga could be the next victim. They're working on him, but his chances aren't good. I guess we ran out of miracles today." She tried to make a joke through tears and failed.

"There are more miracles in store." Zeb answered calmly, as if it was the most natural statement. "You have one already in the bag."

Touching her stomach, she knew he meant it, but didn't see how it was possible to repair this insane butchery. The complete goodness of the last week was blotted out by a single night of irrational hatred and violence. Her anger made her physically ill.

To think of those children lying dead at her hospital, was more than she wanted to bear tonight.

Mary nestled in Zeb's arms. They clung to each other for a few moments, drifting, dreaming, and drawing strength from each other in quiet surroundings. Neither wanted to end the embrace. They fit together like pieces of a puzzle. He shifted slightly looking into her eyes. He brushed his lips against hers, first lightly then deeply, mouth open, tongue darting, searching, and finding a partner. Breathless after only a moment they parted held hands at arms length and let go. They stood taking each other in quietly, each burning images into memory. Then they moved, and took a last look around.

Finally, Zeb doused the fire, stirred the ashes and watched a cloud of steam-filled smoke curl into the chimney. He looked over his shoulder, and Mary could see his face clearly glowing in the darkness, as if he possessed an internal power source. Later she rationalized her mind was playing tricks, but never lost the image. For the rest of her life she was able to bring it to mind at will, no matter where she was or what she might be doing and it always brought a feeling of peace.

Zeb stood up and crossed the room. They were leaving the cabin exactly as they found it. Time seemed to be moving in slow motion. He reached for her hand and they headed out to her car. He took her in his arms and kissed her long and deep, once more becoming part of her. Stardust and magic exploded in Mary's mind, while Zeb's heart pounded with pent up passion. He drank in each touch, and savored the smell of her.

Releasing her he lifted his arms towards the heavens and she sensed the air become electric. He breathed evenly and deeply speaking quietly then listening for several minutes. At last he smiled, lowered his arms and opened his eyes.

She wasn't surprised or intimidated. Through all the years, exploring different modalities of healing, she witnessed far stranger things than reaching up to God and asking for help. That was an everyday occurrence. Waiting for answers was the tough part most of the time. Zeb, for whatever reason, seemed to get them a little faster.

As she watched and listened, the quiet beauty of their surroundings began to overtake her; the stillness of the snow lying on the ground, covering acres of woods. Nothing stirred until a small gust of wind swirled the mist hanging just above the ground. All was illuminated by a brilliant march moon, suspended, glistening radiant silver in an endless ink blue sky.

She stretched her sixth sense to its limit in the silence and thought she heard. There were a few pleasant words, and then jumbled sounds drifting in and out as she lost focus. She regained it, but she couldn't be certain she heard anything. She thought she might be imagining it, but felt beings very near around her.

"Well?" She questioned as his eyes returned to her.

"We aren't out of miracles just yet, Mary." Zeb answered, and she believed him. They jumped in her car. He turned the key and they roared away into the darkness. Neither of them looked back.

CHAPTER TWENTY-SIX

They worked on Raphael for nearly two hours, and the team was exhausted. Joe Tomlevich and Sam Shulman came and stayed. Lea Tenfingers chanted and burned sage, while Joe and Sam prayed. Brennen Roller, the Rei Kei Master, passed his hands over Raphael searching for energy fields which no longer had measure.

Raphael watched quietly from the ceiling. He stared at Maryann longer than he should. It was time to leave, but he was reluctant. It wasn't that he was unprepared to meet his maker, he was ready; but so much good had been done in Springfield. He felt his part wasn't finished. He felt there was more to do, so he stayed and watched Maryann and the emergency team try to restart his body, while others tried to restore his spirit.

Dr. Provenzano called everyone in the hospital that had any success in healing anything. Before Joe Tomlevich left, he anointed Raphael and gave him his last rites.

"A little lubricant. Just in case he's on his way home. Dr. Provenzano. No offense."

Joe Provenzano chuckled, "None taken, Father. You can grease me up when it's my time too." The little bit of levity served to ease frazzled nerves.

Joe and Nurse Lebrowitz were drenched in sweat and sprinkled with blood. Normally this procedure lasted twenty minutes before calling it quits, but so many amazing things had happened in this building over the last few days, that the staff expected to succeed all the time. They kept at it. Raphael had enough extra adrenaline pumped into his chest cavity to power a football team through an entire season, with no result. The young nurse/technician operating the electrical charger for the paddles nodded to the doctor. Joe lifted the paddles rubbed them together to get them evenly covered with grease, shouted, "Clear" in a tired voice and jolted Raphael for the last time. The line on Rapahael's monitor remained flat. Joe Provenzano dropped the paddles on the tray. He pulled the mask and cap off his head at the same time and stood looking at Raphael for a moment, which stretched into two and three until Nancy Lebrowitz took his hand.

"We tried our best, Joey."

"I know." He said smiling through tired tears. Squeezing her hand he thanked Nancy, and instructed everyone that it was over. He turned away and was greeted by a muffled sob at the rear of the room.

"Mrs. Santiaga?" He noticed her for the first time. She looked at him, eyes wet and frightened, shaking all over, moving her head from side to side, searching his face. Lea Tenfingers watching from the doorway, came into the room and took Maryann into her arms. No one attempted to stop her. The young doctor was exhausted and at a loss what to do or say.

"He's gone. Isn't he?" She questioned, looking timidly out from Lea's embrace. Dr. Provenzano nodded.

CHAPTER TWENTY-SEVEN

Mary and Zeb pulled into the parking lot, as Joe Provenzano yelled, "Clear" for the last time. They sped across the macadam and slammed into the curb in her reserved space. She reached for the door, but Zeb grabbed her arm.

"Zeb, it's a little late to start . . ."

She turned and the look on his face made her pause. "What is it, Zeb?"

"I thought we would get here in time." He twitched violently, as if getting a sudden jolt of electricity.

Mary was concerned and reached for his hand. "Zebedia, are you all right?"

He ignored the question. "Raphael Santiaga is leaving," he whispered. "It's not time. It's not time."

"What are you talking about? Raphael was badly injured in the fight; he's not going anywhere."

Zeb looked into her eyes and smiled. Mary could tell he was thinking deeply and didn't say anything else.

"Look at your watch and remember the time." Mary did as he asked, barely an hour had passed since they left the cabin, but that wasn't possible. They were on the road for nearly two hours. She glanced up at him again and Zeb winked at her.

"Remember the time, Mary. I hadn't intended for you to know this part, but this isn't being done according to my plans." Zeb smiled and settled against his seat, adjusted himself to be comfortable with no distractions, and squeezed Mary's hand. She let go of the door and felt the energy rise in the car. She could feel warmth flowing from Zeb's body and being generated by her own. It was wonderful, peaceful and exhilarating all at the same time. Mary didn't resist, relaxing, closing her eyes, not wanting to disturb the moment. Zeb raised her hand and they were transported. She could hear his voice, but he wasn't speaking to her. He was calling after a figure walking away from them towards a blinding, beautiful white swirling light. There was no reason to move, yet she felt free of any constraint and her mind moved her about freely. Zeb called after Raphael with the words he had spoken before.

"Its not time, Raphael. You must come back. I need your help."

Raphael turned around and hesitated.

"Must I?" Came his reply and Zeb smiled.

"Thirty more years is not so long to wait, Raphael. It is a small request. Please? You are fortunate. You know what is and what was. You can live a short while without fear, because we will be waiting for you. Your place here is secure for all time."

A figure appeared out of the light. Mary couldn't quite make out the face encased in brilliance against the light, but heard the soft voice.

"What do you want with him? They beat him up all the time. They shoot him and stick him with knives and his friends can't even tell anyone he's a good person. He has done enough?"

Zeb laughed, "You are going to argue with me now, Les?"

The spirit smiled, "Look, Zeb. I was given permission to bring him up. He's already had more lives than a cat."

"I need him, Les. Jimmy Rivera needs him, and so do a lot of others."

Mary couldn't believe it. She must be dreaming. The light, their surroundings, everything was magnificent, yet it wasn't overwhelming or frightening. It all seemed so normal, so natural and suddenly she understood something, which had been missing in all her years of training. This journey was as much a part of life as life itself.

"There are two things every human does alone which unite us all." She thought to herself. "We come into the world from the spirit and return to the spirit alone, without worldly possessions.

Our only baggage is a conscience containing the sum of our efforts. If we worked solely for our own personal gain, we create our own isolation in the spirit. We are the sum of our desire and our ability to control it."

Zeb turned and winked at her. She sensed him inside her head as she was in his, and felt very close to him. They were kindred spirits. He in his baggy kacky pants, denim shirt and well-worn leather bomber jacket, and she in her simple skirt and lab clothes. Mary never dressed differently. She saw no point to the effort. Simple and neat was best for her. The only exception was for business meetings to which she wore one of two expensively tailored suits with four-inch high heel shoes, made of soft Italian leather. For some strange reason she wished she were dressed nicer now. Zeb looked over at her and she sensed his thoughts again.

"You are lovely. Clothes are only covering for a beautiful creation."

She answered without speaking, "You should know."

He laughed and shook his head.

The angel protecting Raphael moved towards Mary, staring directly behind Zebedia to where she waited. The angel was tall, and slender with an oval translucent face. She had light olive skin and pale green eyes. Her hair, flowing out behind her in waves, was the color of winter wheat, touched with red flames, by a setting summer sun.

"It has been a long time for you on earth, Zebedia. You've assimilated many human traits and desires." She spoke without rancor, a touch of sadness in her voice, as if she was losing someone very special. "Raphael has earned his peace." She continued strength of conviction filling out her voice again.

Zeb returned quietly, "His peace is secure, and his place here will never be in jeopardy, no matter what he is tempted with. I will be with you to watch over him. He will be aware of more than just his world, and he will never again want for anything. They need him Leslie, now more than ever, because I will not be with them."

The spirit moved slightly, a little surprised, "You are returning to us?"

"For all the reasons you mentioned and more." Zeb glanced at Mary, a look of love that wasn't lost on the angel. Mary sensed his thoughts. Now she understood what he meant when he said he would miss her. "There is much work to be done. In this tiny place I found many people ready to listen. They will spread the word."

Mary watched Raphael turn back towards Zeb and start to move. Leslie retreated into the light. She waved to Mary, who felt an overwhelming desire to remain here, but Zeb turned her away. This was only a glimpse of what was available; something to keep her going.

Then everything seemed to collapse around her. Raphael hurried quickly past her and disappeared. One second he was here; the next vanished, as if he had never been. The light faded and just as quickly as this world opened, it was gone. It was like watching water being sucked out of a giant hole in a dam except they were in the water. Mary felt a little lost and sick at heart. She ached for this to be real, but they were back in the car. She opened her eyes as Zeb was getting out.

Mary leaned over and asked, "Was it a dream?"

Zebedia shook his head, "You know it wasn't."

"How do I get back there?"

"Do you have memories of your home?"

Mary answered, "Of course."

Zeb smiled, "When you allow yourself to, you will remember further back and there is where you will find me."

Mary realized then the feeling of emptiness she experienced at leaving the spirit world, was much the same as the period just before waking from a pleasant dream, when we don't want to wake up, but we must.

Mary explained this to me perfectly a few weeks later, in April.

She came to see me on a warm sunny day. I remember because the weather had changed so quickly and dramatically. My dad arranged the meeting. He knew how much I was missing Zeb. He also knew Mary would understand better than anyone.

I didn't know how he knew, but he did, and he was right. She was annoyed that I was mourning for Zeb. She told me he wouldn't like it. It was evident, she understood Zeb better than I did. I couldn't chase the empty feeling deep in my guts. It was much the same when my Grandpa passed away.

Mary made me understand Zeb wasn't lost to us at all, and neither was my grandpa. I need only close my eyes and search my heart to find them. Even though I understood on an intellectual level, I was still only seventeen. It took me years to get over the feeling of loss. Time is the ultimate healer. Time is the reason I am now able to put all these events to paper. Things I shouldn't know are in my head. I sit quietly at night and events begin to manifest in my conscious, as if I actually experienced all of them. I didn't, but I know what other people saw, felt and said without effort. I would be frightened, but I know he wants this story told exactly as it occurred. I become more aware of his presence in my life with each page I complete. I am feeling better and freer than I ever have. He is near me; so near I could touch him. Nights, sitting at the typewriter, I have felt his breath on my shoulder, but I never told anyone, until now. I was afraid everyone would think me a fool.

Mary Savage was never afraid. Her experience that night was the most extraordinary of her life. She told the story without missing any detail, over and over again. She would never be uncertain or afraid of anything in this world ever again.

"We're just passing through," she whispered to herself that night.

Zeb chuckled, "You have a great way of cutting through to the core."

"Why all the suffering, Zebedia. If we are going home, why all the suffering?"

"Why must children be taught, Mary? Why must they be disciplined? I wish I could give you the answers, but in my years on earth I have lost some of what I once understood. I am less in some ways, but in others, I am so much more." He looked at her and she could see the longing in his eyes.

"When you leave. Will you be very far away?"

"No, I will be very close."

"How close?"

"Perhaps a thought, a whisper or a dream away," he answered.

Mary responded in a deep lusty voice, "I don't know if that's close enough."

Zeb backed out of the car. He leaned across the seat and kissed her softly, good-bye wringing in their ears.

"Remember the time," he said to her. "It will be important to you when you are troubled, or uncertain. This memory will be vivid and easily brought to mind if you give it a specific reference point."

She glanced at her watch. She was startled. It must have stopped but the second hand was moving. It read the same as before.

CHAPTER TWENTY-EIGHT

The blip came on the screen just as Zeb exited the car. Joe Provenzano turned and couldn't believe it, dropping his cap and mask to the floor.

Nancy Lebrowitz was already leaning on Raphael's chest, listening for breath, saying, "C'mon sport, c'mon back to us."

She held her hands above his chest, working in the ethereal layer surrounding his body. Without actually touching him she was willing Raphael back to life. Then she let out a scream as heartbeats filled the monitor. Small ones at first then full and steady.

"It worked! It worked! Oh my God! Oh my God!"

Dr. Provenzano laughed out loud, and mopped his tired face in relief. He reached for Maryann and she took his hand for only an instant. Then he was back at the table.

"We're back in business, ladies and gentleman." They stayed fussing, checking and regulating for another ten minutes, reveling in their success. Then the entire team left the room, exhausted and elated.

Down the hall Zeb moved from room to room with Mary in tow. In each case, they were successful. After securing the wounded, he asked Mary to follow him to the morgue.

She was frightened and he saw her hesitate. "You can't be serious?" She questioned.

"After everything you've seen, you still doubt the possibilities."

"They are dead, Zeb."

"Death is a natural progression. These are not natural deaths. Your watch has not moved, check it against any wall clock. Is that possible? These are violent interventions in the order of the universe, affecting the ebb and flow. You asked why all the suffering. Here is your answer. We create it. We sustain it. We relish it. Evil is not permanent. What we call the devil is real, but not part of our original order. No matter now, because today is special and we always have hope, Mary. You must never stop hoping.

"C'mon there is a lot to do for these children, and I need your help. Add your chi to mine, and who knows what might happen. Would you give your life to have their lives returned?" She nodded and he smiled. " I thought so. We interceded for Raphael perhaps we can again."

"Leslie could have refused to let you take Raphael back."

"It was Raphael's choice, but if you hadn't believed, Les might have been more convincing."

"I didn't do anything."

"Your presence was the difference. You must begin to trust in your spiritual ability, as much as your physical dexterity. You need them both. You will use them both more extensively than you ever dreamed possible. Your body and mind are a melded entity. There is no separation. Just as light flows into dark. Energy flows into tissue."

She followed him through the hospital halls. News of Raphael's miraculous return from the dead spread like fire in a pile of dry leaves.

Mary whispered to herself, "Oh boy, wait till everyone gets a load of this next performance."

Zebedia turned, "Did you say something?"

"Just mumbling to myself, Zeb. Lead on."

He knew every word she whispered, the same as he heard me the day he fixed my dad's car on the day we met.

When three supposedly dead youths showed up on the surgical floor in rooms the next morning, the wire services went crazy. Published reports the day before were mistaken. It was too much to believe three children returned from the dead, so they figured that there was misinformation circulated in the confusion. Now they searched for answers to questions of their own making. They refused to believe what actually happened. It was impossible, though many strange and wonderful things had occurred here. Dead was still dead even to the sensation seeking soothsayers of the media world. But not in the halls of Community Medical. Many of the staff saw the wounds, examined the three youths, and speculation was rampant.

Parapsychologists' phones started ringing all over the country. Miracle cures were one item the staff could take credit for. Resurrections were a different matter. The several referred to in the Bible suddenly had modern credibility.

Throughout the day, questions were asked. Little by little, the media watch began to focus on the real possibility an unnatural occurrence had taken place. Something outside the realm of human understanding, –almost impossible to conceive in linear thought–was at work. It was beyond sensational, therefore, it wasn't believable.

Three children returned from the dead; Six others wounded were healing quickly; and a young police officer awakened and alert after his own bout with death. The world wouldn't hear any of this good news. It wasn't news fit to print, because it wasn't believable. It wouldn't sell papers like the youths' violent deaths had. This was news reserved for the tabloids.

Mary Savage left Zeb down in the basement cleaning out the hazardous waste material in the incinerator room. He was whistling his now familiar tune. As she moved upstairs she felt anxious at leaving him, finally understanding why.

She sung quietly, "Baby, baby I'll go down on my knees for you. Barumph, barumph, barumph bump . . ."

She had no physical way of knowing Zeb felt a flutter in his own stomach. As she disappeared down the hall he watched her move and noticed the curve of her calves and the swing of her hips. He stored the information quickly so she wouldn't sense him staring and went back to work. But her mind was very quick. She picked the warmth of his affection out of the air, just as waves of his energy washed through her. A small smile creased her lips. She didn't turn, but he knew she felt the same about him. I think "I love you" popped into his head, then she was gone.

Frank Johnson was in a foul mood when he came upon Zeb, "Nice of you to show up. I've been calling you for hours at home and at the Crowley's." He noticed Mary Savage moving down the hall and looked from her to Zeb.

Then he smiled, and softened. "I was calling her, too." He rubbed his chin. "I'll be darned. You are one amazing son-of-a-gun."

Zeb looked at him with a crooked grin men get when they are caught at something, but he didn't answer and Frank didn't press.

"No matter. It's two in the morning and we will be here until two tomorrow. With all the extra attention and people, this place is a mess. Can you handle three shifts in a row?"

Zeb finished tying the double plastic container, then sealed the lid. "You've been here a day and a half without sleep already. That's why you're cranky. We'll manage the best way we can, Frank. As for whether I can handle it or not, I'll let you know tomorrow at two in the morning."

Frank slapped him on the shoulder. "Can't ask for more than that, son. How about we get a coffee and something to eat."

"You go ahead, Frank. I want to finish up here. I'll see you in your office. Get me a cup of tea to go, please."

"You got it," Frank returned his mood rising.

Zeb hurried about, gathering the rest of the waste, which had spilled, on the floor. He cleaned the entire mess, then locked the door to the room before heading for Frank's office and that cup of tea. When he reached the door it was ajar so he pushed it open. His tea stood on the corner of Frank's desk in a Styrofoam cup. Frank was sound asleep on his couch. Zeb removed the plastic lid and blew lightly as steam rose from the piping liquid.

Sitting down in a chair, Zeb made certain not to disturb his sleeping boss. He sipped his tea thinking about his friend, watching him rest. Frank pushed himself beyond the limit of his endurance day after day without complaining. Zeb raised his cup to salute Frank. Then he became still, lying his head back against the overstuffed chair. Events of the past two weeks played in his mind's eye.

Elizabeth and Ben dancing together, me, my brother and sister; the people at Jack's candy store and the gangs on the streets: Each piece part of the fabric of our lives. All of it intertwined dependent on the other like patches on a quilt. Our weaknesses were apparent, while our strengths, we had only begun to examine.

People are capable of such joy and laughter, yet we are unable to get past distractions to express it to one another except on rare occasions.

Zeb let his mind roam. "We are hopeful, fragile sensitive creatures, but we cannot express softness, because hate controls our daily existence."

He sat there thinking about all of us for a long time. I know he expected us to do well. He told me so on several occasions. Judgment didn't enter into his thought processes, but he observed everything. He loved without reservation, asking nothing in return. This was unbelievable to us. He wished everyone well. Its that simple, perhaps too simple. This is the observation of a young man nearing thirty years.

I experienced these events with a seventeen-year-old's understanding, and insecurities. I grasped much of Zeb's message, but it took years for me to comprehend the depth of his love for all of us. At seventeen, I wanted to know how he did it. I wanted to know why he did it. I wanted to be him, because he was better than me. I didn't see it was possible for all of us to be like him. That was his most important lesson. I was absorbed with needing to know the source of his peace and power. I wanted to attain it for myself and become better than Zeb. I didn't realize he was sharing it with us everyday a little at a time, so we all might accomplish exactly what I wanted. His capacity for love and forgiveness was beyond my comprehension. As much as he wanted us to learn we felt threatened by the depth his simplicity. We couldn't trust completely. He wanted us to be happy, in love and at peace. Not bad wishes for any time or any place.

Love changes the way the universe operates. It easily changes the way we operate. I wanted to pick and choose the parts of his personality important to me.

There were so many things I didn't understand. All knowledge already exists. We don't create it. We uncover it. We didn't create electricity, we found it in the air. We didn't build atoms, we learned of their existence. By challenging our potential, and testing the unknown, we find things hidden by our ignorance. Technological advances are part of the natural progression Zeb talked about. We find answers, but we cannot create worlds. The more we learn the more we realize there is more to learn. Not knowing isn't frustrating, it is liberating. We enter the field of universal intelligence, with unlimited possibilities.

I didn't understand any of this before my friend was gone. I missed an opportunity, which never returned. I made a concerted effort to find out what made him tick without him knowing. All I had to do was ask him.

CHAPTER TWENTY-NINE

Zeb worked at the hospital for two days straight. The atmosphere was like a carnival. Patients, staff and guests were jovial and pleasant to each other all the time. Celebrity newscasters came and went on a daily basis. Famous individuals from movies and television arrived too; some seeking notoriety, others seeking solace, or a cure. All sought something missing inside them.

People from every walk of life came. The tiny chapel in the hospital was full every minute of the day with lines extending out into the parking area. Rich and famous waited in the same lines as everyone else. Stars appreciated the lack of attention they received. Nothing more was expected of them than anyone else. All during this commotion, the staff continued to function at near normal efficiency. No deaths occurred. Healings occurred, but at a slower rate. No more resurrections took place.

Zeb was removed from the flow for a few days. He worked constantly, and was nearly exhausted. With the steady influx of negative people the positive energy advantage was disappearing.

Zeb kept hard at work, his head still spinning from his night with Mary Savage, unable to get her out of his mind. He laughed at himself, because he felt giddy, alive and wonderful, but he couldn't concentrate. Every time he saw her, his heart raced. He would find himself walking past her office just to catch a glimpse of her. His emotions ran free. He understood why people got lost in their emotions and how difficult it was to maintain some continuity and balance. Mary seemed unaffected. It was maddening, until Zeb realized, he was jealous.

He savored each and every emotion. He came to understand how easily jealousy built into rage.

There are many wonderful parts to humanity. Surviving each day and being good is very difficult, much more difficult than Zeb ever imagined. He wondered if his Father and the ancient ones were concerned over the powerful assault evil inflicted on humanity. Zeb was aware Satan's hold was growing stronger. That battle wasn't his to fight. Zeb's purpose was to teach people to see their unlimited possibilities. He was free to help with any trouble as best he could. With that thought in mind, he raised his hands and asked for the strength that he needed to complete what he started. The answer was simple. Evil cannot win as long as one person is hoping and loving.

Each journey begins with a single step and each effort to do good, no matter how small, affects the eventual outcome of the eternal struggle with evil. Zeb saw a larger picture, beyond this town, where each of us helps a little each day. Love continues growing, out from and beyond our town.

I watched the beginning, and am grateful to have been directly involved. Even as I write these truths, I am aware of the astonishing, unbelievable nature of what I am writing. If I were reading it, I would have doubts as to its veracity; but, it doesn't matter what I think or believe. Ultimately, you and I, and everyone around us matter. As long as I care more about the people I try to reach than I do about my position, everything will fall in place. You and what you believe are the issue. Placing my ego aside, hoping you will reach for your dreams with expectation of them coming true, is all that matters. Touching lives of people I will never know, because I wrote this down is what was expected. In completing the task, I hope someone sees some glimpse of wonder, which they share with a loved one. This is payment beyond any monetary compensation.

It is something like walking seventy-five miles joyfully, after helping a stranger with your carfare.

After ten years of running away from his lessons, I can begin saying I've started to understand. Good is inside each of us. We need only look for it in each other. Be careful, because you may fill a heart you never expected to.

CHAPTER THIRTY

Pain lingered in Grace's arm for two days. She was sweating more than usual and felt sick to her stomach. Ignoring it, as she did most pain in her ancient body, she became concerned, and finally called Lea, who came to stay with her. Normally, she would have called John and Cathy Sullivan, but she didn't want to put them through watching her die, and she knew it was time. Today, she felt as if a mule was seated on her chest, repeatedly kicking her left shoulder. Lea was with her. She helped her lie on the kitchen table, no mean feat for two older women.

"I haven't been up on this table since Charlie died." Grace quipped through a grimace.

"Don't start with your dirty mouth, old woman, or I'll let you suffer." Lea replied, eyes twinkling with mirth, at the image of Grace and her husband making love on the kitchen table.

After getting her a pillow for her ankles and knees, Grace settled back on the table. Lea placed two books under her head then asked her to close her eyes and breath deeply. It was a little cool in the kitchen. Lea, shivering from a cold draft, decided to fetch Grace a blanket from the linen closet.

Outside the sun was setting. Its last rays streamed in the window across the floor and up the wall as it sank behind the houses at the base of the hill, across the street. Grace's home sat at the top of a rise overlooking almost the entire town. She liked watching life all around her from the comfort of her porch. She had chosen the piece of property more than a half century before. Grace was wearing a loose fitting, brightly colored dress covered with purple and orange flowers. Lea removed Grace's bright red shoes, chuckling at her outrageous friend.

"I think you had better taste in clothes when your mind was missing."

Grace laughed and tried to answer, but the pain in her chest stifled a response. The crushing weight on her chest made it nearly impossible for her to get a breath, let alone speak.

"It begins, there is little time," Lea said quietly. She moved across the room easily, mixing with and becoming part of the shadows. Like a wisp of wind, she returned with two candles, lit them, removed her own shoes and started to massage Grace's feet. She worked steadily from point to point pressing and relaxing, relieving tension and soothing muscles up along Grace's legs to her sides. She was in no hurry. Her only purpose was to make Grace more comfortable as she slipped beyond this realm of existence. Lea wondered in her own mind what new adventure might be in store for someone as accomplished as Grace. Lea was sure it would be wonderful.

She chanted an old Indian tribal song softly, as she worked. It was a war dance, which she believed quite appropriate. Grace's life had been a series of glorious battles and triumphs. A small silent draft caused the candle flames to flicker and dance, throwing shadows everywhere in the mounting darkness. When Lea reached Grace's abdomen she was very gentle contacting her hara lightly, and breathing deeply. She continued smoothly up and down Grace's arms and shoulders, feeling the tension melt away.

Resting her hand over the older woman's heart, she felt the fire raging inside the old chest. Great heat burned in and around the dying muscle, while it struggled to continue, as it had for more than a century. Grace witnessed extraordinary events in her lifetime. When she started out, few people even knew what a car was. Those funny little contraptions with wheels would never replace horses. Now men walked in space, communicated around the world in less time than it took Grace to speak to neighbors around the corner, and horses were for betting, or recreation. Lea's fingers glided up Grace's neck, stretching and caressing gently yet firmly. Lea finished her work in short order then moved down Grace's body again, sliding her right hand slowly and easily along the arm back to Grace's hara.

Lea combined a classical education with Indian tradition passed down to her through many generations. Her investigations into related cultures, and Oriental philosophy, shifted and settled her ideas. She believes to this day, the soul resides near the hara, the traditional Oriental center of "Chi," or life force, in the body. The hara is located three-fingers-width below the navel. From there the life force, Chi or energy, spreads out through channels filling the entire body. Breathing into hara nurtures all our organs; each breath is a renewal of life or rebirth.

In ancient time, Lea believes Indian, Mexican, and Oriental cultures were all one, separated by disharmony, and shifting landmasses. The search for harmony is on going and will end with final reunification of the entire human race as one culture. Lea knows we are missing only information. She told me once in a private moment, "Our bodies are perfect pharmacies creating everything we need in perfect proportion. We interfere and confuse and throw everything out-of-whack. If we didn't we might live forever."

I remember being astounded by the shear magnitude of the thought. Discord hatred and violence are parts of the whole, just as night flows into day and the river drains into the sea. All are separate, yet dependent on one another. In balance they cannot destroy us. When we alter the original balance of our inner terrain everything is at risk. We tend to expand the imbalances exponentially. After ruining our interior environment, we began to alter the environment we live in. For some strange self-destructive reason, we can't leave things as they are. We can't be as we are and accept bliss. The Vedic scientist said it best, "Grass doesn't try to grow, it just grows. The river doesn't try to flow. A child doesn't try to be in bliss, the child exists in bliss."

To explain her theory, Lea sites examples like Tahiti, where races have reunited for centuries producing some of the gentler and more physically beautiful people in the world. She speaks often about the importance of harmony, and believes the ability to focus on God's essence in our own physical make-up creates a positive energy flow unrelentingly propelling us towards the outer limits of our human potential. A favorite saying she offered which I never forgot is, "In coming times, humans will be able to communicate telepathically with other beings in the universe."

That raised some eyebrows until Zeb seemed to be able to do exactly that. It is now one of her favorite themes. She knows her forefathers had this ability and some of the visionaries of present time are the inheritors.

After Zeb left us, I would go to hear Lea speak as often as possible. The people in Springfield became knowledge junkies, reading everything, exploring every avenue. Knowledge and hope became a central focus in our town. No one remained untouched by our gain and ultimately our loss. As with many things in life, we didn't appreciate what we were presented until a major source of it was gone.

Zeb taught us to believe the power to heal is in all of us. He showed us the power of love and hope. He forced us to see the good in the bad, experience forgiveness in the anger and use our power of love constantly. He showed us how liberating being non-judgmental is, to the point where if we are able to judge no one and nothing we would automatically eliminate envy, greed and war from the planet. All power would then be centered, focused universal in intent, Godlike.

Looking back now, with twenty seven-year-old eyes, I wonder how I missed it; how I questioned everything Zeb did. Most importantly, I wonder why I questioned Zeb at all. He lived openly, hiding nothing. If I wanted to know something, all I needed to do was ask. Zeb held no ulterior motives. He wished the best for everyone. I judged everything he did. He wasn't hard to believe. He was too good to be true. At any rate, I didn't get it then and neither did a lot of the adults who could have changed things more quickly. Change takes time, but not a lot of time. If it is more than a human lifetime we consider it a long time, but is it? Zeb did get the notion of eternity to sink in. My grandpa exists in the time continuum; I will see him again.

Lea focused her energy, creating a powerful healing force not unlike an electromagnet, able to draw on the forces of nature without full awareness of why. She wasn't here to physically heal Grace Abernathy, her friend and soul mate of so many years. She was here to help her relinquish her physical body. This was a send off party. Grace was excited and a little frightened at the same time. Her journey into the unknown, across the universe, to become a different part of it was about to begin. Her earthly stay was complete. She was ready. Her life provided a wealth of knowledge for generations to come. Her work created no hatred, no demons to exorcise. John Sullivan and Raphael Santiaga would administer her wealth in the best way. Grace gave to life more than she was taking out — a positive exchange. Now the universe was hers for the asking.

Lea's task that evening was easy. Fifteen years earlier she would have taken Grace out along the side of the river on a cold winter night. They would have sat and talked until Grace went to sleep forever. Now, Lea found other dimensions and moved in mystical circles far beyond those early days. She was fortunate to work with people open to new ideas and ancient wisdom, without thinking her delusional. It amazed her, how rigid organized religions are, controlling their members with ancient teachings without understanding, ancient ways.

She questioned an old priest one day if he would have a diseased kidney removed or place leaches on his stomach, after listening to him give a particular vile sermon, which openly targeted several young parishioners. Their main crime was to disagree with a church law, but Lea's analogy was lost on him. He didn't know there is a difference between church law and God's law. She hadn't pressed him, and wouldn't try to change him. It had saddened her, because he was a good man, misguided, but good.

For years he ministered to the sick and distraught late at night, while others slept comfortably. It was a shame he couldn't connect to and draw some peace of mind from all the positive energy he created. He spent too much of his time focused on the dark and couldn't accept it as part of the light. His exalted position, due to his status as priest, was much too important to him. He needed people to be aware of how good a man he was. Love and affection were missing in his life making him extremely insecure. He needed to be patted on the back often.

Lea understood his frailty. He could never walk in the light without seeing the darkness. Where Lea looked for the joyful side of people, this man dug into their wounds. Where she strove to lift them up, his ego needed to hold them down. Part of her gift was an innate wisdom about and a gentleness towards people.

So much was happening, so much good was occurring. The ancients benefited from sharing their knowledge long ago. They were unafraid of consequences. It cost them dearly in the physical world, but it didn't matter. They existed only to move through this world back into the spiritual plain. That was key. They understood the transitory nature of materialism. They know more than we do. They did not seek power or control over each other. They know it doesn't last past one lifetime, which is a narrow period.

Nowadays, many are afraid to move past a lifetime. They cling to this life, afraid to relinquish control, because their hardened hearts see no further. They cannot admit, even to themselves, control is an illusion, or at best, a momentary aberration in the relentless march of time. The ancients were willing to share their secrets for the good of all. Lea wasn't sure when greed and suffering replaced sharing and happiness, but the results were evident¾disease, poverty, despair, gluttony, anger to name a few. The list is long and growing, but it can change. Zeb made Lea aware it can change. As the circle turns seeds of good sprout up among evil weeds, light forces its way into dark corners, and hope comes into view on the horizon out of the depths of despair.

"We need to learn yin and yang all over again," Lea mused. "Time collects all. It is the master mechanic."

Lea smiled at her simplified view of the Great Spirit. Years ago she envisioned Great Spirit as a giant all encompassing being. Now, a simple craftsman, like a mechanic sufficed to organize worlds, universes and wisdom beyond her comprehension. The entire Yin in the universe condensing into a Yang repair shop made her laugh out loud and Grace asked, "What's funny?"

She answered, "We are, love. We are."

She rested her right hand on Grace's hara. Her left lay lightly on her shoulder. In the darkness beyond the candles, Lea could sense spirits gathering. She felt the room warming. Her hands began to glow slightly as her own auryllic energy increased. She recognized only one. Grace's troublesome son had come to greet her.

Lea refocused her attention on Grace, who opened her eyes. "You should have been a doctor, Lea."

Lea shrugged. "We are all doctors after a fashion, my friend. Your energy has soothed my path for today, and healed me for days to come. I will carry it with me until I see you again. I would like to stay with you, as you cross over, if that's all right."

Grace clutched Lea's hand. "I'm a little frightened."

Lea smiled, "Think of all you've seen and accomplished. Your fear is unfounded. You are a child of immortality, beginning a new life. Your soul has much to teach and much to learn. I envy you."

Grace chuckled, relaxing, "You would."

They laughed together for the last time. Grace closed her eyes. Lea felt Chi emptying from Grace's hara. Then her heart simply stopped beating. She wasn't able to see her leaving. When she opened her eyes she was alone. Her eyes had been closed the entire time, and she hadn't known it. The entire scene had played, clear as sunshine in her mind.

Grace's magnificent one-hundred-and-four-year-old machine lay in front of Lea; quite still, empty of Chi. She examined it with mixed emotions. This body-machine served her friend well for so long, and she would miss her, but it was never Grace. It still resonated reflecting light and appearing as Grace appeared, but it was never Grace.

A chill ran down Lea's spine when she realized someone was touching her shoulder. In her mind words formed like someone writing on a chalkboard. Grace placed them there, "I'm free, Lea. I feel marvelous. Thank you." The words faded. She was gone, and Lea was more certain of her beliefs then at any other moment of her life. She added this experience to her growing repertoire, she would share this story and write it down. Whether others believed this happened was not her concern. Her ministry was to explore and expand wisdom, and tell the stories, as her ancestors had along rivers and in sweat lodges covering North America completely not three-hundred-years ago.

Lea is the one who finally convinced me to write this all down. Much as my Grandpa and Zeb convinced me of things, she told me stories, made me feel good and let me decide for myself. I am more fortunate than most. Most depend on faith. I was there and still it took me ten years. Lea scoffed at the ten years. She said was a warm up period, like a bullpen for pitchers in baseball. She had me laughing when she made it seem like I was the relief pitcher in the World Series. In a certain sense I imagine I am. She and some of the others are getting extremely frail. I am the fresh voice. She will become my ancestor.

Lea feels my voice added to hers and the others is of tremendous importance. Mine is the voice of the cynic who needed to see to believe. I suppose that is why Zeb chose me. She shared the events while they were occurring. She extolled their importance to anyone who might listen, during and after, encouraging everyone to believe in something.

It never mattered to her what they might call the Great Spirit. He was and is many things to many different people, Buddha, Jehovah, Allah to name a few. A gentle belief is what matters. Great Spirit is all of these at once and more. Lea knows God can be anything to anyone, all at the same instant. She is a conduit and a coupling of worlds, never to be part of one without flowing into another. This is her Karma.

Her ancestors quietly expected everything to be good. It was as her ancestors' intended. Zeb was a manifestation of their expectations. Our journey continues. A time for sharing, nurturing and reflection is upon us. It is the bottom of the ninth inning God is trailing by three runs, but has runners in scoring position. It is time to take stock of our efforts. It is a time to take heed. We learned so much while Zeb was here. We missed so much.

CHAPTER THIRTY-ONE

Mary explained recent cures to the press, for the tenth time that day. As she passed Zeb in the hall she shook her fist at him and smiled, but didn't stop. He felt his heart surge, then plunge. He was a little hurt, because she hadn't even slowed to say hello. He smiled at his own jealousy.

The media mongrels following her paid little attention to Zeb, leaning on his waxing machine. He fixed his gaze on Mary moving down the hall holding court. She was totally in command, happy and at ease. He followed her flowing hips until she rounded a corner and was gone. Sighing to himself, regaining his composure, he set his machine to the side, and slipped into Margaret O'Brian's room. The child was sitting up in bed, playing with several dolls, which appeared in her room over the last few days. She was talking evenly to her favorite, a petite little rag doll with freckles, flaming red mop hair and a huge smile. Margaret appeared, as if nothing ever happened to her.

Zeb looked up at the ceiling, mouthed a silent, "Thank you."

Then he looked back at the happy little girl. "Hello, Margaret," Zeb greeted her warmly.

Margaret stopped pretending, and looked up at him. He was dressed as usual in tan shirt and loose pants.

"Why aren't you dressed in your doctor clothes?" she questioned.

"Because I'm not a doctor. I'm a janitor."

Margaret digested this, adjusted her dolly's dress, and then stopped again. A look of concern came over her small features. She looked at Zeb then back at her doll and spoke sternly, "I have to ask him, Sally."

"Sally, Margaret can ask me anything she wants," Zeb interjected. Neither noticed Jim and Claire come to the door. They stopped and listened without entering, wondering what was going on.

"How did you help me wake up, if you're not a doctor? Are you a doctor sometimes?"

Zeb was momentarily at a loss and then whispered, "If I tell you a secret, you must promise not to tell anyone."

Margaret shook her head up and down. Her eyes grew wide and she leaned closer to Zeb. She adored secrets as much as any four-year-old.

Zeb leaned back, drew an imaginary cross on his chest, then said, "Cross your heart and hope to live forever. You won't ever tell."

Margaret nodded and Zeb sensed her parents behind him, but he wouldn't stop now. Margaret would tell everyone anyway, also the same as any four-year-old.

"Okay. You know your mommy and daddy love you very much, and they didn't want you to be sick."

Margaret shook her head up and down, a very serious look on her face, which almost made Zeb laugh.

He continued, "They brought you here, because no other place was good for you. Everyone wanted you to get well, everywhere else, but they didn't believe you could. Here is different. Everyone believed you could get well, they just didn't know how. When I came and saw all these people cheering for you, I just knew it was meant to be. I came in your room, while your mom and dad were sleeping and prayed a special prayer. That prayer added to all the others and your mom and dad's, was like magic, Margaret."

"Like Santa or the Easter Bunny," Margaret piped in.

Zeb nodded in agreement, exaggerating his serious look and she matched it.

"Just like Santa, and we got a special present. We had enough of Santa's magic to reach your mind."

"What did you ask Him for?"

"I held in my heart what I wanted and what I thought your mom and dad wanted."

"What's that?"

"More time with you, of course."

"How did I wake up?" she asked setting her doll aside and placing her hands on her hips.

Zeb almost laughed again at her posturing. "Your brain is very powerful. All the love surrounding you gave it the boost it needed to return to work. It had to adjust your immune system to a new frequency. It was like switching channels on television and then tuning in again."

"You mean like switching from Barney, to . . ." she thought for a minute, then said, "to Sesame Street."

"Exactly!" Zeb exclaimed clapping his hands.

Margaret was positively gleaming.

"Did you hear Mommy? I switched the TV channels in my head."

"Yes, I heard," came the quiet reply.

Now Rodney Fisher was standing at the door with Jim and Claire. Lea Runningwater stopped too, wondering what was happening.

"May I give you a hug, doctor."

Zeb smiled and answered, "You certainly can."

He bent and she squeezed him tight as she could around his neck. Zeb felt how weak and frail she was and centered himself for just an instant to give her another boost. He spoke to Margaret for a few more minutes, then turned to face the growing crowd.

Claire stopped him. She didn't know what to say. She just looked at him, a mixture of love and compassion playing on her face. He took her hands and brought them to his lips.

"Tend to your child, Claire. All your love, and hope brought her back." He patted Jim on the shoulder and moved towards the hall. Rod Fisher already had his pad out, ready to pounce.

"Did you mean all those things you said in there?"

Zeb nodded.

"Can you heal any disease?"

"I've had some success giving people tools with most problems."

"AIDS too?"

Zeb nodded, "I said most problems."

He was going to add that everyone in the hospital possessed the power to heal in some degree. He was going to say that his own healing energy was more developed, because he used it often. It developed with practice, just as most capabilities do. But it was too late. Rod was gone. He was a man in a hurry, running down the hall scribbling in his pad talking to himself. Zeb shook his head, and smiled. It didn't matter. It was almost time and he wasn't in control any longer. The master mechanic was hard at work here. The rest of those gathered inundated him with questions and Zeb held up his hands. He was tired and felt it.

"I was going to tell Rod before he ran off, that all of us contribute to the healings in this hospital. I have a slightly greater gift than some of you because I use it, believe in it, and thank God often for it. We are all responsible this wonderful success. Let your feelings flow. Listen to the wind, the rain and the silence around you. Fill these halls with, love, knowledge and energy for a long time to come. Continue to do your darndest and keep your humility. Not only will the so-called miracles continue, but also a homogenization of talent will crystallize in your minds. Your mental capacity will expand. Your collective healing ability will multiply. You will see things more clearly than ever, and understand each other as you never thought possible.

"There is special chemistry here. All of you are in touch with past knowledge, present problems and future concerns. Immortality stretches before you. You can almost touch it. I say to you, reach further, grasp for it and hold on. The ride is unbelievable. Keep trying. Keep reaching. Most of all, keep loving."

"I knew you weren't only a janitor." The statement came from the rear of the group.

Frank Johnson moved through to confront Zeb, "Are you leaving?"

Zeb smiled at his boss with tired eyes.

"Right now I'm going downstairs to clean out a storeroom I haven't finished rearranging. Does that make me a janitor?"

"That qualifies you as a custodial engineer," Frank answered beaming. "You can be a philosopher or a goat herder later if you want to, but right now, I need you, boy. That old man you recruited is down there waiting for you."

Zeb clapped Frank on the shoulder and they started to walk away. The crowd at the door dispersed. There were mixed emotions and different thoughts among them, but one theme was constant. Each wondered at the sense of loss they felt.

Lea hung back having just returned from Grace's home. Zeb and Frank were moving away when she called to him without opening her mouth. He turned and smiled.

"I'll be along in a minute, Boss. I want to speak to Lea."

Frank said, "Don't be too long, Zeb. There is an awful lot to do."

Zeb looked directly at his friend, a simple man, who worked joyfully and willingly at every task.

"I've learned a lot from you, Frank Johnson. Thank you."

Frank ignored the comment, a little embarrassed by the compliment.

"Don't keep him to long, Lea. We have work to do." Frank remained unaffected by all the sensational things happening around him. He reduced life to a very simple philosophy, "Keep at it," He was living proof the philosophy worked.

People passed back and forth in the hall while Zeb and Lea stood silently facing each other. Lea didn't try to hide the tears streaming down her cheeks. She wasn't sobbing or falling apart, but she was troubled and saddened by what she saw in her thoughts.

"They will come for you now. As soon as this hits the papers they will not leave you alone." Zeb nodded.

"You will be pawed and clawed and attacked for a charlatan and a fraud."

He nodded again. "You are worried about me. That is very nice of you, Lea."

"This is larger than you, Zeb. It can't end here."

"My dearest, Lea. You mustn't worry. The order of things continues as it always has. Everything will occur as you sense it. You will continue without me."

"You will be sorely missed." She no longer felt drained. Just being near him was like a plugging into some sort of cosmic transformer.

"My energy, like my soul, is immortal. It is all around you as yours is around me. You and others will work to enhance your own ability. You all understand what is possible. You can feel it inside you. You, personally, have searched the spiritual world for years. The others are in their spiritual infancy."

"I could learn so much from you."

"And I you Lea. We will work together. I will never be far from you. I have a special job when I leave the physical world. I will be sort of the Johnny Carson of the spirit, and you are my medium. We will make people laugh. They will learn from you. After you, I will move on to your son. He is very wise, Lea, but he is confused. He has studied every philosophy and every religion trying to find his roots. He is lost. Why did you let him wander so far from the truth?"

Lea smiled. "Because I, too, was uncertain. Until a few days ago I wasn't sure of a lot of things. I hoped, but wasn't certain."

"And now?" Lea chuckled and took him in her arms. She kissed his eyes, cheeks and nose, ending softly on his lips. It was a kiss transcending centuries. It wasn't an old woman kissing a young man. It was a first kiss. Soft and sensual, a smorgasbord of delight. Lea stepped away a little shocked and breathless.

Zeb was slightly embarrassed. "The possibilities are quite phenomenal, eh, Lea?" he quipped.

She let out a small laugh.

"Grace is on her way."

He grew serious. "Where is her body?"

"It will be cremated. Her ashes will be placed in Arlington National Cemetery."

"Where is that?"

"It's near Washington, D.C. Many of her friend's remains are there and she deserves the honor."

"I don't understand."

"It is a cemetery for warriors, heroes, and dignitaries."

"She is certainly all of those. I have to go, Lea. Frank is short of help, as usual."

"Will I speak with you again?"

"Often."

With that he turned and hurried down the hall. Lea watched him go, feeling no loss, just a great sense of completion. This was the last time she would see him in this world, and she felt full and joyful. All the things she believed, wished and dreamed were happening around her. She could reach out and touch all of it. There was no reason to fear death, because there was no loss. Life was precious and death was an extension of life.

She turned and walked away in the opposite direction, humming a familiar tune. Then for no apparent reason she broke into song. Everyone stopped and stared, but it didn't matter. She sang with all the joy she felt in her heart. That joy touched everyone who heard her.

CHAPTER THIRTY-TWO

The mob found him in a bathroom scrubbing a toilet. A young medical journalist fired the first salvo.

"They say you are a miracle worker. Is it true?"

"Can you see with your heart?" Zeb asked.

"Of course not"

Zeb smiled, "Then I can never answer your question."

"You're going to answer a few questions whether you like it or not," the arrogant young man fired back.

"I didn't say I wouldn't answer questions. I said you wouldn't hear the answers, because the answers won't sell papers. You will twist my words to sell papers. My time and energy will be wasted. I have little time and no energy to spare on you."

"Are you crazy?"

"Crazy enough to believe in miracles. How about you?"

"Do you perform them?" Maria Gonzalez asked quietly and Zeb smiled at her, warmly. He liked the young television reporter. She had seen this through from the beginning.

"I help them along, as well as any person created in my Father's image. We all have the ability, Maria."

"People are saying you brought the dead children back to life, is that true?" She continued.

"I requested their Chi be returned and the request was granted."

"By whom?"

"By the one you call God."

"What do you call Him?"

"He has many names. Some call Him Allah, some Buddha, some Yahweh and some the Great Spirit. Does it really matter? He is all these and more. I call him Father and friend. At a certain point you will understand the mechanism, which restarts the machine you call your body. We are all no more than reflections of light, anyway."

There was nothing more to add. They thought he was crazy and the papers were full of lies about him over the next few days. I saw him portrayed as a womanizer. He was romantically linked to several, including my mom and Mary. They wrote he was a fraud. They said he staged everything that happened at the hospital on the night he and Mary returned to find Raphael and the others dead.

Raphael Santiaga knew Zeb spoke the truth. He remembered where he had been and so did Mary. They each tried to tell the media, but their voices were lost in the feeding frenzy of a sensational story. It reached a crescendo when religious groups attacked Zeb. He was held up to public scorn and questioned at length by public officials. The pressure from organized religions became so great that Zeb was arrested and thrown in jail for conspiracy. What conspiracy was never explained, but it didn't matter. Any excuse to get him off the streets, away from people was good enough.

Their greatest fear was Zeb's greatest asset. He spoke the truth. Through the entire ordeal, Zeb never complained. He seemed more at peace than the day I first saw him. I still see him now wiping the filth off his clothes without anger.

On the day he was dragged into court I was asked if I knew him. I was happy to say I did. I told the story over and over of how we met. In fact, during the days he was being investigated many people told stories about him. None was more pertinent than Jack's telling of his imaginary dog, Emma, showing up at his store after meeting Zeb.

They wrote us all off. We were brainwashed and not responsible, some sort of cult members. Expert sources, which had not been involved, knew better. A bishop and a minister, who never saw Zeb or spoke to him, condemned him publicly. Their litany appeared on page one of the *New York Times*. According to them Zeb was a cult leader, akin to Charles Manson.

Maria Gonzales cut through all the garbage and reported the truth. Often her stories were given little airtime, but an underlying phenomenon was occurring.

In Oriental thought all things are necessary. Good cannot be defined without evil. Light depends on darkness; life on death.

The more the media tried to disparage Zeb, the more they tripped over their own bias. Pieces of truth began to come out, Maria Gonzales began to get more airtime because people called and requested it. Switchboards lit up when she was on the air.

The major media failed to convince anyone Zeb was evil. People were drawn to him. With each story the media twisted, Zebedia's reputation grew. He continued to comfort and heal any that came to him. Maria reported these stories and her popularity soared.

The line of visitors waiting to see him in jail stretched for miles. People camped overnight rather than lose their place. The police sent Sulli and Raphael to see if Zeb would address the entire crowd and ask them to disperse. The traffic problems and sanitation problems were too much for them to handle.

Zeb obliged beleaguered police officials, convincing the crowds he was one with all of them, but it was time to leave. Again avoiding a media circus, he waited until all of them dispersed to concentrate on their problems. Calls came in by the thousands with testimonials the day after he spoke to the crowd.

The constant blitz of sensational media coverage made it inevitable the Federal Government would get involved. Headlines like, "MIRACLE CURE MANIA" and "HEALINGS OR HOAX" served to heighten the already astronomical curiosity about Community Memorial. Thousands flocked to the hospital and a constant stream of healings occurred.

A government contingent arrived in town barely disguising their belief Zeb was some sort of alien. Their ignorant assumptions grew out of a need to explain miracle cures using linear logic. The members of the staff baffled them with discussions of inter dimensional worlds and cross currents of vibrational creation. Mental time travel left them shaking their heads.

Zeb taught me a little Oriental philosophy, which accepts the flow of universal interconnected energy. Things that occur in nature and work continually need no explanation. The fact that they work often and consistently is proof enough. Some call it faith, others Yin and Yang. Our western minds, held prisoners by a psychotic need to control and explain everything with finite knowledge, have trouble with acceptance. Western science will never be derailed by faith.

I must admit I doubted. I am lucky to have witnessed these events first hand. I would not believe otherwise and make no claim that I would. So few of us are able to accept and rejoice in life without explanation. I take no comfort knowing I am one of this group. We lose our childlike wonder much to soon and spend the rest of our days searching for it. I know, now, why I feel good when my mom puts her arms around me. I remember what it means to be encouraged to learn and love. I will never lose my ability to hope, because I was there. I saw all these things happen. I know they are real. The government personnel know too. They saw with their own eyes and distorted the truth beyond recognition.

Media and medical experts couldn't bring themselves to back away from their anti-God position no matter what they witnessed. All present felt the presence of energy, beyond human explanation, operating. None had the courage to challenge their collectively held position. They attacked Zeb as a homeless, migrant worker, labeling him, "A no-account maintenance man. A charlatan, trying to capitalize on the misfortune of others."

Frank Johnson blew his cork. "He didn't know that the job he had done well for so many years was of no-account." He was quoted on national television by Maria Gonzalez, saying, "Each and every institution in America had an awful lot of no accounts cleaning their toilets." This brought a roar of laughter. The head of the lobbying group, who made the statement, was quickly replaced, and the onslaught resumed.

Zeb remained unconcerned by the hoopla. He concentrated on battling the anger he felt, turning it out and away from him. Several members of the, so-called, legitimate press began to print his thoughts correctly. This angered leaders of several faiths. Rabbi's, bishops, and ministers questioned him at length. None could find fault with his humility, honesty or message. The simplicity of his philosophy and depth of understanding were irrefutable. In the end, it was left to Congress to dispose of him. His legend continued to grow, expanding geometrically, beyond control. Mary Savage appeared on several national talk shows, with Raphael Santiaga, who appeared more like a Latin movie star than an under-cover police officer. The scars over his eyes added to his rugged good looks. The scars inside his heart would take much longer to heal. Little by little the slant of the media stories changed. The angle became, Zeb might be telling the truth.

Each day, those of us who knew him believed he would be released. That was before the head of the Senate Ethics Committee asked Zeb whether he was a citizen of the United States. Zeb answered that he was not. His goose was cooked. They would hold him until he told them where he was from.

Day after day he was interrogated. Patiently he explained his background was not a concern. The issue was whether healings occurred at the hospital. The panel was not interested in the issue. Their job was solely to discredit Zeb. Day after day they failed and Zeb appeared stronger, but his patience was waning. The constant exposure to selfish interest and innuendo took its toll. He began to attack their stupidity openly. He objected to being held for no reason publicly. Everyone knew the healings occurred, all of us spoke in his defense, but it didn't matter. They weren't interested in truth. Politicians were interested in looking good on television for as long as possible.

I really can't blame them. They asked the same questions publicly, which I asked privately. My mom never doubted Zeb a moment and neither did my dad, but I was young and easily swayed by public opinion. I won't say I denied him, but I did waver. I will regret it my entire life. Each doubt harbored by someone Zeb counted as a friend affected Zeb, much like Raphael's wife's thoughts affected Raphael when he teetered between this world and the next.

While the effort to publicly humiliate him continued, healings at the hospital increased ten-fold. Zeb continued to understand us better than we do ourselves. Even in the midst of all this proof we failed to believe. He had done all he could. There was no more time. There were no more quiet conversations. He took his smile, and his gentle attitude, and left us wondering. There was no reason to stay. We didn't have enough courage right then and there, but we did hope. We saw change was possible. We didn't have the courage to set him free, but time would take care of courage. For the first time in a long, long while, goodness became a sensational topic worthy of news coverage. Our humanity actually was showing. He never asked more than that.

Maria Gonzalez reported every positive story she could find. She would never have a bleak topic for her entire career. Rod Fisher's career would mirror hers on the printed page. They have kept our town and the events alive for more than ten years.

EPILOGUE

Through the remainder of his last drunken haze, he remembered Zeb asking him if he was sorry for all the pain he caused himself over the years. He vaguely remembered saying, "Yes". He asked for the ability to do some kindness for children before he died, and Zeb hugged him through the bars. He just hugged him and the prisoner in the cell next to Zeb felt better than he had in years. His body grew stronger and his mind more alert. He decided then and there that he was never returning to jail. He had been in and out of them for most of his adult life.

He never even knew who Zeb was, only that he cared. Zeb didn't judge the man's life or tell him how stupid he was. He just hugged him and said, "Be as good as you are able. Go with God."

He must have fallen asleep, because he told me he thought it was all a dream until he woke up and found Zeb's clothes neatly folded by his bed. Zeb left him a note and my name and address.

"The children will always hope if you give them reason. Do your best and be kind to yourself. The damage you've done exists only here and now, not in my home or yours. Envy, hate and greed will pass. Fear will never again touch your heart or control your mind. Look after the children and the child in you will bring you home. Have faith. See you soon. Zeb."

On top of his clothes Zeb left a wooden statue of a child at play. It was nearly perfect except for an unfinished hand. My mom and I smiled when he gave it to us. We gave it to Mary Savage. She placed it in the entrance of the hospital. It became a symbol of our work. The statue was never completed.

Zeb showed us the joy in learning from everyone. It is an

integral part of life's great excitement. As Frank Johnson likes to say, "Life is your own creation. Just keep at it." I intend to until, I see Zeb again. If you see him before I do tell him hello for me, and one other thing. Tell my grandpa, I love him. He knows, but it doesn't hurt to remind him how special he is.

BVG